Christie Barlow is the number one international bestselling author of twenty-two romantic comedies including the iconic Love Heart Lane Series, *A Home at Honeysuckle Farm* and *Kitty's Countryside Dream*. She lives in a ramshackle cottage in a quaint village in the heart of Staffordshire with her four children and two dogs.

Her writing career came as a lovely surprise when Christie decided to write a book to teach her children a valuable life lesson and show them that they are capable of achieving their dreams.

Christie writes about love, life, friendships and the importance of community spirit. She loves to hear from her readers and you can get in touch via Twitter, Facebook and Instagram.

facebook.com/ChristieJBarlow
x.com/ChristieJBarlow
bookbub.com/authors/christie-barlow
instagram.com/christie_barlow

GN00598336

Also by Christie Barlow

The Love Heart Lane Series

Love Heart Lane

Foxglove Farm

Clover Cottage

Starcross Manor

The Lake House

Primrose Park

Heartcross Castle

The New Doctor at Peony Practice

New Beginnings at the Old Bakehouse

The Hidden Secrets of Bumblebee Cottage

A Summer Surprise at the Little Blue Boathouse

A Winter Wedding at Starcross Manor

The Library on Love Heart Lane

The Vintage Flower Van on Love Heart Lane

Standalones

Kitty's Countryside Dream

The Cosy Canal Boat Dream

A Home at Honeysuckle Farm

A POSTCARD FROM PUFFIN ISLAND

CHRISTIE BARLOW

One More Chapter
a division of HarperCollins*Publishers* Ltd
1 London Bridge Street
London SE1 9GF
www.harpercollins.co.uk
HarperCollins*Publishers*
Macken House, 39/40 Mayor Street Upper,
Dublin 1, D01 C9W8, Ireland

This paperback edition 2024
3
First published in Great Britain in ebook format
by HarperCollins*Publishers* 2024

ISBN: 978-0-00-870801-6

Printed and bound in the UK using 100% Renewable Electricity
by CPI Group (UK) Ltd

This book contains FSC™ certified paper and other controlled
sources to ensure responsible forest management.

For more information visit: www.harpercollins.co.uk/green

For Woody,
You are simply my best friend.
I love you.

Puffin Island

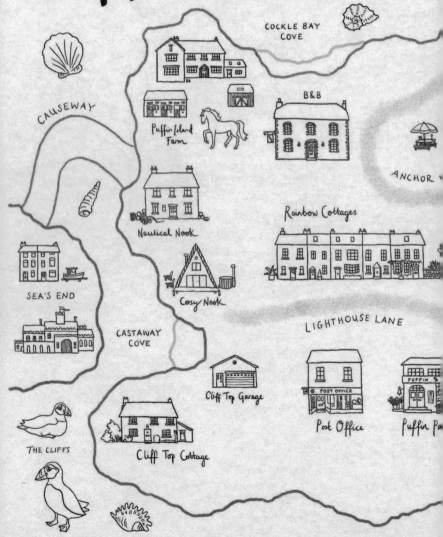

COCKLE BAY COVE

CAUSEWAY

Puffin Island Farm

B&B

ANCHOR

Nautical Nook

Rainbow Cottages

SEA'S END

Cosy Nook

CASTAWAY COVE

LIGHTHOUSE LANE

Cliff Top Garage

POST OFFICE

PUFFIN

THE CLIFFS

Cliff Top Cottage

Post Office

Puffin Po

Chapter One

'That is the longest screw I've had in a while.'

Hearing the gravel path crunching behind her, Verity Callaway felt a blush flood her cheeks. What on earth had possessed her to say that out loud? Spinning around she came face to face with Kev, the local postman.

'Sorry, I didn't mean that; it's not true at all. Well, actually it is, but I don't need to overshare my love life, especially now it's non-existent. Hence the reason I'm off travelling.'

She raised her eyebrows as Kev sang out 'Hit me baby one more time' whilst attempting a risky dance move that looked like he was having some sort of spasm.

Alarmed and not quite sure what was going on here, Verity was relieved when Kev pulled out his phone then took an AirPod out of his ear.

Grinning, Kev said, 'Sorry, Verity, did you say something? I had music blasting. Britney.'

Her smile was bright. 'If I had to guess your favourite idol, I'd guess Britney any day of the week.'

Switching off the music he slipped the phone back in his pocket. 'What did you say?' he repeated.

'It's okay, Kev, I was just talking to myself,' she replied, glad to have been spared embarrassment…for once.

'What exactly are you doing?' He looked towards the toolbox lying on the ground next to her.

Verity pointed towards the postbox that was attached to the wall outside the front door of her cottage. 'The new tenants want it removed. I think their exact words were "It's an eyesore". Not that I can blame them. It's rusty and has been sealed up for as long as I can remember.'

Kev pointed. 'There may be hidden treasure in there. You never know, maybe you'll find a letter from years ago telling your grandmother she'd won the lottery.'

'Now wouldn't that be the dream?' Verity sighed wistfully.

'You're coming back, aren't you?' Kev took a glance over the road to number 50.

'He obviously just can't let me go,' Verity joked, wishing her ex, Richard, lived on the opposite side of the world, not the opposite side of the street. She had discovered his infidelity six months ago, and to add insult to injury, he'd decided just two months later to move into the house right opposite on her street – with the woman concerned, his university sweetheart. If it had just been a matter of sowing his wild oats one last time before their wedding, she might have been able to forgive him in time, but no, it turned out he'd been sleeping with her for a number of years, after they'd reconnected on social media.

Verity and Richard had been together ten years when his cheating was exposed, and suddenly Verity had two choices. She could believe him when he claimed he would give the other woman up and never cheat again, or she could walk away. She had chosen to walk away and she was still questioning if what she had felt for Richard had actually been love. Last year, she'd been happy to marry the man, but now that feeling had turned to contempt. She had been deeply humiliated by his betrayal and hated him with every bone in her body.

'It beggars belief that she would want to live in the same village as me, never mind on the same street. But not for long! I'm off on an adventure and have six months of not seeing them to look forward to. Remember, Kev, I'm just going to slip away in the early morning tomorrow and you know nothing until the new tenants move in. That's in approximately two weeks.'

'My lips are sealed. But I'll miss you.' He handed her a couple of letters.

'Now, you get back to Britney, before I get all emotional. I'm no good with goodbyes.'

'Have a safe journey and just for the record, Richard was always punching.' Kev gave her a wink.

'I can't argue with you there.'

Verity wasn't usually the adventurous type, but right at this moment the ferry ride to Amsterdam, where her best friend Ava would be waiting for her, couldn't come soon enough. She'd been employed at the local vet's for the last five years and loved her job, but after Ava had talked non-stop for the last couple of months about her upcoming travels, Verity had found herself questioning what was actually preventing her joining Ava.

After Googling 'International Veterinary Assistants Vacancies', she'd discovered that there were jobs available all over the world, and with her references in her bag, she knew that, if necessary, she could always find work on the road. She could rely on the rent from the tenants to fund her trip, but a bit of extra cash would certainly come in handy.

Still, she could worry about that once her trip was underway. For now, she revelled in the thought that this town would soon be far behind her. The ferry to Amsterdam from Newcastle upon Tyne was leaving tomorrow and she was going to be on it.

The last few days had been bedlam as she prepared to make her escape to Amsterdam. She had spent the week working her way through a list of things that needed doing for the new tenants: fixing the leaking tap in the bathroom, securing the catch of the upstairs window, undertaking a mammoth spring clean. Now, most of her clothes and personal things were safe in storage, and her rucksack was packed and waiting in the front room.

The van had been her secret project for the past two months. Through blood, sweat and a lot of tears Verity had converted her battered old van into a cosy comfort space of floral quilts and plush rose cushions, inspired by TikTok videos. Verity named the van 'Hetty', after her grandmother, Henrietta, who had passed away twelve years ago. She'd had a huge impact on her life and Verity cherished her memories of Hetty with all her heart. She was looking forward to making new memories with Hetty the van.

Verity couldn't wait for the ferry to leave. Her toiletries and clothes were packed in drawers in the van, along with essentials like a camping stove, kettle and copious amounts of tea. The cupboards were bursting with baked beans, soup and a huge supply of toilet rolls. She didn't need to think about the expense of hotels; she had everything she needed right there, inside her travelling home.

Turning back to the claret-red postbox covered in rust spots, Verity sprayed WD40 on the tarnished old screws, which soon began to turn. Once the screws were out, she lifted it off the wall. Thankfully, it looked heavier than it was. After taking it into the house she laid it on the kitchen table, then switched on the kettle. Leaning against the sink, she glanced around. The kitchen had never looked so tidy; everywhere was spick and span, ready for the tenants, who'd signed a six-month lease.

The house had been left to Verity's mother, Alison, in Hetty's will, and Verity had bought it from her mum seven years ago, when Alison decided on a whim to move to a warmer climate, after continuously watching *Escape to the Sun*, a TV programme she'd been obsessed with for years. She'd been sunning herself in the South of France ever since, and after meeting Pierre, a Frenchman obsessed with art, she'd never looked back or come back.

Hearing her phone ring, Verity smiled as Ava's name flashed on the screen. 'Are you ready to glamp with no glamour?' she trilled before Verity even had a chance to say hello.

Ava had been her best friend since the age of eleven when they started high school together. Even though they'd clicked straight away, they were like chalk and cheese and

5

nothing had changed in the intervening years. Ava was a free spirit, floated from job to job, and didn't have any ties except a goldfish that had almost reached the age of fifteen by the time it finally stopped swimming. Ava winged everything and worried about nothing, whereas Verity always liked the stability of a steady job and a home.

'I'm ready, born ready,' chirped Verity, knowing she'd heard that line in a movie.

Ava laughed. 'I can't quite believe safe Verity has resigned and is coming on a six-month adventure.'

'Hey, I'm not safe, as that suggests boring,' she protested, but she didn't entirely disagree with Ava: she wasn't usually one for taking risks.

'You're never going to look back. We're going to have the best six months. I promise.'

Verity thought back to how life was six months ago, as she looked around the home she'd thought she'd share with Richard. She now couldn't fathom why she'd stuck it out with him so long. Maybe it was because of other people's expectations. Her mother had drummed the conventional way of life into Verity from an early age. Leave school, find a job and a man – it didn't matter in what order – get engaged, married and then have children. The worst possible outcome, according to her mum, was to end up on the shelf, because then people would start to ask what was wrong with her. Verity had had no idea who these 'people' were or why their opinions mattered.

She could still remember her mother's words when she heard from Verity that the wedding was off, and they rang loud and clear in her ears now. 'He would never do that. An affair? It must be your fault somehow. You need to find a way to make it work. You'll never find anyone as good as him.'

All Verity could think now was, thank God she hadn't listened. Because if Richard was considered 'good', she never wanted to date anyone 'good' again.

'Happiness is more about mindset than marriage' had been Verity's parting words to her mother. When she was growing up their relationship had always been strained. She had never been her mother's first priority, and her father was a topic her mother refused to even talk about. When she moved to France it was a relief.

After the disastrous phone conversation when she'd told her mother that the wedding was off, Verity had made a difficult decision. Even though they were related by blood, her mother was no good for her mental health, and it was time to take a step back from their relationship. She'd never encouraged Verity, never shown her any true compassion, and always left her feeling like a huge disappointment to her. Enough was enough. Neither of them had rung each other since that conversation.

'Hetty is full of petrol, my clothes and food are packed and tomorrow can't come soon enough.'

'I'll be on a different ferry, but I'll meet you at the port in Amsterdam as planned. Then the world is our oyster. Any plans for tonight?'

'A long hot shower, as we have no idea when our next will be. Though I have pinched one of those portable pet washers from the surgery. It's like a huge petrol can that you fill up with water, then you pump the water and it comes out through an attached shower head.'

Ava laughed. 'If the worst comes to the worst, we can

always take a dip in the canal. After all, there is a lot of water in Amsterdam.'

'Eww, over my dead body! And no doubt there will be a few dead bodies in there along with bicycles.'

'Twelve thousand bicycles a year on average,' confirmed Ava, full of knowledge as ever. 'All we need to do is find a good coffee shop when we get there, and then the rest of the day will be a daze.' She laughed.

'You mean drugs, don't you? I'm beginning to worry I've given up my stable existence for a life of body odour and weed,' Verity joked.

'One last adventure before we're thirty and only then should we consider growing up a little.'

'In my case that's only a month away!'

'Then we need to make the most of that month! Our adventure is going to be epic. See you tomorrow!'

After hanging up the phone Verity looked at her reflection in the mirror that was hanging on the living-room wall above the fireplace. She looked tired and emotionally drained. She needed this change of routine and was determined to enjoy every second of this trip. Verity always thought this house would be her final destination in life, but now she was open to the possibility of change. She was grateful for the opportunity to have some fun with her oldest and best friend and take her time planning exactly what she wanted from her future.

She opened the fridge. The shelves were empty except for a ready meal for one, a small bottle of prosecco and a pint of milk for her morning brew. Verity pierced several holes in the film of the ready meal and placed it in the microwave for five minutes. As soon as it pinged, she stared disappointedly at the least appetising meal she'd ever seen. Washed down with the prosecco, though, it was just about bearable.

After she finished eating and washed up, there were only two things left to do: put the bin out ready for tomorrow's collection then take a shower. Tomorrow would be an early start and a long day. The journey from Staffordshire to Newcastle upon Tyne was over three hours, but with numerous audio books loaded on to her phone, and a playlist of all her favourite songs queued up, hopefully that and the excitement would carry her through the fifteen-hour boat ride she had ahead of her once she arrived at the ferry terminal.

With one last wipe of the kitchen worktops, she left a flask by the kettle ready for the morning. She opened the back door, pulled the bin around the side of the house and left it on the pavement, knowing that when Kev delivered his letters on his round tomorrow, he would kindly put the emptied bin back at the rear of the house. Hearing another bin being scraped along the ground, she looked up and locked eyes with Richard. She quickly looked away without a flicker of acknowledgement on her face. She only had another few hours before there would be five hundred miles between them and he would become nothing but a distant memory.

Back in the kitchen she remembered the toolbox needed to go into the van. It was resting on the floor next to the kitchen table and she was just about to pack it into Hetty when her gaze caught on the rusty old postbox still lying on the table. Kev's words came back to her and, even though she knew there was probably nothing inside, curiosity was gradually getting the better of her. There was a strong barrel lock on the front, which had rusted over the years, and not having a key, Verity grabbed a screwdriver and managed to prise the door open a little. She then swapped the screwdriver for the claw end of a hammer. With one almighty pull she wrenched the door open, and, surprised, she stumbled backwards.

To her amazement, the postbox contained mail! There were various local business leaflets, from handymen to painters, an outstanding week's milk bill written in shillings and pence, and, right behind the rest of what she would call junk mail, a postcard.

Holding it in her hand, she took in the colourful picture on the front, which featured two puffins sitting on a rock, looking out over the sea.

'Puffins!' she said, smiling, memories flooding back to her. The stocky, short-winged, short-tailed birds with their bright orange webbed feet and white faces, their large, triangular parrot-like bills of bright red and yellow, had been a huge part of her childhood, appearing frequently in the bedtime stories that her grandmother had told her. A natural storyteller who never read from a book, Hetty took her for endless exciting adventures on a place called Puffin Island. Verity could vividly remember the images her granny had described of the quaint island with its colourful cottages and sandy coves.

Verity gave a tiny gasp, feeling her heart beginning to race as she traced her fingers over the gold foil print on the front of the postcard. It had faded but she could still clearly make out the words 'Puffin Island'. Her granny's words started ringing in her ears. *Puffin Island, where there's always a good dose of sun, sand, sea air and a puffinry of puffins.* As a young child, Verity had always burst into a fit of giggles whenever Granny had said the word 'puffinry'. She'd thought it was a made-up word until she became a veterinary nurse and stumbled across the word in a textbook. That took her by surprise then, and this took her by surprise now. Verity turned over the postcard and saw the date on the postmark: 1972.

'Surely you can't have been stuck in the postbox for over fifty years?' Verity said aloud before reading the words written on the card.

> *My Dearest Henrietta,*
> *I know the secret must have been too much to bear but I*
> *can't imagine my life without you.*
> *Always and forever,*
> *W x*

Perplexed, Verity turned the postcard over, then turned it back and read the words again. She racked her brain trying to think of anyone in her grandmother's life with the initial 'W'. Then it suddenly struck her – she'd seen the picture on the front of the postcard before! She hurried down the hallway to the snug and opened the door. Even though this room had changed over the years, Verity always remembered the sight of her grandmother sitting in her armchair in front of the bay window – her favourite spot – usually knitting and watching the comings and goings of the street. The decor had changed when her mum had inherited the house, and again when Verity bought it, but after all these years her grandmother's favourite picture was still hanging on the wall. Richard had never liked it, claiming it looked like something out of a junkshop, but Verity had refused to take it down. She loved it and it reminded her of her childhood.

Staring at the framed photo on the wall now, she saw that the image was exactly the same picture as the one on the postcard.

'W, who is W?' Rummaging through the drawer of the dresser underneath the photo, Verity found exactly what she was looking for: her granny's old address book. Sitting down she quickly began to turn the pages, looking for any name beginning with W. She wasn't sure what she was expecting to find or what she was going to do about it.

When she reached the end of the address book, she sat back, a little disappointed. Sliding the address book back in the drawer, she stood again in front of the framed picture hanging on the wall.

Who was W and what secret was too much to bear? Were they friends, lovers? Taking the photograph off the wall she laid it on the carpet. Carefully bending back the pins, Verity removed the back of the frame, surprised to find a message written on the back of the photograph...in the same writing as the postcard.

The summer of 1972.
W x

Quickly doing the maths, she realised her grandmother would have been twenty-two years old in the summer of 1972. More importantly, her daughter, Verity's mother, was born in 1973. Verity immediately thought of her grandfather, Alf. She was almost sure her grandparents were married just before her mother was born but she couldn't be certain. Both of them had passed away – her grandfather twenty years ago from lung cancer, which was not surprising as Verity had never seen him without a cigarette in his mouth, and her grandmother unexpectedly in her sleep twelve years ago. She remembered them as very much in love and inseparable.

So how did W fit into the equation? 'You're overthinking it,' she said out loud, trying to stop her spiralling thoughts. W could be anyone, but the use of the word 'secret' on the postcard intrigued her, as did the fact that both the postcard and the picture that had been hanging on the wall in the snug for decades belonged to the summer of 1972. Taking a photo of the inscription, Verity reassembled the picture and hung it back in its place.

'Puffin Island,' she murmured, taking the postcard into the sitting room and grabbing her iPad from her rucksack. She typed 'Puffin Island' into Google.

'No way.' Verity was astonished. According to Google, Puffin Island was a real place!

> *Puffin Island gives a distinct and spectacular character to the north Northumberland coastline just off the town of Sea's End. The island is approximately 2.5 miles long and 9 miles around.*

Still not believing that this island really existed, Verity clicked on the images and immediately felt the familiar comforting warmth that the childhood stories told by her beloved granny had always conjured. Independent shops lined the charismatic old high street, and charming restaurants and bespoke shops were dotted along the picture-postcard harbour beside a pretty lighthouse. Verity had always been fascinated by the famous rainbow cottages her granny had described, and insisted that when she grew up, she would live at Cosy Nook Cottage on Lighthouse Lane, which was a stone's throw from Blue Water Bay. With its dramatic coastline, soft stretches of caramel sand and a puffinry of puffins, Verity was inordinately pleased to find that the island was real and not just a figment of her granny's imagination.

'You're actually a place. I can't quite believe it,' she whispered, trying to digest the information.

Puffin Island is a tidal island linked to the tiny hamlet of Sea's End by a long causeway. Twice a day the tide sweeps in from the North Sea to cover the road, affected by the phases of the moon. The causeway crossing times are forecasted as safe, but all travellers should remain vigilant.

Again, exactly what her granny had told her.

Looking back at the postcard, Verity suddenly realised that there was a huge possibility that *all* the bedtime stories that Granny had told her were true. She racked her brain trying to remember if Granny had ever mentioned any names beginning with W, but no one sprung to mind.

Chapter Two

Verity was woken at the crack of dawn by the sound of her alarm. She took a moment to rally herself, then realised she had no time to stay in bed. It was today her adventures started. Arriving in Amsterdam was hopefully going to be all flowers and museums, food and coffee shops. Organised as ever, she'd laid out all her clothes the night before, opting for a simple pair of denim shorts, a white T-shirt and her faithful, comfy, worn-out trainers. Already packed in her rucksack were a raincoat and jumper as she didn't know how chilly it would be on the ferry.

Within seconds she'd jumped out of bed and straight into the shower. Welcoming the warm jets of water that cascaded over her body, she stayed in longer than necessary, knowing that tomorrow morning she would probably be washing with a portable pet shower.

Fifteen minutes later she blasted her hair with the hairdryer, tied it up in a messy bun and applied minimal makeup. Just as she was about to slip her feet into her trainers she heard rain start to patter against the windowpane. Late last night, dark clouds had rolled in, torrential rain had given the town a drenching, and it seemed the storm wasn't quite done yet. Verity checked the weather app on her phone, finding that a thunderstorm was currently raging in Newcastle upon Tyne. Hopefully, by the time she arrived, it would have passed. Pulling back the curtains for the last time, she stood for a moment, breathing deeply and taking in the view she wouldn't see again for at least six months. The last few months of her life had been full of turmoil, but since she'd made the decision to take off in her travelling van, it had felt as if a weight had been lifted off her shoulders. She was relieved that it was almost time to hit the road. She couldn't wait to catch up with Ava.

After making a flask of tea, Verity did a final check of the house, switching off the fridge and all the electrical sockets. She laid all the appliance instructions out for the new tenants and picked up her rucksack.

Just as she was about to go through the door, she hesitated, remembering that the postcard from Puffin Island was still lying on her bedside table. She quickly ran up the stairs to fetch it and slipped it into her rucksack. She couldn't wait to share with Ava the story of the old postbox and see what she made of the message written on the postcard.

Locking the front door behind her, she gave a quick glance around to confirm that there wasn't a soul in sight and she would be able to slip away quietly, just as she'd planned. She deposited the keys in the lockbox, threw her rucksack onto the passenger seat and slipped the flask of tea into the door pocket.

Then she punched a text to Ava.

> I'm on my way! See you soon!

Starting the engine, Verity switched on the wipers and set up the sat nav on her phone.

According to Google Maps she would reach her destination in just over three hours. Verity wasn't a confident driver, and the furthest she'd ever driven before now was to the supermarket on the edge of the town, but she wasn't going to let any doubts creep into her mind. She could do this.

Putting the van in reverse she took her foot off the clutch and started to edge out of the drive.

Bang!

'Shit! What the hell was that?' Verity slammed on the brakes, pulled on the handbrake and jumped out. The rain was coming down hard as she stood at the back of the van and stared in dismay at the black wheelybin now lying on its side. 'Damn,' she muttered, noting the dent in Hetty's back, before hauling the bin upright again. So far there had been nothing quiet about this getaway. She glanced up and down the street. Thankfully, it seemed her little accident had gone unnoticed, but it wasn't the start she wanted, and now she was sodden, the rain having soaked through her T-shirt. After jumping back into the van Verity turned up the heater before grabbing her jumper from the top of the rucksack.

'Let's try again.'

As she switched on the radio the lyrics of 'I Will Survive' rang out, and she smiled.

'Got to love Gloria Gaynor!'

There was only one thing for it. Verity turned up the radio. It was her intention to live up to those lyrics and from now on live life to the max. Reversing off the drive, she took one last look at the house. She'd thought she might feel apprehensive about leaving, might question if she was doing the right thing, but all she felt now was excitement mixed with relief. Driving up the road, she sang at the top of her lungs and didn't even glance towards number 50.

Three hours later, Verity had successfully navigated herself to North Shields and decided to pull over and get a bite to eat from the greasy spoon café parked in the layby, before entering the ferry port. Outside the glorified caravan stood plastic chairs and tables, each with a laminated menu standing between a ketchup bottle and a container full of plastic knives and forks. Most of the tabletops also came with free grease, or spilled salt.

Thankfully it had stopped raining, though the sky still looked threatening.

As soon as she stepped from her van, Verity was hit by an aroma of bacon, sausage, fried onions and coffee. Suddenly feeling a lot more than peckish, she joined the queue of bikers and truckers to the sound of wolf-whistles. Feeling a crimson blush upon her cheeks, she focused on the counter and tried not to make eye contact with anyone. Amongst the hungry customers she spotted a man standing at the head of the queue who looked even more out of place than her, if that was possible. He wore a designer suit of navy twill cloth, with a contemporary fit, natural shoulders and pick-stitched lapels. He turned around, and she couldn't help but stare; he was drop-dead gorgeous, looking as though he should be dining at an exclusive fancy restaurant, not a greasy spoon by a ferry port. His curly blond hair was wild at the top. She guessed he was in his early thirties – so, around her age. His eyelashes and deep blue eyes were to die for, his face was tanned and he had that unshaven thing going on. As he walked away from the counter, taking a bite of his sandwich, he caught her eye. He slowed as he approached her, saying, 'And here was me thinking they were whistling at me.' He gave her a wolfish grin and carried on walking.

Verity smiled and glanced back over her shoulder, watching as he climbed into a black four-wheel drive and finished his food before starting the engine. She was still watching him as he pulled out of the parking spot, and he glanced over in her direction again and paused. They stared at each other for a moment. Verity's stomach gave a little flip – a feeling she hadn't felt in a very long time. She wondered who the handsome stranger was and whether he would be on her ferry to Amsterdam.

'Can I help you, love?'

'Just a sausage bap, please. Oh, and a coffee?' she said, hastily stepping up to the counter.

The assistant nodded and cut open a bread roll then walked over to the fryer that was bubbling with fat and fished out a sausage with a long pair of tongs. He handed her the roll in a napkin, along with a polystyrene cup of coffee. 'There's sauce and sugar on the tables.'

After thanking him and handing over cash, Verity

walked back to her van, the handsome stranger still very much on her mind. From where she was parked she could see he'd driven the short distance to the ferry port. His car stood higher than the vehicles behind him and he was now queuing for passport control. As she juggled her keys to open the van door, her phone vibrated and flashed on the passenger seat. Quickly she balanced the food and cup on the bonnet and hastened to open the door.

Five missed called from Ava were showing on the screen and Verity immediately had a sinking feeling that something was very wrong. Returning her friend's call, she waited for Ava to answer.

'There's nothing to panic about,' Ava quickly reassured.

'Thank God for that. I thought you were ringing to tell me you've changed your mind and were about to leave me stranded at the ferry port.'

'Not quite, but there is a tiny blip. But don't worry, all will be back on track in forty-eight hours.'

'What kind of blip? Because your blips are usually quite catastrophic.'

There was a pause on the end of the phone.

'Ava!'

'I'm not going to be with you today or tomorrow, but I'm coming.'

'What do you mean? Why not?'

'I tripped over my rucksack at the top of the stairs, lost my balance, and chipped my front tooth as I fell. I have an emergency dentist's appointment this afternoon and the next ferry I can get on is the day after next, but my ticket is confirmed.'

'What am I going to do for two days on my own?' Verity

realised that the first words out of her mouth were not very sympathetic. 'Sorry, Ava. Let me rephrase that, how are you?'

'A half-smashed tooth is not a very attractive look, and I know it's not ideal but for two days you need to put on your big-girl pants and embrace the situation. You'll be fine and I'll be with you before you know it.'

'I know, I can do this,' Verity said with determination.

'You can. Get yourself settled on the ferry, relax, read a book, watch the world sail by. I'll text you over the campsite details and I'll make my way there as soon as possible. I promise.'

'You'd better! I'm just about to join the queue to go through passport control.'

'Don't have too much fun without me!'

Verity had to admit she was feeling a tad disappointed to be starting this adventure on her own, but Ava would be there as soon as possible and Verity would only need to keep herself occupied for the next forty-eight hours.

Starting the engine, Verity drove into the ferry port and began to follow the slow line of vehicles. Up ahead was a steward who reminded Verity of a flight attendant, his arms stretched in front of him directing vehicles of different sizes into different lanes. The lane in front of her was moving steadily and soon the steward directed her straight ahead, to join the camper vans and the four-wheel drives. Sitting in the queue she looked out towards the long line of ferries. She'd never realised how big they were; she'd only ever seen one on TV. In fact, she had never been on any type of boat before, so this was certainly a first!

Just above the ferry the royalty of the coastal skies was

circulating, the enthusiastic, happy band of seagulls swooping down towards the water, no doubt scavenging their next meal. The car in front began moving and stopped at the kiosk, where the occupants handed over their passports. This was it: as soon as she was through passport control her six-month adventure would start.

Verity switched on the radio and smiled as one of Britney's songs played, instantly reminding her of Kev. Turning up the music she began jigging in her seat, and, taking a sideward glance, she found a pair of mesmerising eyes staring back at her in amusement. There he was again, the gorgeous guy from the greasy spoon, in the next lane. He began pointing at her bonnet and she raised her eyebrows and shrugged, not understanding what he was trying to tell her. He pointed with both hands and Verity followed his gaze.

There, miraculously still balancing on the van's bonnet, was her sausage bap. (The coffee was long gone.) The phone call from Ava had distracted her and she'd forgotten all about it.

Verity laughed, opened the van door and hopped down. Just at that moment the ferry honked its horn, causing her to nearly jump out of her skin. She placed both hands on her chest and dared to glance in the attractive man's direction. He was now shaking his head and laughing. The car in front of her van was beginning to move so she quickly grabbed the sandwich. As she turned, a seagull swooped towards her from nowhere. Verity screamed and threw the sandwich in the air. Not missing its chance, the seagull dived at the food and was soon gliding towards a nearby rock with its breakfast grasped tightly in its beak.

Still in shock, Verity briefly closed her eyes. When she opened them, the man was still watching her. She was totally embarrassed, but a tiny part of her saw the funny side. Trying to shrug it off, she laughed and rolled her eyes, but her heart was beating nineteen to the dozen. She mimed 'you win some, you lose some' by throwing her hands up in the air. His smile was wide, showing a perfect set of teeth, and he gave her a friendly wave before the cars in front of him moved and he looked ahead of him in his lane. Verity jumped back in her van and slowly began to close the gap between her and the car in front. Within what felt like seconds, the man was through passport control and heading for the ferry at the far end of the port. She immediately wondered if it might be the one heading to Amsterdam.

Verity's turn was next. She pulled up at the side of the kiosk, wound down her window and handed over her passport.

The customs officer sitting behind the desk scrutinised the passport then intently looked at her face before looking back at her photo. 'Where are you travelling to today?' he asked. 'Amsterdam or Sea's End?'

Verity stared at the man. 'Did you just say Sea's End? Isn't that near Puffin Island?'

'I did. It's that way to Amsterdam, or that way to Sea's End,' he said, pointing to the ferry at the far right of the port, 'with the onward connection to Puffin Island.'

'Does the ferry dock near the causeway?'

'It does and it's due to set sail in the next hour. So, which ferry are you on? Do you have your ticket?'

Verity's mind was racing. If Ava wasn't going to make it to Amsterdam for another forty-eight hours, could she explore Puffin Island today, then jump back on the ferry tomorrow and take the next ferry to Amsterdam?

Thinking out loud, she said, 'I'm not sure if this is at all doable, but would it be possible to buy a new ticket to Sea's End – sailing today and coming back tomorrow – and change my original ticket to Amsterdam for a day later?'

The customs officer had a sudden look of disdain on his face, clearly annoyed that she was holding up the queue and he'd now have the inconvenience of changing her tickets. But the more Verity thought about it, the more she knew this was exactly what she wanted to do.

'You're cutting it a little fine to change your ticket...' he began.

'But it can be done?' she insisted, taking her chance. 'It's just a mad coincidence that that ferry could take me closer to Puffin Island. I didn't know it even existed until yesterday – actually, that's a lie, my granny used to tell me stories about the place when I was a little girl, but I thought it was all make-believe – when you'll never guess what happened.'

'Enlighten me,' replied the man, now narrowing his eyes.

'I found a postcard stuck in my postbox addressed to my granny. It was sent over fifty years ago from a man called W – I'm saying it's a man because I can only assume it's a man and he said he couldn't imagine life without her and their secret must have been too much to bear.' Verity raised her eyebrows. 'My granny never saw that postcard because the postbox was sealed up with the post inside, so it's fate that I'm now so close. I *need* to go to Puffin Island and see if I can find W and discover the secret they shared. It's like

24

something out of a movie, with romance and intrigue. Look, I have the postcard.' She reached into her rucksack and held up the postcard towards him. 'A postcard from Puffin Island.'

The customs officer held up his hands. 'Okay, I'm invested! Who am I to stand in the way of secrets and possibly romance?' He turned to the computer behind him and began tapping on the keyboard. 'It's your lucky day. There are a couple of tickets left. The return ferry is coming back mid-morning tomorrow, and the next ferry to Amsterdam leaves two hours later, but there will be a cost to change your ticket.'

'That's no problem.' Verity couldn't believe her luck. She could spend a day and a night on Puffin Island and then arrive in Amsterdam around the same time as Ava. The timing couldn't be any better.

The man tapped away again and the printer next to him began to whirl, spitting out new tickets. 'Hang this on the mirror of your van'—he handed over what looked like a paper coat-hanger, which she hung on the mirror —'and here is your return ticket to Sea's End, and a new one-way ticket to Amsterdam. The extra cost is ninety pounds.'

Verity handed over her credit card and as soon as the transaction went through, he handed her back her card and passport.

'Thank you so much.'

'If you join the queue of cars going that way'—he pointed to the right —'they're just starting to board the ferry. Oh, and good luck.'

'Thank you,' replied Verity, smiling. Placing the tickets on the passenger seat, she gave him a nod of appreciation before making her way to the ferry. 'Puffin Island, here we come!' she said to herself, excitement fizzing inside.

She joined the long line of vehicles driving towards the ferry. She stared at the colossal vessel in front of her. She'd never seen a ferry this close. There were stewards along the way waving flags, directing them onto the ferry and into the next available parking space.

The large ramps made a clanging noise as she drove over them onto the boat, manoeuvring carefully through the tightly packed vehicles. Taking the next available space, she parked the van and gathered everything she might need for the ferry ride. Just before she stepped out of the van, she pinged a text to Ava.

> Change of plan for me too! But I'll still be there before you! I'll tell you all when I see you. X

With her phone still in her hand, Verity jumped as the steward knocked on her window, encouraging her to vacate her vehicle as quickly as possible. Over the tannoy, an announcement sounded. 'Please take all your belongings you need for your journey as there will be no return to your vehicle possible during this sailing.'

Purse, check, Kindle, check, phone, check. Verity had everything she needed. Once the van was locked, she slipped the keys into her rucksack and turned to follow the long line of passengers who were weaving through the parked vehicles towards a flight of metal steps at the far end of the ferry, with a sign reading, To THE DECK.

Verity immediately recognised the car parked opposite her as the four-wheel drive belonging to the handsome stranger. Her pulse began to race, knowing he was actually on the same ferry as her, though at the minute he was nowhere to be seen. Verity couldn't resist a peek inside his car as she walked past. The interior was immaculate; it looked like it had just been driven off the showroom floor. The only thing visible inside was his suit jacket hanging up in the passenger window. Walking past the steward who was directing the passengers towards the stairs, she asked, 'Excuse me, how many passengers are on this ferry?' She wondered how difficult it might be to track down the stranger.

'One thousand five hundred passengers, four hundred and seventy-three cars, two hundred and forty-seven cabins, seven hundred and eighty-six beds, three hundred and thirty-seven reclining seats, a self-service restaurant, a bar, a café, a gift shop, two cinemas, a video game arcade, a children's playroom, a reading lounge and WiFi. These ferries cover forty-five thousand miles per year,' the steward finished in a rush before she finally came up for breath.

'Wow.' Verity was impressed. 'I'm guessing that's not the first time you've said that this week?' she replied, smiling.

'I've lost count. It's that way to the deck and everywhere is signposted once you're up above.'

Calling her thanks as she was swept along by the crowd, Verity was soon up on deck, where she found a cabin with rows and rows of seats, most of them already occupied, huge windows looking out over the water. At the back of the boat was an outside deck where passengers were leaning against the safety rail waiting for the ferry to set sail. The queue to the café was already long and even though Verity was feeling hungry she found herself a vacant seat in the cabin and made herself comfortable.

Hearing her phone ping she looked at the screen to find a message from Ava.

> Tell me more!

> I'm chasing a secret romance on an island full of puffins!

After slipping her phone back into her rucksack she glanced around the cabin, but the handsome stranger was nowhere to be seen in the crowd. Feeling a little disappointed she turned towards the window and thought about what exactly her plan should be when she arrived on Puffin Island.

She'd boarded the ferry on a whim, chasing a secret and a romantic dream, excited at the prospect of exploring the island her granny had told her about. The burning question was: would anyone remember her granny? It was probably unlikely but she remained hopeful that she might find some answers and a new connection to the grandmother she'd loved so deeply.

The horn sounded and the ferry slowly began to move, the gulls still circling above. The rain had stopped for the moment but if the colour of the sky was anything to go by, that wasn't going to be for long. Taking a glance towards the queue at the café Verity saw that it wasn't dwindling fast, so with nothing but time on her hands, she pulled out her phone and Googled Puffin Island again. She knew from her granny's stories that the causeway was the main route on and off the island, and that it was closed at certain times of the day when the tide was high. According to the online timetable, the next time Verity could cross the causeway to Puffin Island would be just after two o'clock that afternoon.

Verity wondered whether village life on the island was exactly like in her granny's stories. She smiled to herself. Whenever she'd had a sleepover at Granny's she'd always wanted to go to bed early so she could listen to the next instalment of what everyone got up to on Puffin Island. The tales started coming back to her now. Beachcomber Bakery, which made and sold delicious cake. The 'to die for' (according to Granny) afternoon cream tea from the tearoom on Lighthouse Lane. Verity racked her brain trying to remember its name but eventually gave up and Googled 'tearoom on Lighthouse Lane'. And there it was: the award-winning Café by the Coast. The thatched Grade 2-listed cottage, offering traditional clotted cream teas, tasty sandwiches and scrumptious cakes, lay at the end of Lighthouse Lane overlooking Blue Water Bay.

As with Puffin Island itself, Verity couldn't believe the tearoom's owner, Betty Rose, was real, but there she was, proudly standing in front of the teashop on the front page of its website. In her seventies now, Betty apparently hadn't quite retired, still working three days a week alongside her granddaughter, Clemmie, to welcome thousands of tourists every year. According to their website, to avoid disappointment it was recommended to book a table in advance to sample the delights of their award-winning cream teas. So that's exactly what Verity did: booked a table for one at three o'clock that very afternoon.

The picturesque Lighthouse Lane, the main street of

Puffin Island, had camera-worthy credentials and had no doubt graced countless postcards, keyrings and chocolate boxes in its time. Pastel-painted houses and timber-framed buildings lined the gently winding cobbled lane, with its numerous bespoke shops and boutiques including a second-hand bookstore, Beachcomber Bakery, and Puffin Pantry, a delicatessen that sold local jam and chutneys alongside meats and cheeses.

The lane took its name from the lighthouse just off the harbour adjacent to Puffin Island, which guarded shipwreck shallows. Docked in the nearby bay, The Sea Glass Restaurant, with its spectacular glass bottom that showed the clear blue waters underneath the tables, was a favourite place to dine for locals and visitors alike. The next street, Anchor Way, also cobbled, offered the finest in fashion, and all seaside essentials. The B&B, along with Smuggler's Rest, the island's hotel, was located here, a stone's throw from the pub, The Olde Ship Inn. Anchor Way led into a small square where you could discover local whimsical contemporary art in the gallery, and aged treasures in the antique shops.

Puffin Island had one hundred and sixty residents, and attracted over six hundred thousand visitors a year – and Verity was about to become one of them! Moving on to Google Earth, Verity zoomed in on the map to follow the small path leading from the end of Lighthouse Lane to Blue Water Bay, which had a sandy shore, clear blue water and a breathtaking scenic coastline. Across the bay, was the harbour and further on the sand dunes which led you to another secluded cove, Castaway Cove, where the rocky coastline leading up to the cliffs housed the forty-three thousand pairs of puffins that made their home on Puffin

Island between April and June every year. As Verity zoomed in further she noticed an isolated cottage, which looked exactly how she'd always pictured the cottage that often featured in Granny's stories.

According to her granny, Cliff Top Cottage, nestled amongst the puffins' dens, was the most beautiful and sought-after cottage on the island, with stunning views over the harbour. Taking a glance out of the ferry's window, Verity saw that the coastline was diminishing in the background and the ferry was gathering speed. Once more, the heavens opened and the rain began to lash against the water and window. The sea looked choppy and Verity's stomach flipped. All of a sudden, she began to feel a little queasy and her whole body felt warm. Her stomach churning, she turned towards the café, finding the queue was now only five people deep. Taking her chance, she left her rucksack on the chair and slipped her phone into the pocket of her shorts.

'A bottle of water please,' said Verity, once she'd reached the front of the queue. Only an hour ago she was ravenous but now she was doing her best to hold on to last night's ready meal.

'Anything else?' asked the shop assistant with a smile.

Verity looked towards the menu on the blackboard behind the assistant, then scanned the sandwiches in the glass cabinet. Her stomach lurched and she felt herself pale. 'I'm not quite sure, I'm suddenly feeling very unwell.'

The assistant looked sympathetic. 'Is it your first time on a ferry?'

Verity nodded. 'I was feeling absolutely fine five minutes ago but now…'

'Try and stay distracted, I always find nibbling on a biscuit helps to take off the edge.'

'I'll take those ginger biscuits then. Thanks.'

'Good choice – and don't look directly at the water, it'll make you feel worse. When I first started working on the ferry, I used to have an emergency bucket by the side of me, but I found it helped going out onto the open deck and taking in the fresh air.'

Glancing out of the window, Verity saw the rain still looked heavy.

'There's a cover so you won't get soaked, though maybe a little sprayed,' the assistant said kindly while ringing the items up on the till. After Verity paid, she gingerly made her way back to her seat. The first mistake she made was to look at the water as she sat down. Her stomach flipped again. Closing her eyes, she tried to think of anything to distract herself, but it wasn't working. Her stomach had decided it was competing in gymnastics at the Olympics as it lunged into a triple somersault. With her eyes still closed she took a sip of water and nibbled on the biscuit. It was no help. Fearing she was going to vomit, she grabbed a sickbag from the pocket of the chair and looked towards the seats in the middle of the ferry. It appeared it wasn't just her who was feeling the effects of the stormy seas, as there was a long line of people sitting with their heads back and their eyes closed, clutching a sickbag.

Feeling her body temperature rising, she desperately wanted fresh air. Up on her feet she staggered on the unsteady floor, brushing against numerous other passengers as she made her way towards the open deck. As soon as she opened the door Verity welcomed the blast of fresh air. She walked to the stern rail and grabbed onto it for dear life. Gulping air, she was grateful for the light spray of the rain. Keeping her eyes closed and her head down, Verity breathed in deeply and filled her lungs with air. But still it wasn't helping. No matter how hard she tried not to think about how she was feeling, the nausea swirling in the pit of her stomach was only intensifying.

'The joys of ferry rides, eh?'

Verity lifted her head slowly and opened her eyes.

The handsome stranger from the greasy spoon was standing right next to her. His timing couldn't be any worse. Verity swallowed hard, trying to think of anything except the bile rising from her stomach. She didn't trust herself to speak.

'You look kind of green.' He gave her a lopsided grin. 'I suspect that seagull did you a favour as it means you haven't got a sausage sandwich swirling in the pit of your stomach.'

The very thought made Verity heave but somehow, she'd mislaid the sickbag on the walk to the outside deck. Her eyes began to water and she feared she couldn't hold back for much longer. Raising her hands, she frantically wafted them in front of her face.

The handsome stranger looked horrified. 'You're about to be sick, aren't you?' He didn't wait for an answer. Quickly leaning behind him he grabbed a sickbag from the holder on the wall and thrust it into Verity's hands. Mortified, but thankful for the bag, she threw up.

As soon as she stopped heaving, he passed her a tissue. 'Sam Wilson,' he shared. For a moment they stared at each other in an awkward silence. 'We meet again. First you get me wolf-whistled and second, well, you throw up. It's not often those two things happen to me in the space of a couple of hours. As Monday mornings go, it's been eventful!'

Still feeling green, Verity managed a laugh. She liked his sense of humour.

'I have to say, though, there are other ways to get a man's attention. Just a normal "Hello, I'm…" would have been enough.' He had a glint in his eye and Verity's stomach began to flip again, this time for all the right reasons.

It had been a long time since she'd flirted with anyone, and that's all it was, because the last thing on her mind was the possibility of getting involved in any romantic entanglement, no matter how sexy he was. The next six months would be all about finding out who Verity Callaway was, and what she wanted from life. But from the way he was looking at her, it was clear that he found her just as attractive as she found him.

'Hello, I'm Verity…Callaway.' She smiled but suddenly felt a little shy.

'There's a little bit of colour coming back to her cheeks.'

She knew she was blushing and wiped her mouth with the tissue hoping to hide that very fact. 'I'm really sorry. The second the ferry started moving, that was it, my stomach no longer belonged to my body. Would you excuse me?' She wrinkled her nose as she held up the sickbag. 'I think I need to dispose of this.' She leaned behind Sam and dropped it into the bin.

'How are you feeling now?'

'Kind of dizzy.' Verity wobbled.

Sam put out his hand to steady her. 'Keep drinking water and breathing in the fresh air.' He looked at his watch. 'You'll be over the worst now.'

'Thank God,' she replied. 'One thing I've learned from my very first ferry trip is that I'll never want a job in the Royal Navy. In future, my feet are staying firmly on land. I'm not sure I'll make the fifteen hours to Amsterdam.'

Sam's eyes widened. 'You do know it was the other ferry going to Amsterdam, not this one?' Panic was evident in his tone.

'I know,' she rushed to reassure him. 'That's where I should be heading right now but I got distracted.'

'Distracted?' Sam raised an eyebrow.

'Don't go getting any ideas. I didn't see a perfect handsome stranger in the queue at the greasy spoon, then follow him to the ferry port and decide to change my ticket at the last minute because his four-wheel drive was getting on a different ferry from myself and Hetty.'

Sam looked over his shoulder. 'Hetty? Do you have company?'

Verity smiled. 'Hetty is my travelling van. This is our first adventure after...' She paused.

'After?'

'After my separation.' Verity couldn't quite believe she was sharing all this information with a complete stranger. 'She was my old works van and when I resigned, I decided it was about time I did something out the ordinary. So I converted her into a camper. It took a couple of months but now she's just perfect. Tonight, we'll be sleeping under the stars.'

Sam looked up at the sky. 'I don't want to burst your bubble, but with a sky that dark…'

Verity laughed. 'You have a fair point.'

'Shall we get back to your story? You were saying something about a perfect handsome stranger in the café queue…' Sam teased.

She arched an eyebrow. 'Café is a very loose term.'

Sam laughed. 'So why the change of destination? And can I just say I'm a little disappointed that it wasn't because you were chasing the perfect handsome stranger? That's the stuff of movies and we all know how those stories tend to end.'

'And how do they end?'

'The couple fall in love and live happily after ever.'

She smiled at him. 'The perfect handsome stranger is a bonus,' she replied, happily flirting right back. 'I'm travelling for six months with a friend. We should have been meeting in Amsterdam but she's had an emergency and can't make it for another forty-eight hours.'

'Her loss, Sea's End gain.'

'Definitely her loss. Apparently she tripped over her rucksack, and chipped a tooth.'

'Ouch.'

'And when the customs officer informed me this ferry was going to Sea's End, which is right next to Puffin Island, it was fate.'

'Fate?'

'I just had to visit because when I was a little girl my granny told me bedtime stories about the island and I've just discovered it's a real place.'

Just at that moment an announcement informed them

that the ferry was docking in five minutes, and asked the passengers to gather all their belongings and make their way back to their vehicles.

'You do know you won't be able to drive across the causeway until this afternoon?'

'I do. How long is the causeway?'

Sam pointed. 'A little under three miles. That gorgeous harbour at Sea's End is where we're docking. It's the nearest town to Puffin Island and it looks like St Tropez on a sunny day. Not so gorgeous in the rain though.' He held up his hands. 'But it does look like it's clearing.'

In a steady stream the passengers began to vacate the deck. 'After you,' said Sam. 'You look a little brighter.'

'I'm actually feeling quite hungry now.'

'You won't find a greasy spoon in Sea's End as it's a little more upmarket, but the seafood restaurants around here are to die for.'

'I think I'll wait for my stomach to settle a little more first.'

'Good plan.'

They made their way down the stairs towards the lower deck. Numerous passengers were already sitting in their cars with their engines running, waiting to drive off the ferry.

'I hope your ferry ride to Amsterdam goes a little more smoothly,' he said with a smile. 'My car is here,' he said, pointing.

'My van is here.'

'As soon as you come out of the ferry port, the causeway is clearly signposted, as is Sea's End.'

'Is that where you're heading?'

'I am, until I can cross the causeway.'

'It was lovely to meet you,' she said as she climbed into her van.

'You too.' He pointed at the car in front of her, which was already moving. The car behind her also had its engine running, waiting for her to move forward. 'Have fun on your adventures, Verity Callaway.'

They stared at each other for a moment.

'I don't suppose…' Feeling impulsive, she was just about to ask whether he would be free for dinner tonight, when the car behind began to impatiently beep. The driver wound down his window. 'Come on, we're moving.' He gestured irritably.

'You'd best get a move on.' Sam turned and walked around to the driver's side of his car and climbed inside. He took one last look in Verity's direction and gave her a sexy smile as he started the engine and began to follow the long line of vehicles in front of him.

'Damn, double damn,' she uttered under her breath. Thanks to the impatient motorist behind her she'd missed the opportunity to ask Sam out, but there was nothing she could do about it now. With the handsome stranger still very much on her mind she drove off the ferry and followed the exit signs. Sam's car was nowhere in sight, but as she knew he would be crossing the causeway as soon as it was safe, she hoped that she might bump into him there. There was something about Sam Wilson that had her wanting to know more.

Chapter Three

Verity glanced at the spectacular view out of the window as she followed the signs to the causeway. The dark clouds seemed to have been left behind for now and the sun was breaking through over the picturesque harbour.

The coastal town of Sea's End was of outstanding beauty, with its colourful waterfront with stunning white sands bordering the small harbour, watched over by the castle on the hill. In the distance, Puffin Island was surrounded by the glistening sea. Taking a right turn she followed the road signs towards the seafront car park and pulled into a space. Just in front of the car park was a slip road where cars were already lining up, queuing to cross the causeway as soon as the tide turned.

Immediately behind the car park was a row of shops including a bakery. Now her sickness had totally subsided, Verity was ravenous. As she walked into the bakery, the delicious aroma transported her back to the traditional

French patisserie she'd visited with Ava on a girly weekend away in Paris. Spoiled for choice, her eyes swooped over the mouth-watering single-portion quiches, freshly made sandwiches, crusty loaves and buttery pastries. She made a selection, knowing she could keep some of it for later this evening and possibly the next morning.

Sitting in the front of her van, she tucked into a crusty ham baguette and admired the view, completely different from this morning now that the storm had abated. Hearing a notification of an incoming text message, she grabbed her phone. It was Kev, letting her know he'd replaced the dustbin in the garden during his postal round. Quickly, Verity snapped a photo of her view and pinged it to him. His reply landed almost immediately.

It's all right for some!

His return photo was one of the puddled street with black bins standing in a long line, like soldiers on guard. But they weren't the first thing Verity noticed in the photograph. No, the first thing she noticed was her ex, standing on his drive. She swallowed and studied the photograph.

How was it you thought you knew someone when all along they'd been leading a double life? The number of lies he must have engineered... It floored her. And she'd believed every one. His trips 'away with work', the 'residential training courses' he'd attended. He'd been away for the same week every year for the past few years and it suddenly dawned on her that it was more than likely he'd been on holiday with *her*.

All she'd ever wanted was to settle down, have a family and live the fairytale, but that was now the last thing on her mind.

Determined to make the most of the next six months whilst she figured out exactly what she wanted from the future, Verity deleted the photograph then flicked over to her Instagram. Within seconds she'd scrubbed her profile clean until there was no trace of the past or her ex. Good riddance. It was not like there was anything to mourn as she'd apparently never really known him at all.

Feeling surprisingly relaxed, she watched the world go by from the driver's seat of the van for the next ten minutes. There was something about watching the water lap against the sand that brought a sense of calm. After finishing her baguette, Verity decided to join the queue of vehicles lining up to cross the causeway. As soon as she was in the line, she cut the engine. Feeling a bit tired after the long drive and the ferry crossing, she climbed into the back of the van and snuggled on top of her duvet. Within moments, she was asleep.

The next thing she knew, she was waking up to the sound of knocking on the van window. Startled, she jumped up and popped her head through the curtain into the front of the van. Standing there was a policeman. Verity quickly wound down the window and began apologising profusely. She'd clearly been asleep for a couple of hours and the line of cars in front of her had disappeared. She was now holding up the long traffic behind her.

Through the open window, the policeman called, 'Have you driven the causeway before?'

'I haven't,' replied Verity.

'Shallow water or seaweed might cover numerous potholes. There's been quite a few flat tyres recently, so drive carefully. All that said, some drivers lose themselves in the excitement of driving the causeway for the very first time and drive exceeding slow. Can I ask you to keep the traffic moving.'

Verity nodded and he waved her on. At the start of the causeway there was a short bridge and next to it a refuge shelter for drivers of vehicles that had been caught out by the tide. 'Well, we aren't that daft to be getting caught out, are we, Hetty?' said Verity, taking in her surroundings, which were a little surreal. The causeway was around three miles in length, the first mile through the sea, the next two snaking along the side of the island. The mainland was about a mile from the western end of the island as the puffin flies.

As she drew closer, there was a sign welcoming everyone to Puffin Island. The sign was of course decorated with a couple of puffins. It was incredible to think all of her granny's stories were genuine and that once she stepped onto the island everything would be familiar. Verity felt a wave of emotion.

With the postcard from Puffin Island still dominating her thoughts, she took in the island itself. The whole place looked like a little piece of heaven and she was confident that she'd made the right decision to divert her plans. She followed the signs to the island's car park and soon found a vacant space overlooking the sea under the trees. Just ahead there was an information hut, and attached to a board outside was a poster with the tide times. She grabbed her bag, locked up the van, then walked on to study the poster. She needed to make tomorrow's ferry to Amsterdam, and according to the tide crossing times, it would next be safe to cross at 3.30 a.m. Staring at the poster she realised she needed to make a choice: sleep on Puffin Island and get up extremely early, or head over to Sea's End and find a safe place to park there. Looking towards Hetty, she smiled. Whatever she decided, she knew her time on Puffin Island was going to be special. She was re-living a part of her granny's past.

Henrietta Callaway had been a huge part of Verity's life. In fact, she was more of a mother to Verity than Verity's own mother had been. Verity's relationship with her grandparents had been one of love and warmth, and as a child and a teenager she had spent more time with them than with her own mother, whose priority had always been herself. Granted, Alison Callaway had been eighteen when Verity was born, but she had chosen to carry on living her life without any responsibilities and always did what was best for herself.

With the rain stopped and the sun breaking through, Verity suspected it might be a clear night. She made the decision there and then. Even if it was only for a few hours, she would stay on Puffin Island, open up the skylight in the roof and sleep under the stars in her travelling van.

Checking her watch, she saw she had one hour to explore before sampling the scrumptious afternoon cream tea she'd booked at Betty Rose's Tearoom. On the side of the information hut was a map of the island and Verity took a quick photograph with her phone before setting off along the shallow stream that ran at the side of the cobbled pavement. Within seconds, she found herself on Lighthouse Lane. As she took in the magnificent view, she realised that the Google images of Puffin Island hadn't done it justice. The majestic lighthouse towered in the distance, standing tall against the cerulean sky over Blue Water Bay. Puffin Island was utterly perfect.

Up ahead, the row of rainbow cottages lined Lighthouse Lane, while here at the very beginning of the lane was Cosy Nook Cottage. Verity gave a tiny gasp. It was real, the cottage she had always claimed she would one day live in, every time her granny mentioned it in her stories. The whimsical storybook cottage was charming, and captured her imagination just as it had when she was a child. The asymmetrical shapes, the mismatched windows, the deeply pitched thatched roof, the oak archway with tumbling blush roses...it was everything she'd ever dreamed of. She wondered if the place even had a secret room, revealed by pulling a book on the bookshelf, just as her granny had told her. She smiled at the notion; some things in her granny's stories had to be made up. Wondering who was lucky enough to live there, she carried on walking past the line of rainbow cottages, each with a gorgeous name and just as Instagram-worthy as the one before it.

The cobbled lane was busy, with people milling in and out of the independent shops, and children laughing and running towards the cove, waving fishing nets above their heads. Verity stopped outside The Story Shop, Lighthouse Lane's second-hand bookshop. A couple of trestle tables on the pavement were piled high with boxes of classics. Verity stopped and picked one up.

The book still in her hand, she stepped inside the bookshop. Every shelf was packed with books – travel books, classics, thrillers and romcoms. In the corner an old-fashioned till stood on a wooden counter, and sitting behind the till was a girl who Verity guessed was in her early twenties. 'What a fabulous bookshop,' said Verity, placing the book on the counter and looking around with admiration.

'Isn't it just,' the assistant replied with a smile. 'Are you visiting for the day or staying on the island?'

'An unplanned day trip but leaving in the early hours. I can't wait to explore.'

The girl smiled. 'First time on the island?'

'It is.'

'I can guarantee it won't be your last. You've made a good choice of book, it's actually one of my all-time favourites.' The assistant wrapped the book in old-fashioned brown paper, tied it with parcel string and placed a pink sticker in the top right-hand corner.

Verity read the message on the sticker aloud. '"With love from The Story Shop." And a picture of a puffin, too.'

'Just a small personal touch.' The assistant smiled again as she rang up the sale.

Verity smiled too as she handed over the cash.

'I'm a local, so if there's anything you need to know about the island, just pop back. I'm always here, writing away and selling books, the best of both worlds.'

'Writing? Are you an author?' Verity asked in awe. She'd never met a real-life author before.

The assistant extended her hand. 'Amelia Brown. A name to remember. One day, I hope my name will be on a front cover standing proudly on one of those shelves.' She held up her hand and crossed her fingers.

'I'll have to come back to buy a copy,' confirmed Verity, taking the parcel from Amelia.

'I'll hold you to that,' replied Amelia with a smile. 'And what do you do?'

'I'm Verity Callaway, not a writer, just a relationship escapee – though a happy escapee. Anyway, I've upped sticks, thrown caution to the wind and left my job as a veterinary assistant in order to roam the world in my travelling van for the next six months.'

Amelia raised her eyebrows. 'Woah! How exciting! Six months of travelling. I take it the relationship didn't end well? You don't need to answer that, but I do need a villain's name for my book, so...'

They both laughed.

'Don't tempt me!' said Verity.

'And this travelling van of yours has brought you to Puffin Island?'

'Yes, I left this morning from Newcastle upon Tyne. My first stop was meant to be Amsterdam, but my plans took a slight detour so here I am on Puffin Island. The ferry trip wasn't kind to me.' She shuddered.

'Sea sickness?'

'The worst ever. I'm beginning to wonder how I'll manage to get to Amsterdam.'

'Bands, you need travel bands. They sell them on the counter at the Nautical Nook, the gift shop, and at the Cosy

Kettle, the tea hut at the cove. They might be a placebo but...'

'Anything's worth a try.'

'Exactly and if you do decide to stay around tonight and want some company, you'll find me in The Olde Ship Inn. Wannabe writer by day, barmaid by night.'

'I might just do that.' Verity gave her a smile and wondered if there was a possibility she might bump into Sam as well. She hoped so.

Chapter Four

Situated at the end of the cobbled lane, just metres from the path that led to the bay, was Betty Rose's Tearoom. The pink thatched cottage was everything a tearoom should be, as well as boasting breathtaking sea views. It looked even more magical than the online images, with its pastel triangular bunting hanging across its front. Outside, the tables draped with floral tablecloths were all occupied, the whole place full of life. Verity was glad she'd booked and couldn't wait to sample the delights. Opening the wooden gate, she made her way down the path. As she opened the door, the old-fashioned bell above her head tinkled and Verity was enveloped by the mouth-watering aromas floating all around her.

The inside was just as vintage as the outside. Homemade pastries on the open counter lined the way to glass-domed cake stands filled with the most scrumptious-looking cakes Verity had ever set eyes on. Antique dressers lined the wall, displaying vintage teacups and teapots, and behind the counter was a chalkboard with today's specials. The whole room was packed to the rafters and Verity suspected this place was the heart of the community.

'Welcome to The Café by the Coast.' The girl behind the counter smoothed down her white pinny as she hurried over. Verity recognised her straightaway from the pictures on the internet. It was Clemmie, Betty Rose's granddaughter.

'You must be the girl in the travelling van booked in for a cream tea at three o'clock.'

Verity was hit with surprise. 'How do you know that?'

Clemmie grinned and pointed to the brown-paper-wrapped book in Verity's hand. 'Everyone knows everything on Puffin Island!' She laughed. 'My best friend is Amelia. You think she's sat there typing away, creating her first novel, but the nine texts I've received in the last ten minutes would suggest she has time on her hands in that bookshop. She's not a gossip but she told me that if a girl – so tall, messy bun, wearing shorts – walks in with a twinge of green to her complexion, then I need to be extra-special nice. I take it the ferry crossing got you?'

Verity laughed. 'Good and proper. I'm not sure I can face it again so soon but I'm due back to the port tomorrow to catch a fifteen-hour ride to Amsterdam.'

'I have to say I don't envy you, but there is a simple solution.'

'Which is?'

'Just stay on Puffin Island! Park your van at the bay. What could be better than waking up to the waves crashing against the sand and the gulls circulating up above.'

'You make it sound so appealing and easy.'

'It is easy. We have a hundred and sixty residents on the island, but we're always looking for more recruits. Unfortunately, it's very rare that a property comes up for sale.'

'Is everyone this lovely on Puffin Island?' Verity replied, her imagination running wild. 'It would be living the dream, waking up to that view.' She glanced out of the open window towards the bay.

Clemmie pulled out a chair for Verity at a table in front of the window. 'This is the best seat in the tearoom and as your visit to the island is a short one, you deserve it.'

'Amelia really didn't miss anything out, did she?' said Verity with a smile, taking the seat. 'Apparently it won't be my last visit.'

'Everyone comes back.' Clemmie smiled. 'I can't ever imagine living anywhere else.'

'It's utterly stunning and picturesque. I honestly feel like I'm on a movie set.'

'It is a very special place.'

'But I have to say I've not seen a puffin yet, which is a bit disappointing.'

Clemmie pointed. 'You head over that way before you travel to your next destination and you won't be disappointed any longer. Believe me, there are thousands. Though I've always thought that when you've seen one, you've seen them all. I can't tell them apart. Now, you're booked in for a traditional afternoon tea, so there's a choice of traditional finger sandwiches, freshly baked scones with strawberry preserve and Puffin Island clotted cream made right here, along with delicate sweet treats and for the touch of elegance, we can add a glass of prosecco.'

Verity's mouth was already watering. 'That sounds like the perfect plan.'

'In that case, all that's left for me to say is welcome to The Café by the Coast, aka Betty Rose's Tearoom. I'll be back with you very soon.'

Verity watched as Clemmie walked behind the counter and pushed open the swinging kitchen door. This had been a good choice. Pulling on the string around her recent purchase, Verity opened the book and read the opening paragraph before turning to the window and watching the people wandering down Lighthouse Lane towards the sea.

Clemmie soon reappeared, holding a tea stand with three individual floral china plates.

'Woah! Look at this! This can't be for one person.'

'It sure is! You take your time though, the table is yours for as long as you'd like it. Sit back and enjoy the best afternoon tea I can guarantee you'll ever have. I'll bring you a pot of tea and a glass of prosecco, but is there anything else I can get you?'

'I think you've covered everything,' replied Verity, taking a cucumber finger sandwich from the plate. 'This is definitely the life,' she murmured as Clemmie hurried off, soon returning with the drinks.

Verity held up the prosecco glass. 'Cheers, and thanks for making me feel so welcome. I'm so glad I decided to jump on the ferry to come and check out the island. Would you believe my granny used to tell me stories about Puffin Island when I was a small girl? I thought it was make-believe and it was only yesterday I discovered that this place actually existed. My granny described it so well I actually feel like I've been here many times.'

'Wow! How did you discover we aren't all make-believe?'

'Funnily enough, a postcard from the past! I've rented out my house for six months and in preparing it for the renters I removed an old, sealed postbox. Inside I discovered a postcard from Puffin Island that had been lying there, unread, for decades.'

Clemmie's eyes widened. 'A postcard from Puffin Island. Decades old. Wow!'

'And that's when I realised this place must be real and my granny must have been here at some point. I don't know whether it was for a holiday or whether she stayed for a while, so I was hoping to do a little digging whilst I'm here.'

'Who was the postcard from? Everyone knows everyone here so it shouldn't be too difficult to find out.'

'That's the thing, it doesn't really say. But whoever it was from apparently can't imagine their life without her.'

'That is so romantic. Was there no name at all?'

Verity shook her head. 'That's where the mystery deepens, it's only signed with the initial "W". But whoever it was, it seems he may have thought my granny was his one true love.'

'And what does your granny say about it all? Does she know you're here?'

'No, she passed away.'

'I'm so sorry to hear that.'

'That's okay, it was a long time ago. Still, I'm intrigued to know who W is. I know this is a long shot, but do you know of anyone, at a guess possibly between the ages of sixty-five and eighty, that lives on the island and has the initial W? I've got the postcard with me. Would you like to take a look?'

'I would!'

Verity delved into her bag and pulled out the postcard, which she handed over to Clemmie.

'I recognise this! This postcard is still sold in the Nautical Nook, the local gift shop. But the initial W isn't ringing any bells. Let me have a think.' Clemmie wafted the postcard in front of her face whilst looking deep in thought. 'No one springs to mind but now I'm just as intrigued as you are to know what the secret is.'

'It could possibly have been a holiday romance, in which case I've not got a cat in hell's chance of discovering anything, with the number of tourists that must pass through here each year. I just thought that if my granny had stayed here for a while...it's a long shot but someone may remember her.'

'If there's anyone who knows everything about this island, that would be our very own Puffin Island Google.'

Verity looked at Clemmie, puzzled.

'My grandmother Betty. Believe me, she knows *everything* that goes on on this island and what she doesn't know isn't worth knowing. Someone could walk through that teashop door from fifty years ago and she would still recognise them, know their name and remember all their past history. Sharp as a knife and nothing passes her by. What's your granny's name?' Clemmie took out her pen and pad from the front pocket of her pinny.

'Henrietta Callaway, Hetty for short.'

Clemmie scribbled down the name on the pad. 'And when are you leaving?'

'I'm heading for Amsterdam early tomorrow morning.'

'So, we have less than twenty-four hours to solve the mystery of W. Unfortunately, my grandmother is away for a couple of days. Shall I take your number? If, on her return, she knows anything, I could drop you a text.'

'Would you? That would be perfect.'

Clemmie was poised with her pen as Verity gave her the number.

'I'll let you know one way or the other as soon as I've spoken to her. Now, you enjoy your afternoon tea and before you leave you do have to go and see the puffins. It's unbelievable when you see them for the first time…'

'I will and thank you.'

Clemmie placed the pen and pad back in the pocket of her pinny before returning behind the counter. Verity devoured the finger sandwiches in a matter of minutes and as she sat back in her chair sipping prosecco, she watched the world outside the window pass her by and wondered if Betty Rose could shed any light on the postcard from the past. And if she could, what exactly she might say.

Chapter Five

An hour later, Verity walked towards the bay and kicked off her shoes. Paddling at the water's edge she embraced the sunshine that had finally followed the dismal weather of the morning. She looked across to the lighthouse that was guarding the scenic coastline and wondered whether it was still in use. She began to walk across the bay towards the sand dunes, which led to a coastal path that meandered to the top of the cliffs where the puffins could be found.

Thankful for the sea breeze, Verity powered her way to the top of the cliff and stood in amazement. Clemmie was right. She hadn't seen anything quite like it before. Thousands of comical creatures, each in its glossy black dinner jacket with a crisp white bib and a brightly coloured, parrot-like bill, and with orange feet, covered the rocky cliffs. A sign informed visitors that they couldn't touch or feed the puffins, and it was clear that this part of the island belonged to the puffins and the puffins only. Verity was in awe. Perching on the edge of a rock she pulled out her phone and began to video them so she could remember this moment. This was the first time she'd ever seen a puffin up close. They were incredible. She sat still, watching the adults return from fishing at sea, sand eels hanging from their mouths, to feed their pufflings. She could happily have sat and watched them for hours, but she wanted to stretch her legs and she knew exactly where to head. She was curious to discover the real-life Cliff Top Cottage, which, according to her map research, should be just a little further on up the cliff path.

The most sought-after cottage on the island (according to Granny's stories) stood three hundred metres above the sea with fantastic views of the Puffin Island coastline, including Blue Water Bay and Castaway Cove, where lobster boats and fishing boats bobbed on the waves. Fish were clearly plentiful in these waters, something welcomed by puffins and locals alike.

Verity took the gravel track towards the top of the cliff, excited to be greeted by the most gorgeous-looking cottage, just like in her granny's stories...but was surprised to find there wasn't much picturesque about Cliff Top Cottage. In fact, it looked as if it had been abandoned years ago.

It definitely lacked tender loving care. The garden around it was a little overgrown, the front door and windows rotting away but miraculously still intact. Verity knew this could be transformed into a place of beauty as it once had been, according to descriptions from the past. Knowing she was trespassing but too curious to pass up this chance, she walked up to the front window. Surely it wasn't possible for anyone to still be living here? Cupping her hands against the grimy window she peered into the gloom.

The room was sparsely furnished. A battered old sofa and an armchair stood beside a rug in front of an open fire. Verity nearly jumped out of her skin when she noticed an elderly gentleman asleep in the chair, a flat cap on his head and what looked like a glass of whisky in his hand. She took a deep breath and watched him for a second. Then, just as her pulse began to settle, his eyes flicked opened and he stared straight at her. She stumbled backwards as his eyes widened, and before she could do anything he was up and out of the chair. The look on his face wasn't welcoming but she couldn't blame him. She shouldn't have been snooping. Within seconds the front door had been flung open and the man was charging towards her. 'You tourists think you can come onto my land whenever you like but you can't!' He pointed to the wooden sign hammered into the ground. 'Private Property, Keep Off. Just like it says. Now shoo.' His voice was gruff, and he wasn't anywhere near as welcoming as the other islanders she had met.

Verity began apologising profusely. 'I'm so sorry, I was just curious to see this place.'

'The path is that way.' He dismissed her with his hand. 'You people think you can wander up here but this is my space. You tourists have the rest of the island. Be on your way.'

He stormed back inside and shut the door with a slam. Verity was thankful it didn't fall from its hinges.

She knew she'd overstepped the mark but she hadn't meant any harm, and there was a way of speaking to people. Turning and walking away she dared to look back over her shoulder. The man was standing in the window watching her. Verity couldn't help wondering what had happened here. Cliff Top Cottage had featured many times in the stories her grandmother had shared. Henrietta had described it as cosy, with oak beams and a log fire, certainly nothing like the dilapidated cottage of today. In her stories the wild cliff top flowers grew all around, and a garden gate led to a lawned garden with a patio area to the side of the cottage for sitting in during the summer months. Racking her brain, Verity couldn't remember who her granny had said lived there. Still, those stories were from a long time ago and it was possible the previous occupants had moved on since. Verity knew the upkeep of any property was a massive commitment and cost. The man who'd shooed her away looked as if he might be in his seventies, so perhaps age had prevented him from returning it to its former glory. Or maybe he liked how unwelcoming the property had become. It was obvious from the few seconds she'd spent in his company that he didn't welcome visitors.

'But what a view,' she murmured, welcoming the light breeze as she headed back towards the harbour. This might be her only chance to wake up to this view so she made the decision there and then: she would drive the van down to Blue Water Bay and park for the night. She'd watch the sunset and enjoy every second sleeping under the stars, even if it was only for a few hours before she drove back over the causeway. Taking a breather, she sat down on a rock. She took one look at the puffins, then briefly closed her eyes and tilted her face up to the warmth of the sun.

She suddenly felt as if she were being pushed. Her eyes sprang open and she screamed, then made a strangled noise as she was met with a pair of huge eyes. A wet tongue swiped across her face and two gigantic paws pounded against her chest, causing her to lose her balance.

'What the…' she shouted, stumbling backwards. 'Get off me. Get this dog under control.'

There was a sound of footsteps hurrying along the path. Verity was trying to get up off the ground and to keep the dog licks at bay. The dog managed to give her another lick before his lead was clicked into place.

'Jimmy, get down.' Sam attempted to reprimand him but all he could do was laugh. 'I'm so sorry. I've tried to tell him he can't go kissing every new girl in town, but in our defence, he's just a friendly guy.' There was a spark of humour and a glint in Sam's eye.

Verity's mouth fell open. She knew she was catching flies but she couldn't help it. Here he was again, Sam Wilson, making her heart thump twice as fast as he extended his hand to pull her up. She was secretly pleased. 'He's your dog?'

'He is, and, as you can see, he's a little excitable. But don't worry, he's very friendly.'

'I know he's friendly, I've never received so many kisses in such a short time.' Verity smiled as she ruffled the fur on top of the dog's head.

'I find that hard to believe.' Sam caught her eye, and the blush upon her cheeks darkened slightly. 'But we're sorry, are you okay?'

'Dented pride and dirty shorts, but I'll live.'

'Glad to hear it. We couldn't have death by kisses on our conscience, could we, Jimmy?'

The giant chocolate curly labradoodle danced around for a moment before sitting down by Sam's side.

'He's the size of a Shetland pony. Who exactly is taking who for a walk?'

Sam laughed. 'He's taking me. Let me introduce you properly. Jimmy, this is Verity, Verity, this is Jimmy…Jimmy Chew…because he likes to chew shoes and usually no shoes are safe. He's seven months old and still growing into his paws.'

Verity stared. 'Wow! Seven months. Look at the size of him.'

'He's like a mini human but has the most lovable nature.'

'I can't argue with that.'

'He doesn't normally take such an instant liking to just anyone, he's got good taste. Isn't that right, Jimmy?'

Verity noticed Sam biting his lip to suppress a smile.

'Clearly,' she replied, embracing the playful banter.

'And what are you doing on this part of the island?'

'I wanted to see the puffins before I left.'

'They're an incredible sight. What did you think of them?'

'So fluffy and I love their waddle.'

'They're certainly special. I'm heading that way, do you want to walk with us?' Sam pointed down the path.

Verity looked between Sam and Jimmy. 'Okay, as long as I don't get swept off my feet again.'

'I can't promise that,' replied Sam. The air crackled between them.

As they began walking, Verity looked back over her shoulder towards the cottage. 'Who lives there?'

Sam followed her gaze, and she was sure he bristled.

'Pete,' he replied. 'He looks after the wildlife on the island and is in charge of the puffin census.'

'Puffin Pete,' said Verity. 'I bet he's not heard that before.'

Sam smiled. 'Have you ever thought of being a stand-up comic?'

'Humour is one of my talents... You're kidding about a puffin census, right?'

'Nope, the puffins get counted every year. It used to be every five years but now they keep a closer eye on the colony so they can see what's changed season to season. It allows them to make important decisions to help protect the puffins.'

'Because with no puffins it would just be called "The Island". But how do you know which ones have already been counted? They all look the same.'

'I'm not quite sure. Pete is in charge of the census, overseeing the rangers.'

'How many rangers?'

'Usually around six to ten.'

'I've just had the pleasure of meeting Pete.' Knowing how close-knit communities could be, Verity decided not to share that it wasn't the best first impression.

Sam nodded. 'We don't cross paths that often as we don't have anything to do with one another.' He looked as if he was going to add something but had changed his mind.

They carried on walking in silence. As soon as they set foot on the sand of Blue Water Bay, Sam unclipped Jimmy's lead. He woofed as he chased the gulls off the sand and followed them straight into the water.

'I wouldn't like to be in your shoes, trying to get him in the bath. Have you ever tried one of those portable pet showers? I've got one in my van.'

'I'm lucky if I have any shoes left, at the rate he likes to chew them! Why do you have a portable pet shower?'

'I didn't like the idea of not knowing when my next shower would be, so I pinched one from work.'

Sam raised his eyebrows.

'I'm a veterinary assistant,' she filled in quickly. 'Well, I was up until yesterday. Now I'm officially unemployed, but by choice. I've thrown caution to the wind, rented out my house and am travelling with my friend Ava for the next six months.'

'Oh right. I think you mentioned you were going to Amsterdam?'

'Yes, that's right. I'm catching the ferry early tomorrow morning.'

'Make sure you stock up on sickbags and don't eat anything after midnight.'

'Good advice. Look at Jimmy! He's heading towards that boat. Is that the restaurant?'

'It is, The Sea Glass Restaurant, the glass-bottomed boat. Always making waves.'

'I see what you did there.'

'The interior is just as pretty as the outside. It's got a nautical theme – polished wood, a blue and white colour scheme, a grand piano, and a private terrace at the bow with stunning views of the lighthouse, the ocean and the gorgeous harbour.'

'You sound like an advert.'

Sam grinned. 'I never miss an opportunity to sing its

praises. It's a shame you aren't around a little longer to sample the experience, but we're fully booked tonight.'

'We?'

'I'm the proprietor. I renovated the old boat. It once belonged to my grandfather and when I was eighteen it was given to me by my mother. She called it junk and couldn't wait to get rid of it. I knew exactly what I wanted to do with it – create a floating restaurant. It's now booked up three months in advance and even a few celebrities frequent the place.'

'I bet your mum is proud of what you've achieved.'

'I wouldn't think so.' Sam stared out towards the restaurant, his cryptic comment leaving an awkward silence.

Verity sensed that his relationship with his mother might just be as unhealthy as the one she had with hers. Jimmy was now clambering out of the water and up onto the ramp. After shaking his body several times, he barked at the restaurant door. The door opened and a woman appeared. She waved across at Sam before letting Jimmy inside.

'Wife, girlfriend?' asked Verity, the words leaving her mouth before she could stop them.

'That's Robin, owner of Beachcomber Bakery. She's dropping off the freshly baked bread for this evening.'

'I'm a little disappointed that I won't get to eat at the restaurant.' What Verity didn't add to that was that she was also a little disappointed that it was more than likely she wouldn't see Sam again before she left, if he was working at the restaurant tonight. 'I'm leaving in the early hours of the morning. I was thinking I'd park my van here tonight in the meantime.' She pointed to a parking space just in front of the bay.

Sam looked up at the sky. 'Now the black clouds have moved on, you should have the perfect view. It's an amazing view at night, the harbour is lit up with fairy lights along with The Sea Glass Restaurant, it sparkles like diamonds on the water. I bet you won't get any sleep – the view will be just breathtaking.'

'Then I'll try and sleep on the ferry tomorrow. It's going to be a very long crossing.'

'If you need a coffee and an early morning croissant, the Cosy Kettle is open throughout the night because of the early morning crossings.' He pointed towards the coffee hut on the edge of the bay.

'I'll remember that.'

They both stared out to sea in a contemplative silence before Verity finally spoke. 'It's been lovely meeting you, Sam,' she said. 'Maybe I'll call back at the island on my return journey and book a table at your restaurant.'

'Maybe you should do that.'

Savouring the moment, Verity briefly closed her eyes and inhaled his woody, masculine aroma, which made her heart beat a little faster. When she opened her eyes, his blue gaze flashed towards her.

'It must be nice knowing where you belong, especially in a place like this,' she murmured. 'I bet you want for nothing.'

'I wouldn't quite say that,' he replied, running a hand through his hair, but he didn't elaborate.

'I'd best be off.' Reluctantly, Verity turned and walked away with a little sashay. She suspected he was watching, so she gave him something to remember her by. When she dared to look back over her shoulder, she saw she'd been right. Her heart thrummed with adrenalin, a feeling she hadn't experienced in ages. For the first time since planning her trip, Verity found she didn't want tomorrow to come. In fact, she wished she could stay on the island for a little longer.

Chapter Six

Verity was parked for the night in a great spot overlooking the harbour. It was such a different view from her living room back home, which overlooked nothing more than number 50 on the other side of the street. For a little under an hour, she'd been sitting in a deck chair in front of the van, hugging a brew, staring out over the water and thinking what a difference a day makes.

The whole place had a sense of calm about it and for the first time in ages she felt happy being exactly where she was. She was no longer on edge, she could walk about freely without feeling anxious about bumping into her ex, she'd left the old street behind, and now, without the constant reminder of the ex's betrayal, he was beginning to slip firmly out of her thoughts. Puffin Island was already beginning to heal her.

She planned to walk over to the pub a little after seven p.m. but for now she carried on people-watching. Along the beach children were running in and out of the sea, squealing with delight as the cold water splashed against their legs. Further on people dived from the boats that were moored a little way from the harbour and there was activity around the lighthouse – it looked like some sort of lifeboat drill. Verity couldn't believe she was sitting here. She wondered once again what had brought her granny to Puffin Island in the first place. She wished she could find out more about the past. She hoped Clemmie would be in contact as soon as she'd spoken with her grandmother.

Meanwhile, she wondered if there was any other way to find out the names of the residents of the island in 1972, in case there was an islander whose initial was W. She also thought of Pete. He wasn't the most approachable character but maybe she could blame that on herself for being nosey. He seemed around the right age to have been here that summer. Perhaps, if she took a stroll back to the cottage and apologised again, he might soften and they could chat about the postcard. But the more she thought about it, the more she feared a second shouting-match, and she decided against it. No, her main hope was Betty, as Clemmie had been adamant that she was a person who remembered everything.

Taking the opportunity to enjoy the warmth of the sun, Verity grabbed a small bucket from the back of the van and kicked off her shoes. She wanted to hunt for keepsakes along the sandy bay to remind herself of her first visit – first, because she already knew she would be back one day. It was like a treasure hunt, walking up and down the shore edge, scanning it for glass gems. Dozens of beautiful sea gems sparkled at her. It reminded her of a time her granny had taken her to the beach. They spent the afternoon on the sand and after a picnic they'd collected a bucket full of sea glass. To Verity's amazement, her granny had turned those gems into a bracelet. She glanced at her wrist, which that very bracelet still clasped. She treasured that day; it would always be one she remembered. Even though her granny had passed a long time back, she was suddenly awash with emotion. In this moment, here on Puffin Island, she felt so close to her.

———

A couple of hours later, Verity had changed her clothes. She opted for a simple striped summer dress that stopped above her knees, along with a loose cardigan, and slipped her feet into her battered white Converse. She enjoyed the walk to The Olde Ship Inn, chirping 'Good evening' to everyone she passed. Outside the pub, the wooden tables and benches were full of people enjoying the last of the sun before the warmth ebbed away. The clear azure sky was a perfect backdrop for the traditional pub, with Blue Water Bay in the distance, and Verity took a moment to stop and admire the view before stepping inside. The pub was exactly as she'd imagined it, full of nautical charm and olde-worlde character, with its low oak-beamed ceilings and open fireplace, which no doubt roared all day every day in the height of winter. The ambience was perfect, a proper pub, with tourists drinking the local beer and dogs sprawled out at their owners' feet under the tables.

She immediately spotted Amelia at the bar, serving customers. Amelia beamed and waved her towards an empty stool at the end of the bar.

'We've saved you a seat here next to Clemmie.'

'We're glad you've made it,' Clemmie said warmly.

'A night in the local? I wasn't going to miss that.' Verity climbed onto the high bar stool as Amelia slid a couple of beers over the bar towards them. 'Puffin Island beer, not just for puffins, and on the house. I've already cleared it with the owners, Cora and Dan. I know your trip to Puffin Island is a short one, but have you enjoyed your day?'

'Thank you, that's very kind. I have! And this is the perfect end to my visit. I actually don't want to go home. Not that I'm going home for six months, but you know what I mean.'

'This place captures the heart,' agreed Amelia. 'I don't want to wake up anywhere else in the world. I see you've parked over at the bay. You've picked a great spot.'

'I didn't know what to expect when I made my detour this morning but I can honestly say that, apart from being sick on the ferry, I've really enjoyed my time here. Let me make a toast…'

They all held up their glasses. 'Mine is water, I can't drink on the job otherwise I'll be sacked,' Amelia said, looking over at Cora and Dan, who were setting up some sort of audio equipment in the corner of the pub.

Clemmie leaned in towards Verity and whispered, 'Don't believe her, I'm sure there's a vodka in there.'

'A toast to a fabulous day and a stunning island with breathtaking scenery. Thank you for making me feel so welcome. I already feel like I've made new friends.' They clinked their glasses together.

'You have made new friends. That's what I love about this place – year after year visitors come back here and we see the same familiar faces because they just love our little island so much. We hope you'll be back.'

'I will, I already know it.' It had crossed Verity's mind a number of times throughout the day that she could extend her visit, but knowing that Ava would be making her way to Amsterdam, and that she herself had technically gate-crashed Ava's adventure in the first place, she felt she couldn't let her friend down. But there was still a tiny niggle in the back of her mind. She wanted very much to throw caution to the wind and stay for at least a few more days.

'Are you hungry? Can I grab you anything before I go and serve the other customers? There's lots of delicious dishes – seafood platters, locally sourced fillet steak, and of course the pub's speciality, fish and chips.'

'I could smell the fish and chips as soon as I walked through the door. I'll go for that.'

'I'll have the same,' added Clemmie.

Amelia wrote the order down on the pad before taking it through to the kitchen, then she disappeared to the other end of the bar where she continued to serve drinks.

'It's lovely to see you again,' said Verity, turning towards Clemmie. 'I'm assuming this is your local?'

'It is – and tonight you're in for a treat.' She pointed towards the makeshift stage that had been erected in one corner. 'It's open mic night. It's usually very entertaining. There's everything from comedians to singers.'

'And we have a prime viewing spot right here. How good is the talent?'

Clemmie looked dubious. 'Sometimes it can blow you away and sometimes it's that bad you wish you were blown away.'

Verity laughed. 'Do you ever get up there?'

Clemmie shook her head. 'No, I'm the shy and retiring type.'

Amelia interrupted as she walked past. 'Do not believe a word she says. There's nothing shy or retiring about that one.'

'Hey,' replied Clemmie, pretending to look hurt.

'How do you two know each other?' asked Verity, admiring their jovial friendship.

'Our great-grandmothers were friends, our grandmothers were friends, and our mothers were friends. Unsurprisingly, that friendship has slipped down to the next generation – and of course, with such a small population on the island, I can't get rid of her.' Clemmie gave Amelia a wink.

'I heard that!'

'That's just wonderful.' Verity thought about her own family. Her grandparents were the most stable people in her life and she'd loved them dearly. They'd taken over her upbringing from a young age when her mother showed more interest in her social life then in caring for her. By the time she went to school it was her grandparents who took her there, and to her extra-curricular activities, and soon their home became hers on a more permanent basis. From time to time she stayed with her mother, usually when she'd been let down by yet another man. In her early teens that sense of abandonment had had a huge impact on her self-esteem, not helped by her mother's determination to keep secret the identity of Verity's father. Verity could only assume he was a married man with his own family or was serving time at His Majesty's pleasure. Of course, she had asked her grandmother about her father, but Granny had been just as much in the dark as she was. Verity had done a DNA test but it was still sitting on the Ancestry website, as there had never been a match. So her father remained very much a mystery.

'I bet living in the island is just like a close-knit family.'

'It is. The island is that small that everyone knows everyone and we can't avoid each other. We aren't without our difficult relationships and family feuds, of course, but I suppose any family falls out occasionally…and in a time of crisis we all band together.'

Verity wondered what Clemmie meant by 'difficult relationships', but just then Amelia placed a plate of fish and chips in front of each of them, and the conversation moved on.

'Woah! Look at the size of the fish. What are you feeding them around these parts? It looks more like a whale.'

'Fresh from the bay this morning.' Amelia grinned. 'We often joke that we must have the fattest puffins around these parts, what with the size of the fish.'

'I've seen the puffins this afternoon. I couldn't believe how many you have here.'

'Thousands and thousands. It's not called Puffin Island for no reason!' Amelia said, grinning as she went to clear the plates from a table in the far corner.

'And I met the man who lives in Cliff Top Cottage. I think I upset him.'

Clemmie raised an eyebrow. 'Pete. Why, what did you do?'

'I thought the cottage was abandoned so I peered through the window.'

'And you survived?' She laughed. 'Pete's harmless but he likes his privacy.'

'What's the story there?' asked Verity. 'Does he actually live in Cliff Top Cottage all by himself?'

'He does. He's lived there all of his life.' Clemmie stabbed the chunkiest chip with her fork.

'Alone?'

Clemmie nodded. 'Never married or had children. He was the island's vet but has now retired and the nearest practice is over at Sea's End, which can be very trying if you can't cross the causeway. But Pete is an animal person through and through. He adores those puffins, watches them for hours. And if any domestic animals are poorly, he'll go out of his way to get them back to good health.'

'The cottage doesn't look how I remember it.'

'"Remember it"?' quizzed Clemmie. 'I thought this was your first visit?'

'It is. I remember it from my granny's stories when I was a child. In her tales it was beautiful, the most sought-after cottage on the island. Everyone wanted to live there.'

'Your granny was right. My grandmother told me the same. But sadly it's been dilapidated for as long as I can remember. For some reason, it seems Pete just fell out of love with his home. He may like his privacy up on the cliff but he's still a big part of this island and, believe me, if he has something to say, he doesn't hold back. His voice is heard within the community if he wants to put his point across.'

'I'd love to have met your grandmother,' said Verity.

'Which means you must come back and visit us again. I've messaged her about the postcard. As soon as she replies, I'll let you know. She can bake the best scones and cakes but trying to get her to answer a text is a totally different ballgame. Doesn't like any sort of technology. It took me the best part of a year to talk her into trying an electronic till instead of writing every order on a piece of paper and skewering it.'

'But you still have an old-fashioned till in the tearoom.' Verity remembered the till and how vintage it looked.

'The electronic till lasted a week. Puffin Island is prone to power cuts and on the very first week the till went down – so we had to return to our prehistoric accounting method of balancing the till at the end of the day. You can imagine my grandmother's delight. We've never changed back again. Still skewering those receipts and using a calculator.' Clemmie rolled her eyes.

'Clemmie told me about the postcard. How intriguing,' said Amelia as she rejoined them, folding her arms and leaning on the bar. 'Tell me everything.'

Clemmie shot Verity a playful but warning look. 'You just remember that whatever you say now could end up in a book.'

'That sounds like it's happened before,' said Verity.

'On many occasions,' replied Clemmie.

Verity retold the story of finding the long-lost postcard and how it had led her to Puffin Island. 'And I just thought that maybe I could track down who'd sent it. But the more I think about it, the more I suspect it will remain a mystery.'

'And there was a secret,' added Clemmie.

'What kind of secret?' asked Amelia, totally absorbed in the conversation.

'That we don't know, but the postcard suggests the secret was too much to bear.'

'Do we think it was a resident? Had your granny visited on holiday?' Amelia was throwing out the questions that Verity had already asked herself.

'Again, we don't know.'

Amelia looked like she was thinking hard. 'Who's our oldest resident? It has to be Betty. What she doesn't know about the comings and goings of this island isn't worth knowing and she remembers everyone.' Amelia looked at Clemmie.

'I said exactly the same thing,' Clemmie replied. 'Not that we're implying my grandmother is nosey and makes everything her business…' Both women were quiet for a second.

'But that's exactly what we're implying,' they chorused in unison, making Verity laugh.

'And what about the record book?' suggested Amelia.

'I thought about that, but surely that stopped long before 1972?'

'What's the record book?' asked Verity.

'It was a record that anyone coming on or off the island used to sign,' Clemmie replied. 'I suppose it helped to count how many visitors came to the island each year. But it ceased many years back, as visitor numbers increased, so we're probably clutching at straws.'

'What are you going to do about this postcard?' asked Amelia.

Verity shrugged. 'I don't think I'll ever get to know who sent it or what the story is behind it.'

'This place must have meant something special to your granny if she told you so many stories from her time here.'

'You're absolutely right. Even after all these years there's still a framed picture of the puffins hanging in our living room. The same picture that was on the postcard. It's been hanging there for as long as I can remember.'

'The plot thickens.' Amelia put her hands on her heart. 'Maybe it was some sort of forbidden love, just like Romeo and Juliet.'

'When the postcard came, and I realised it was the same picture, I took the picture out of its frame. It was signed "W" in the same hand as on the postcard, and also dated 1972.'

'This is full of intrigue.' Amelia's eyes were wide.

'Well, at least I've visited Puffin Island and, in a matter of hours, fallen in love with it. I've had a chance to see for myself why my granny loved this place so much.'

Just then a voice was heard over the microphone in the corner. They swung their heads in the direction of the makeshift stage. Cora was standing there with a smile on her face. 'Welcome to open mic night at The Olde Ship Inn. Sit back, enjoy a beer and the entertainment. First up, we have a stand-up comedian who is holidaying here all the way from Cornwall. Please put your hands together and give our first act, Cam, a very warm welcome.'

The pub burst into rapturous applause as a confident-looking man took to the stage.

After finishing their food, Verity and Clemmie whirled around on their stools, drinks in hand, and continued to watch the entertainment.

'How often does this happen?' asked Verity.

'Once a month. It's a very popular night amongst the locals and the tourists.'

'It's a very talented island,' observed Verity, finishing her drink a while later. 'And I have to say I'm feeling very tipsy. No more for me.' She glanced at her watch to find that time had flown by. Knowing she had to be up in the early hours, she needed to head off soon and try to get a few hours' sleep. 'I've enjoyed every second of tonight, but I suppose I need to make a move.'

'Believe me, you need one more drink for the road.' Amelia was insistent. 'There's only one more act and it's the act that the whole island is waiting for.' Amelia nodded towards the door, which had just swung open. A group of giggling girls sauntered into the pub and walked towards the makeshift stage. 'That's the fan club.'

'Fan club?' queried Verity.

'Every open mic night they arrive from Sea's End.'

'But why?' asked Verity.

Amelia nodded towards Cora. 'Because the last act is not to be missed.'

The girls began to whoop and cheer as Cora stepped up to the microphone. 'I don't think this last act needs any introduction.' She smiled at the girls. 'And open mic night would not be the same without the talent of Puffin Island's very own singer-songwriter. Please welcome to the stage the gorgeous and uber-talented Sam Wilson.'

Verity's mouth fell open. She hadn't been expecting to see Sam again before she left the island. The crowd went wild and, as a thought suddenly hit her, she turned towards Clemmie.

'Wilson.' Verity's eyes widened. 'W... Wilson begins with a W.' There was excitement in her voice. 'Is it possible...? Does Sam have any relatives on the island?'

Clemmie shook her head. 'No father, and his grandfather was killed in a tragic accident before he was born.'

Verity's excitement at a possible lead deflated. 'Oh well,' she said, trying not to let her disappointment show, 'it was just a thought.'

She turned back to the stage and watched the pub go wild. Like his screaming fan club, she couldn't take her eyes off Sam. She knew he looked super sexy in a suit, but here he was looking just as good, if not better, sporting a casual look: a snug, faded vintage T-shirt that showed off every muscle of his chest and arms, tight denim jeans and battered boat shoes.

'Bloody hell, he fits into that T-shirt perfectly,' Verity mused. 'Sex on legs – and he sings.' The words had left her mouth before she could stop them.

'Another tourist in love,' teased Clemmie, leaning in and nudging her elbow.

Raking his hand through his shaggy blond hair, Sam sat on a stool and rested the guitar he carried on his knee.

'He might rub people up the wrong way sometimes, but my gosh, he's super sexy. Women dream about running their fingers through that hair,' whispered Amelia.

'Or getting their hands on his body,' added Clemmie.

'What do you mean, he rubs people up the wrong way?' asked Verity.

But Amelia didn't answer. Sam strummed his guitar and again the girls screamed.

'They think he's the Harry Styles of Puffin Island.' Clemmie grinned.

He strummed again and looked up from under his fringe at the audience. As he scanned the room his eyes met Verity's and every inch of her body erupted in uncontrollable goosebumps. She already knew the main reason she would return to Puffin Island; it might have something to do with those goddamn sexy blue eyes, which were currently locked with hers. And then there it was again, that wolfish grin that had her heart racing faster than a Formula One driver completing a qualifying lap. 'Your Sam Wilson fantasies are written all over your face,' quipped Clemmie, clearly noting that Verity's eyes had not left him since he took the stage.

'I can't deny the thoughts I have right now,' said Verity with a laugh. 'Like, how many times a week must you work out to get a body that toned?' She barely knew the man but from the moment she'd spotted him outside the greasy spoon he'd crept more and more into her thoughts. She wanted to know all about him.

As he began to sing, the whole pub fell silent, lost in the mesmerising talent that was Sam Wilson. All eyes were fixed on him. The group of girls in the corner were holding up the torches on their phone and swaying back and forth as if they were at an arena concert.

Verity tilted her head and dreamily put her hand on her heart. 'He's definitely singing to me.'

'You and every other girl in the pub are thinking exactly the same,' jollied Amelia.

Every now and then Sam's eyes danced in Verity's direction and she found herself trying to tame the smile on her face. The air was charged and she felt a buzz under her skin, her body parts suddenly waking up after being fast asleep for what seemed like years. Sam Wilson had got her attention, and the feeling of wanting was definitely back.

'He should be a professional singer.'

Clemmie agreed. 'He should be, but his true love is his restaurant. He lives and breathes The Sea Glass Restaurant and in five minutes' time he'll be back over there.'

'Does he have a girlfriend?' Verity was intrigued. Of course, she'd checked for a wedding ring the minute she set eyes on him at the greasy spoon café. There wasn't one, but surely a man like Sam must be loved up with someone.

There was a glance between Amelia and Clemmie that didn't go unnoticed by Verity. 'What? Tell me!' she insisted.

Amelia shrugged at Clemmie, waiting for some acknowledgement that it was okay to share whatever it was they knew.

'Sam's decided that he's better off on his own, even though every girl in this pub thinks they're in with a chance.'

'And why would someone decide they're better off on their own?' Verity thought about her own life and why she was here and realised she shouldn't be quick to judge.

Before she arrived on Puffin Island, being on her own for the rest of her life had looked like a very desirable option. 'He's had his heart broken, hasn't he?'

Clemmie nodded.

'Islander or tourist?'

'Tourist turned islander, but unfortunately Puffin Island wasn't enough for her. She's been gone for over a year now.'

'And does she have a name?'

'Alice,' shared Amelia.

Sam began singing the chorus, delivering the words from the heart, making everyone in the pub believe them. He was singing about heartache and for a second Verity thought she saw sadness flash across his eyes. The song resonated with her and she hung on every word, remembering how, when she discovered Richard's betrayal, it had felt as if a huge knife had been stabbed through her heart. Then she had been at an all-time low, thinking her life had ended, questioning herself, especially after the unkind words of someone who should have wanted to protect her at all costs – her mother. But it was true, time was a great healer, and even though she was still on that healing journey, she no longer wanted to hit the self-destruct button. Richard had shown exactly who he was, and that wasn't her person; her person would be honest, would look out for her needs, and they'd encourage each other's growth. Thanks to her short visit to Puffin Island, it felt as though brighter days would soon be coming. The moment she drove across that causeway, she'd realised she had full control of her life, thoughts and feelings.

Still not taking her eyes off Sam, Verity sipped her drink.

When he finished, he looked up from under his fringe, his blue eyes briefly locking on hers. There it was again, that burst of adrenalin that was electrifying her heart.

'He's looking at you.' Amelia gave Verity a playful poke in the back.

'Don't be ridiculous, he was just looking in this direction,' she replied, playing it down. But something inside her told her they had just shared a moment.

Standing up to rapturous applause, Sam bowed, smiled and once more caught Verity's eye before disappearing out of the back door.

'Wow, he can really sing.' Verity was still looking at the closed door, a part of her hoping he would walk back through so she could tell him how fantastic he was, hopefully without sounding like another groupie. 'And look at them all,' she added, glancing towards his fan club.

'Can you believe they travel in for just one song?' said Clemmie.

'The song was beautiful. It was captivating.' Verity was still in awe.

'He writes them himself. Very talented individual. He always finishes off open mic night for Cora and Dan.' Clemmie twirled back round on her chair. 'I suppose I'd better settle my bill and head to bed. I'm up at the crack of dawn, ready for the breakfast run at the tearoom. Where's Amelia disappeared to?'

'She's just gone out the back door. And I suppose I should try and bed down for at least a few hours before I go.' Verity heard her voice wobble.

'Aww, don't get emotional.' Clemmie leaned in and gave her a hug.

'I don't know what's come over me,' she replied, fanning a napkin in front of her face.

'It'll be a combination of things: the postcard, finding out we're actually real, knowing this place held a special place in your granny's heart. She's probably even had a drink at this bar.'

That thought had already crossed Verity's mind. She'd also pictured her granny ambling down Lighthouse Lane, collecting sea glass from the beach, paddling at the water's edge.

'It feels a little surreal. I really do hope your grandmother might remember her.'

'We hope so and you'll be back.'

'I will, I know I will.'

Amelia had returned to the bar. Clemmie paid her bill then turned towards Verity, giving her one last squeeze. 'Have a safe journey and I'll be in touch.' She headed out.

'I need to pay my bill, too,' said Verity.

Amelia grinned. 'Your bill has been taken care of.'

'Oh no, did Clemmie pick up the tab?' Verity looked towards the door but it had just swung shut behind her new friend. 'I didn't thank her. That was very kind, I wasn't expecting that.'

'It had been taken care of long before Clemmie left.'

'Huh? I don't understand.'

Amelia leaned in towards her and gave her a delightful gaze. 'You'll be the envy of every girl on this island. Sam settled your bill.'

'Why would he do that?' Verity's pulse began to race and she couldn't stop smiling.

'Because it's a nice gesture...or did I miss something?'

Amelia narrowed her eyes at Verity, who shrugged and repressed a smile.

'Mmm, how long have you been on this island? You're already crushing on one of the locals, and it seems like it's reciprocated.'

'You've either got it or you haven't.' Verity laughed. Getting involved with a sexy restaurant owner was not part of her plan when she left Staffordshire. Even a fling on a very small island was probably not a good idea. But Sam had given her an all-over warm, fuzzy feeling, she'd liked flirting with him, and of course it helped that he was drop-dead gorgeous. And when he gave her that wolfish grin of his, it had made her wonder what it would be like to spend the night in the arms of Sam Wilson.

'It's a lovely gesture.'

'I've worked behind this bar for a fair few years and the only bill I've ever known him to settle is his own.'

'That little piece of information is good to know.'

'I still think there's something you aren't telling me.' The sound of curiosity was evident in Amelia's tone.

'I have no clue what you're talking about.' Verity jumped down from the stool. 'Now give me a hug.'

'Look at you, you can't stop smiling.' Amelia lifted up the bar hatch, walked towards her and stepped into her arms. 'Whilst you're travelling the world we'll try and uncover the mystery of the postcard, but I've got a feeling you'll be back very soon.'

'I think you may be right. Thank you for this evening. I'll keep in touch.'

Verity followed the crowd out of the pub. Outside on the cobbled street everyone dispersed in different directions.

Still smiling, Verity walked back towards the harbour, taking in the amazing view. It was entirely lit up and looked enchanting. Everywhere was peaceful. All she could hear was the gentle lapping of the waves on the sandy bay, their rhythm seeming to slow as the day drew to a close. Fairy lights draped between poles twinkled all along the harbour front, all the way to the Cosy Kettle, where a café board advertised their speciality hot chocolate. From there the lights led on to the small wooden jetty and up to The Sea Glass Restaurant. A couple was walking hand in hand from the floating restaurant to the bay.

The travelling van was parked in a prime position. Verity perched on a rock just in front of it. It was dusk, and in the clear sky one star was shining brighter than the rest. 'I reckon that's you, Granny,' she murmured. 'And I reckon you'll be happy I'm here. But what I want to know is what you were doing here.' Unless Betty could shed any light on the postcard, she might never know.

This time tomorrow she would be in Amsterdam.

Verity was beginning to wonder exactly how she wanted her future to look. Suddenly the thought of going home wasn't filling her with excitement. She knew she wanted more than the same old same old.

Looking at her phone, she saw a text message from Ava, which she'd missed whilst she'd been in the pub.

Not long until our proper adventure begins.

Verity had counted down the days, crossing them off on the calendar that hung on the kitchen wall, wanting nothing more than to get away from the street and her past. All she'd wanted was to breathe freely and begin to live again, without feeling uncomfortable or worrying when she was going to bump into the new residents at number 50. Today she had found that freedom for the first time in ages.

She inhaled the sea air. Even though she was happy, the night held a feeling of sadness, and Verity knew exactly why. In less than twelve hours, Sam and the island had both cast a magic spell over her, and she couldn't get either of them out of her thoughts. She didn't want to leave the island, but tomorrow she would be gone.

Chapter Seven

For the next thirty minutes Verity sat on the rock in front of the van with a blanket wrapped around her shoulders. She knew she should be trying to get some sleep before her early start but she was wide awake, her mind whirling from her time on the island.

'It's a beautiful sight, isn't it?'

Verity jumped up and spun around.

'Sorry, I didn't mean to startle you.' Sam was standing behind her holding two drinks. 'Here, one's for you, hot chocolate. I always get one from the Cosy Kettle on the way home.'

'I didn't hear you at all.'

'You were lost in your own little world there for a moment, I thought you'd be fast asleep by now.'

'I should be but here I am, wondering what tomorrow will bring.'

'Clogs and windmills are my guess.'

Verity smiled, taking the hot chocolate from his hand.

'Thank you, and thank you for paying my bill at the pub, that was a really nice surprise.'

'I thought it was the least I could do, especially as the start of your day wasn't as good as the end.' He pointed to the sky. 'I caught the sunset when I was walking to the pub. It was stunning tonight, the warm blaze of golden orange stretched far and wide as the sun dipped behind the horizon. I never tire of that view. You're lucky you got such a clear night tonight despite that dreadful weather this morning.'

'There are millions of stars. It's so pretty. Do you want to sit?'

Without hesitation Sam slipped next to her on the rock and stared out over the horizon.

'Was it a busy night at the restaurant?' The Sea Glass Restaurant was now in darkness except for the fairy lights trailing the jetty and those entwined around the deck of the boat.

'It's always a busy night, it doesn't matter what time of year it is.'

'I'm not surprised. You're a man of many talents – not only the proprietor of such an exquisite-looking restaurant but also a singer-songwriter.'

'It keeps me sane.' He smiled warmly at her.

'Your fan club seems to like it. You're very popular on this island.'

'Popular with some, not so popular with others.' He didn't look in her direction as he drank his chocolate, instead staring out towards the cliffs.

Verity took a sideward glance at him and studied his face.

'Why not so popular with some?' she asked, taking her chance to satisfy her curiosity about Amelia's comment about Sam earlier, at the bar.

He took a swift glance towards her. 'You can't please all of the people all of the time,' he replied with a shrug. 'Did you enjoy your evening?'

Verity noticed the swift change of conversation, but she went along with it, sensing it wasn't something to pursue right now. 'I did. I'm glad I made the effort to go to the pub. I had a great night. Clemmie and Amelia are so lovely.'

'Very,' he said. 'We all grew up together here on the island so they feel like my annoying little sisters. But Amelia pulls a good pint and Clemmie takes after her grandmother and is a fantastic baker.' Sam pointed to a couple paddling in the shallow waters at the far end of the bay. They held hands, pulling each other along and laughing before they shared a kiss under the moonlight. 'The best time of the day to swim at the bay is after the sun goes down.'

'Very romantic, but probably unsafe and I bet that water is freezing.' Verity gave a tiny shiver at the very thought.

'Bracing is what it is. Have you ever swum in the sea under the moonlight?'

'Isn't that something that just happens in books or the movies?'

'There's nothing more invigorating than swimming late at night. You should try it.' He gestured towards the water.

'Are you suggesting I should try it now?' Verity sounded alarmed. 'I can't get in the sea at this time of night, I'll freeze to death. I'd never make it to Amsterdam.'

Sam laughed. 'Midnight swimming is one to tick off the bucket list.'

'Thankfully I haven't got a list in my bucket, only sea glass, and even if I did, I'm not sure swimming in the sea at this time of night would make the cut.'

'Don't knock it until you try it.' There was a mischievous glint in his eye.

'Are you serious? Are you actually suggesting we get into the water for a swim?'

'Embrace it. Do something spontaneous. Take a risk. Create memories on your last night on Puffin Island.'

'My only night on Puffin Island.'

'One night on Puffin Island, I rest my case.'

'You're incorrigible.'

Verity had to admit, he'd got her thinking. Never in a million years would she do anything spontaneous. Everything in her life had always been planned, even down to the Friday night food shop. Routine was her guiding light, and she realised now it had led her into a rut. Richard had never suggested embracing life the way Sam was now.

'All I can think about is how cold the water will be. I'm shivering just thinking about it.'

'Mind over matter. Cold water improves your mood.'

'And does your mood need improving?' She stared at him. 'I'm not sure mine does.'

'There's always room for improvement.' He tipped her a wink and Verity gave him a playful swipe.

'And what if someone sees us?'

Sam stood up, his eyes glistening as they locked on hers. He took Verity's empty cup and tossed it in a nearby bin, then stretched out his hand.

'You worry too much.'

Verity hesitated for a second. A bright shining star in the sky once again caught her eye. Something was telling her that she'd stumbled upon this island, and adventure, at a time when she needed it most in her life. There was room for lots of new memories. After all, the ones from the last few years hadn't been that memorable. No more sensible Verity – it was time to embrace life and take chances.

Throwing caution to the wind, Verity took his hand. Excitement fizzed inside her as they walked with wide smiles across the sand and along the short jetty towards The Sea Glass Restaurant. Her heart was racing at a pace she hadn't experienced in a long while.

'Do you normally invite strangers for late-night swims?' Verity was intrigued. The girls in the pub had suggested that Sam kept himself to himself, romantically, and to her this was extremely romantic, something you'd do in the first flush of love.

'No,' came his reply.

Walking away from the lights of the bay she dared a sideward glance at him, only to find he was looking back at her with the most kissable smile she'd ever laid eyes on. Her hormones were on fire, that smile had such intensity.

'I swim off here most evenings in the summer. Don't worry, no one can see us from the shore.'

'It's pitch-black. I can't see a thing—'

'Except for the moonlight,' he interrupted. 'And the stars.'

When they reached the back of the restaurant, she saw a private decking area with steps leading down to a secluded lower deck. Sam lifted a small hatch and flicked a switch and immediately a dim light shone across the deck and onto the water.

'Wow! How beautiful.'

'After a busy shift I usually spend half an hour here to wind down before I head home.'

'I think I would too.'

The deck housed a minibar, a table and a small cosy settee with blankets and cushions. It was surrounded by lanterns, and when Sam took a box of matches from the minibar and lit the candles inside them, the deck started to glow.

'It's the perfect setting,' she observed.

'I can happily sit here for hours looking out over the waves.' Sam kicked off his shoes and took off his tie. Within seconds the shirt was off his back.

'What are you doing? You're crazy!'

'It was written in the stars that – in fact, in that big bright one up there'—he pointed—'that I was going to meet a girl with a funny accent…'

'Hey! There's nothing funny about my accent,' she protested. 'And as much as I like to pretend that that star is my loved ones watching over me, that's Polaris, the bright star that is always visible in the night sky.'

He grinned. 'How are you so knowledgeable about stars?' He didn't avert his eyes from hers as he undid his belt and let his trousers fall to the floor. He stood there in his boxer shorts.

Do not look down, do not look down, Verity repeated internally.

'Because I listened at school.'

'Brains as well as beauty.' He grinned.

They were still staring at each other. Verity had to remind herself to breathe.

Finally, she couldn't help it any longer. She glanced down and promptly burst out laughing.

Sam pretended to look offended.

'You have puffins on your boxer shorts!'

'I have twenty pairs of these. They were selling a job lot in the pub and as I live on Puffin Island I thought, "Why not?" It gets better,' he said, turning around and waggling his bum. The boxer shorts had the day of the week written across the backside.

Verity laughed wholeheartedly, then kicked off her shoes.

'In for a penny, in for a pound,' she murmured, thinking there wasn't a cat in hell's chance that Ava would believe a word of what she was going to tell her about her only night on Puffin Island. She slipped out of her dress, and was soon standing in front of him in just her underwear. His eyes still didn't leave hers. The only thought in her head was *Why, oh why, had she chosen the worst possible off-white underwear set?* It had seen better days – but the last thing she'd anticipated that morning was that she'd end the day standing semi-naked in front of the handsomest near-stranger she'd ever seen. Yet here she was, about to take a swim under the stars.

He pointed at some life jackets hanging on the side of the boat. 'Would you like one?'

Verity didn't hesitate; the answer was yes. It wasn't because she wasn't a strong swimmer, more to cover up her shameful underwear and create an opportunity to sneak a glance at his bum again when he turned around. Just like the rest of him, it was toned to perfection.

Sam picked a life jacket off the rack and held it open while she slipped her arms into it. He turned her to face him and zipped it up, then tightened the chest strap. Verity was now standing extremely close to him and their faces were only centimetres apart. 'When you enter the water, your breathing may be all over the place for a moment, so try and keep it controlled and don't panic – it's quite normal. Are you ready? I'll get into the water first.'

Sam climbed down the ladder attached to the side of the boat and Verity watched as he slid his perfect body into the water. He didn't gasp or even flinch, the cold water seemingly having no effect on him whatsoever. He was holding on to the bottom of the ladder, bobbing in the waves, and she saw him take a small, belted loop from the side of the boat and fasten it around his wrist. Then he clipped on another rope that hung over the side of the boat.

'What's that for?' she asked.

'Just a safety measure, so if you get cramp or become too weak you can pull yourself by the rope back towards the boat. It's securely fastened to the deck.'

'You really aren't selling this to me as an enjoyable prospect, you know,' she said, suddenly becoming nervous. 'Cold water swimming is clearly not for the faint-hearted.'

'Once you're in you're going to love every minute of it. Swimming beneath the moon and the stars…what more could you ask for?'

'I'm sure I could come up with something.'

'Less talking, more action. Come on, at this rate the sun will actually be rising by the time you get in.'

'Very funny,' she replied.

Sam moved to the side of the ladder as she descended.

'Now, the only way to do this is to lower yourself in, then keep moving your arms and legs as fast as you can. If you stop or think about it too much, you just won't get in.'

'You're still not selling it to me.'

'How about I make you a promise that when we've finished you can sit next to the firepit and choose a drink of your choice from the bar.'

'Now that sounds more of my sort of invitation.'

'You're stalling!'

'You know me too well.' Verity took a deep breath and braced herself. She remembered a time when she'd been on holiday in Corfu, at a small hotel in the mountains. The scenery was beautiful and the pool inviting. The warmth of the sun had been scorching and she'd jumped straight in the pool, only to jump straight back out after realising it wasn't heated. She spent the next half-hour trying to get warm in the sun. Something was telling her this water was going to be a heck of a lot colder.

'There aren't any sharks, are there?'

'We're on an island in the North East, I don't think there are any sharks.'

'Okay, I was just checking.'

Counting out loud to three, she went to jump but still didn't let go of the ladder. 'I'm going for it this time,' she said, hoping she sounded more confident than she felt. She counted again and, taking herself by surprise, let go of the ladder and slid into the water. She gasped. 'Oh my, oh my, oh my,' she repeated over and over again. 'It's freezing!'

'Cover your neck, you'll start to relax quicker.'

Verity was thrashing around, her arms and legs moving

fast. 'Deep breaths,' said Sam as he pulled her in close and wrapped his body around hers. 'And relax.'

'That does feel better, I have to admit.'

'Now, when you've stopped squirming, look at that view.'

Verity turned herself around, Sam's arms still wrapped around her, their bodies moving together in the water.

Up in the sky the moon shone brightly, reflected in the water.

'Now I don't know whether I should tell you this or not, but this is the shallowest part of the bay. You can actually stand up in the water.'

'You're kidding me, right?'

He grinned. 'As much as I know you want to keep your legs wrapped around my body,' he teased, 'you can stand up. Just like I'm doing.'

Slowly lowering her feet to the bottom, Verity kept hold of him.

He grinned. 'I told you so. Quick, look!' He pointed upwards and the sky lit up as a shooting star streaked across the black velvet of the night. 'Make a wish.'

He hugged her tightly as they watched it disappear.

'What are the chances of that?' she murmured.

'Did you make a wish?'

'I did, but I can't tell you as it might not come true.' Verity knew she'd wasted her wish, as what she'd wished for wasn't going to come true. She couldn't stay on Puffin Island for a while longer. She had promised to meet Ava and she wouldn't let her friend down.

'Let's swim.'

They swam next to each other to the jetty and back

again. To her surprise, Verity found she was enjoying every second of it and the cold water didn't seem that cold at all now.

'I'm actually feeling quite liberated,' she shared, jumping onto Sam's back and wrapping herself around him. The feel of his skin sent new shivers down her spine, but for totally different reasons this time. She leaned backwards and let her head fall into the water. Sam looked over his shoulder, the glint in his eyes catching in the moonlight, his smile melting her heart. This is what she'd imagined life with a partner to be like, fun and spontaneous, full of laughter and experiences and moments like this together.

'See, just up there?' He pointed towards the end of the cove and began walking through the water with Verity still on his back. 'The caves are apparently full of lost treasure. And wait for it... When we get around this side of the restaurant...'

'Woah!'

The bright light from the top of the lighthouse was suddenly shining a path through the sea.

'I could stay out here all night.'

'I knew you'd like it, but we can't stay in too long. I can't have you getting hypothermia on my watch,' he said, swimming back towards the ladder. 'Hold on to my waist whilst I pull us back in with the rope. We're drifting a little.'

Slipping her arms around his waist she closed her eyes for a brief second. It felt good to be so close to someone.

Within seconds they were back up on the private balcony. Sam wrapped a towel around his waist and handed Verity a robe, which she wrapped tightly around her body after taking off her life jacket. She watched Sam attach a gas bottle to the firepit and soon it was spreading a welcoming warmth.

'How did that feel?' he asked.

'I hate to admit it but – amazing. After the initial shock of the cold, I absolutely loved it!'

'I knew you would. It's good for your body and soul. There's something peaceful about swimming in the sea, especially when the sky is as beautiful as it is tonight.'

Verity looked up at the stars. The sky was scattered with their bursts of light. 'The stars are just so scenic. I think I'll remember this night on this island for ever.'

Sam touched her shoulder as he walked past her. 'Let me get you a drink. What would you like?'

'Whatever you're having.'

Sam unlocked a door, which she assumed led into the restaurant. She leaned forward, warming her hands against the dancing flames of the firepit. She couldn't wait to tell Ava all about her trip to Puffin Island. She smiled. This was happiness, feeling relaxed and free.

Five minutes later, Sam returned with a tray and placed it on the table. 'We have a hot mug of coffee, and a whisky. Each will warm you through.' He sat next to her on the sofa and she watched as Sam swirled the amber liquid in the glass and glugged it back. He placed the empty glass back on the tray then picked up the coffee.

'Just like swimming in the sea under the stars, this is also a first for me.' She copied Sam, swirling the liquid around the glass, then swigged it back and immediately scrunched up her face in distaste.

Sam smiled. 'An acquired taste – but it'll warm you through.'

'So what made you want to own a floating restaurant?' Verity asked, picking up her coffee mug.

'My grandfather. He was born and bred on the island and was a keen fisherman. Apparently his dream was to open a floating restaurant on the island, specialising in fresh fish that had been caught that day.'

'Apparently?' she questioned. Amelia and Clemmie had shared that his grandfather had been taken too soon, but she wanted to hear it from Sam himself.

'My grandfather passed away. All I have is what Betty told me – Clemmie's grandmother. She was good friends with my grandfather. They grew up together. He was musical, too,' Sam added softly, looking into his glass.

'I'm really sorry.' Without thinking Verity reached across and touched his knee. 'Is that where you got your musical talent from?'

'I'd like to think so.' He smiled. 'Music is a great escape. I wish I could have met him.'

'It must be really difficult.' Verity had had a great relationship with her grandfather, and it was something she would always cherish. 'What about your parents?'

'My grandmother got pregnant with my mum at the age of fifteen. No doubt at the time it would have been the biggest scandal on the island. My grandparents weren't together by the time the birth came along, which is not surprising, given they were still children themselves, but according to Betty my grandfather took his responsibilities seriously and he used his earnings as a fisherman to provide everything he could for my grandmother and mother for the short time he was alive. He passed when he was only twenty-two, and my grandmother passed away at the age of thirty-five, leaving my mother alone. And then history repeated itself. My mother fell pregnant at an early age, and she didn't stay with my father. He wasn't like my grandfather, though, he never provided anything for her or us. He disappeared off the island one Saturday morning and never came back.'

'Have you ever tried to look for him?'

Sam shook his head. 'He didn't choose me, so why would I ever choose him?' He sounded adamant, but there was sadness in his voice.

'I bet that brought you and your mum closer?'

Sam briefly closed his eyes, stood up and fetched the decanter of whisky. He poured two more glasses.

'You'd think so, wouldn't you? But no, she wouldn't win any mother of the year awards. She moved off the island as soon as I was able to look after myself.' His voice faltered. 'She was barely a mother. If it wasn't for Betty I don't know what I'd have done. She's been a grandmother and mother figure rolled into one for me.'

Verity was silent for a second, thinking of her own situation with her mother. 'I'm sorry you had to go through everything you've been through. It's difficult, isn't it? And yet, somehow, here we are, still standing. Coping and carrying on, doing our best. Even though there's that niggle always in the back of our minds, wondering what we did wrong.'

Sam slightly raised his eyebrows. 'It sounds like you can relate.'

Verity nodded. 'I can, you're not on your own.' She tucked her feet underneath her on the chair as she swallowed a lump in her throat. 'Even now I wonder what the hell I did to make my mother treat me the way she does. Why wasn't I enough? Was it because she was jealous of me, or was it because of my father? If it was, I'd have no idea; she's always kept his identity a secret from me and my grandparents.'

'You don't know anything about him at all?'

Verity shook her head. 'Growing up I asked but she would never talk about it. I've learned to live with it because I know it can consume me if I think about it too much. It can make me sad, sometimes, for days at a time.'

Sam cupped his hand over Verity's and gave it a squeeze.

'It's nice to talk to someone who can relate. I just try to take the positives from the situation. My mother might not have been there for me but my grandparents were the best. In fact, my granny is the reason I'm here.'

Sam smiled. 'Your granny? And here was me thinking it was because you spotted a handsome man outside a greasy spoon and decided to follow him onto a ferry.'

Verity laughed. 'I can neither confirm nor deny.' She knew there was a glint in her eye as she sipped her whisky. 'EW! How can you drink this stuff?'

'You get used to it. Tell me about your granny.'

'When I was growing up she used to tell me stories of this place. I thought it was all make-believe until I discovered a postcard written to her and signed with a W. Apparently the sender couldn't live without her. I had a mad notion that after all these years I could identify who W is or was and discover more about the time my granny spent here and why.'

'If there's one person that will know, it's Betty.'

'That's exactly what Clemmie and Amelia said. But she's away so I won't get to meet her. But Clemmie said she would message me when she got back. I had this daft idea in the pub that one of your relatives might have something to do with the W as your last name is Wilson. But after hearing your story…'

'It would be highly unlikely.' Sam pointed at the star that was still shining brightly. 'I know it sounds silly but I pretend that bright star is my grandfather.'

'It's not silly at all. I pretend it's my granny.'

Sam lightly bumped his shoulder against hers. 'It's a funny old world, isn't it?'

They sat in comfortable silence looking up at the star. Verity was glad they shared an understanding, each of them having been let down by their mother and knowing how difficult that could be to reckon with.

Verity took a sideward glance at Sam and smiled. His company was so easy, yet she was surprised at herself for revealing her own family situation. It was a difficult topic for her to talk about, and a conversation she'd never even had with Richard, despite the years they'd been together, because he just wasn't one for empathy. It was good to finally be able to open up to someone, especially someone who understood exactly how she was feeling.

'You're very lucky to have all this and live in such a beautiful place.'

'I am. There's something special about Puffin Island.'

'I quite agree.' She clinked her glass against his and took

a last swig. 'This should make me sleep for a few hours at least.'

'What time are you leaving in the morning?'

'Around three-thirty a.m., as I need to back on the ferry by five a.m.' She looked at her phone, which was lying on top of her dress. 'It's nearly midnight and as much as I want to sit here all night with you, I should try and get a little sleep.' Reluctantly unwrapping the robe, she got dressed, then shivered.

'Here, take this.' Sam handed her an oversize grey sweatshirt. 'I always have it on hand after a swim.'

'Thank you,' Verity replied, slipping it over her head. 'I've had a really good night.'

'Me too,' he replied. 'Let me walk you back.'

Walking in silence, they made their way around the side of the boat and along the jetty. The only sound they could hear was the water breaking on the rocks in the shallows. Their elbows kept brushing against each other and the mere thought of Sam's touch was sending electricity pulsing through her body.

'And here you are. I have to say, setting off in a travelling van to explore the world is pretty cool.'

'I'm not sure she would make it all around the world, but Amsterdam, here we come.'

For a moment Sam looked at her with such affection. 'Thank you for listening tonight...I've never really spoken about my parents before.'

'Me neither,' replied Verity. Another loaded silence followed, their eye contact saying so much more than words.

Despite barely knowing this man, Verity thought he

might lean in and kiss her, and she found herself wishing he would. It would have been the perfect end to a perfect night. But instead, he merely touched her arm. 'You take care of yourself, Verity Callaway.'

'You, too, Sam Wilson.'

With that, Sam turned to walk away.

'Wait! Your jumper,' she said, crossing her arms, about to pull it over her head.

'Keep it, it suits you. Something to remember your trip to Puffin Island by.'

She smiled and watched him walk back along the shore until he turned left into Lighthouse Lane and disappeared from sight. Feeling a tiny slump in her mood after such a high, Verity opened the van, climbed in and locked the door behind her. Kicking off her shoes, she quickly brushed her teeth and pulled back the duvet. Just as she was about to take off the jumper she took in a fresh hit of his aroma. It smelled exactly like Sam, a scent that would now forever be etched in her mind. A minute later she was changed for bed then slipped back on his jumper, her arms now wrapped around herself, wondering what it would be like to be in the arms of Sam tonight. She'd arrived at Puffin Island on a whim, attempting to get on with her life, and tonight she had felt more sadness watching Sam walk away than she had when her ex did. The realisation startled her.

Living in the moment, not thinking of the reasons that had brought her here – and this was only the start of her personal journey. Tonight, she'd thrown caution to the wind and had enjoyed every moment of it, but now, exhausted, she looked through the window of her van up at the stars one last time. 'Goodnight, Puffin Island,' she murmured. As soon as she closed her eyes, she fell fast asleep.

Chapter Eight

Verity sat bolt upright in bed to the screech of the gulls circling above the van. It was already beginning to get light outside. Scrabbling for her phone, she looked at the screen. It was black. Damn it, she'd forgotten to plug it into the portable charger overnight.

'Shit,' she said, throwing back the duvet and poking her head through the makeshift curtain that separated the front of the van from the living area. She heaved a sigh of relief as she stared at the clock on the dashboard. Thankfully she hadn't overslept but it was time to be on the move. As the kettle came to the boil, she put her dirty clothes in the laundry bag stored underneath the bed, noting that by the end of the week she would need to find a laundrette. Or perhaps there would be a communal washing machine at one of the campsites they would be staying at. After she'd brushed her teeth and put on clean clothes, she pulled Sam's jumper back over her head, not wanting to be separated from it just yet. As she stepped outside the van with a cup of tea, she took in the view one last time. It was just as stunning at this hour of the morning as it was last night.

Taking one last walk near the water's edge, Verity noticed a couple of gulls going head to head at the far end of the beach, no doubt fighting over rich pickings they'd scavenged from the bin. With a last look at The Sea Glass Restaurant, she smiled as memories of last night washed over her. Despite her reservations about the cold water, it had actually been fun, and spending time with Sam was something she was not going to forget in a hurry. Verity couldn't remember a time she'd made conversation with a complete stranger. Her confidence was growing and she welcomed being pushed outside her normal comfort zones.

Her old friendships had dwindled away over the years and she knew exactly why – Richard. When they got together, his friends became hers, but he made it very clear he didn't like hers, which made it increasingly hard to find time for them. He was always cold with her work colleagues at the annual Christmas Party, and heaven forbid she should walk into a pub and began chatting to anyone; she would get the death stare. Realising she had missed out on many opportunities – new friends, nights out – she was beginning to be grateful for his infidelity, because it had at last set her free to explore life.

After one last look over the bay she finished her tea and decided to skip eating in case the sickness kicked in again on the ferry ride. With her bed made and her rucksack containing her essentials sitting on the passenger seat, she started the engine. As she pulled out onto the cobbled street, there wasn't a soul in sight. Driving slowly towards the causeway, she switched on the radio.

The causeway was clear as she pulled on to it, but as Verity continued to drive, that started to change. Further ahead the sea was lapping over the road, which surprised her as she was expecting the causeway to be completely clear like yesterday. Maybe first thing in the morning there was shallow water to drive through? She wasn't worried as she sat up in her seat and carried on, her wheels rolling through the water, because a little further on the causeway became visible again. Then, without warning, Verity's heart – along with Hetty the van – dropped. She let out a scream and gripped the steering wheel as the van nosedived under the water. The wheels were no longer turning and the van had stalled. Panicking, Verity started turning the key but nothing happened. Quickly, she rummaged in her bag and pulled out her phone, frantically trying to get some life out of it, but again there was nothing.

With a racing heart she looked ahead at the miles between her and the mainland. It wouldn't be long before the water began seeping through the bottom of the door and there was a huge possibility the van would sink fast. Trying to stay calm, she knew she had no option but to get out of the van as quickly as possible before it became submerged with her trapped inside. The rising water made it impossible to open the door so, grabbing her rucksack, Verity wound down the window. Having thrown the rucksack onto the roof, she squeezed herself out of the window into the freezing water. She managed to pull herself up onto the bonnet of the van and then clambered onto the roof. Now she had no clue what to do.

'PUFFIN ELL!' she screamed at the top of her lungs.

Luckily, the van seemed to be staying mostly above water. Still, she knew she needed to make a move quickly. Looking back towards Puffin Island, she could see that the causeway was becoming clear near the island; she just didn't know how deep the water was between here and there. It looked like she would have to find out.

With her arms stretched out Verity managed to stand up on top of the van. She pulled her rucksack on to her back, knowing that her passport and phone were going to be ruined the moment she hit the water – but what could she do? Just as she was about to slide off the roof into the sea she heard a continuous beeping. She looked up to see a black and yellow four-wheel drive heading towards her. Help was coming.

'Thank you!' she shouted, even though they wouldn't be able to hear her. The car stopped at the furthest point it could reach before the wheels were fully submerged. The car door opened and the driver got out, opened the rear doors and took out a canoe. Within seconds he was paddling towards her. Verity narrowed her eyes, a smile spread across her face as she recognised her rescuer.

'It's my knight in shining armour. We meet again!'

But Sam didn't look amused as he got closer. 'What the hell do you think you're doing? It's not safe to cross yet.'

'Well, I can see that,' she replied. 'I'm not standing on top of my van for no reason.'

There was still no smile on Sam's face. 'It's impatient people like you that cost the taxpayers tens of thousands of pounds in rescue costs each year. Did you know that sea rescues can cost up to two grand and air rescues up to four?

We're going to have to tow the van out even though it's likely to be written off. And it will cost you as well, as I suspect your insurance company will regard this as contributory negligence and be unwilling to pay out.'

Verity was taken aback by his not so warm welcome. Rescuer Sam was a very startling different person from the warm Sam she'd enjoyed last night. 'Surely she'll start again when she's dried out?'

Sam shook his head in disbelief. 'You're going to have to get wet. Can you slide down the back of the van and slip into the water? I'll try and get the canoe as close as possible. But before you do that, throw me your rucksack.'

Verity did as instructed and Sam placed it on his lap before she slipped off the van, not very gracefully. The shock of the cold water was no better the second time around but she didn't dare voice her discomfort. Pulling herself into the back of the canoe, she looked at the van she had lovingly restored over the past few months and reality hit her. Fighting back the tears, she swallowed a lump in her throat.

'Whatever possessed you to try and cross the causeway at half-past two in the morning when it's not safe? You only had to wait another hour or so.'

Verity was confused. 'It had gone half-past three when I crossed, and I checked the tide times.'

'It's only coming up to three o'clock now and you can see the water is still covering the causeway towards Sea's End.'

'It can't be only three o'clock now. The clock in the van said it was half three.'

'Well, I suggest it's probably not working.'

Verity was quiet. That was actually a strong possibility because, now she came to think about it, it always seemed to be mid-afternoon when she checked the time. 'I forgot to charge my phone because I had other things on my mind.' It seemed her perfect time on Puffin Island had just ended with a very expensive disaster.

Sam was rowing back towards the four-wheel drive.

'How did you come to rescue me?'

'There's a group of island coastguards on a rota. My shift has only just started. I was heading towards the rescue hut to take over when I saw you from the top of Lighthouse Lane. I just thought you were going to park up and when you kept on going, I raised the alarm.'

'What will happen to my van?'

'It'll be towed to the cliff top.'

Verity looked horrified. 'You aren't going to push her off the edge of the cliff, are you?'

'Don't be daft. Just the other side of Pete's place is a small garage owned by Nathan, the local mechanic. He'll do a post mortem.' For the first time Sam had a look of amusement on his face.

When they reached the car, Sam stood up in the canoe and stepped out. Verity felt an utter fool. Looking back at Hetty she felt a sense of panic. 'How am I going to get to Amsterdam?'

'Certainly not in that van, but you can cross the causeway in a taxi and catch the ferry. By the colour of your lips, though, I'd suggest you need to make sure you're physically fit before you go anywhere.'

Verity was freezing, she was wet through and beginning to shiver, probably from the shock of her ordeal.

She knew things could have been a lot worse if Sam hadn't spotted her. 'I can't leave the van here. She's my home for the next six months so I didn't have to pay for hotels.'

Sam looked towards the van. 'I'm sorry to say this, but I beg to differ.' Helping Verity out of the canoe, he opened the boot of the car and pulled out a thermal blanket. 'We need to get you warm.'

'I've got no dry clothes. They're all in ...' She didn't finish her sentence, instead promptly bursting into tears.

'You're not the first and you won't be the last to get stuck in the water. Jump in the car – the seat warmer is on. Clemmie's an early bird so I'll message to see if she has any spare clothes and hopefully she'll pick up the text when she wakes.'

Verity climbed into the seat with the thermal blanket wrapped around her shoulders.

'In the meantime, you'll have to have another one of my hoodies.' This time he smiled. 'Are you okay?' His voice had softened considerably.

'I'm a complete idiot. If only I'd charged my phone, I'd have seen the correct time.'

'I can't argue with that.'

'What happens to me now?'

'There's a rescue hut, where you can sit and wait whilst you decide your next move, but as nowhere opens for hours you can come back to mine and make yourself comfortable. I'm on shift until lunch time. Let me load up the canoe whilst you decide.' Sam pointed towards the mainland. 'The tide has turned.'

Verity could now see the clear causeway leading to Sea's

End. She closed her eyes for a moment whilst Sam slammed the boot shut and climbed behind the wheel.

'If only I'd waited another hour.'

'If only.' Sam radioed in on the walkie talkie. 'Stranded motorist rescued. I'll arrange for Nathan to tow the van up to the garage.'

Verity didn't know who Sam was talking to, but she was so cold that her teeth began uncontrollably chattering.

'Two minutes and I'll get you inside and the fire lit. You need to get out of those wet clothes and warmed up. Your body temperature will be dropping.'

'Thank you. I actually feel really tired and I'm soaked to the bone.' She looked in the sun visor mirror, seeing the tinge of blue to her lips that Sam had mentioned.

'I'm not surprised, you've probably only had a couple of hours' sleep. Any idea whether you're still going to attempt to catch your ferry? Because if you are we'll need to arrange transport to get you there.'

Verity didn't know what to do. The shock of possibly losing the van was swamping her. 'I just can't think... Oh no! Ava. She's meeting me in Amsterdam.'

'Let's get you warmed up and you can have a think about what you're going to do.'

Looking out of the window, Verity saw a steady stream of cars driving towards them. 'That's a lot of people up at this time in the morning.'

'They probably either work off the island or are catching one of the early ferries.'

Once they'd left the causeway, Sam drove straight towards Lighthouse Lane. He slowed down as he approached the rainbow-coloured cottages then swung into the first driveway. 'Here we are.'

Verity's eyes widened. She couldn't believe it. 'You have to be kidding me.'

Sam parked the car. 'What do you mean?'

'You live here?'

'I do.'

'This is unreal. This is my cottage.'

'Have you had a bang on the head, too?'

In her excitement, Verity grabbed his arm. 'When I was a child my granny used to tell me stories about this cottage and I said I was going to live here one day. I can't believe this.'

She stared at the whimsical, cosy storybook cottage. 'How long have you lived here?'

'This cottage has been in the Wilson family for as long as anyone can remember.'

'My granny...she's been here.' Verity pointed to the oak porch with the blush-coloured roses tumbling all over it. 'She always told me the roses around the door were stunning. How long have they been here?'

'For as long as I can remember.'

'Wilson. The W has to be Wilson.'

'Like I said last night, I don't think it's possible. Have you any more information to go on?'

'Only the date stamped on the postcard. Oh, and the picture of the puffins that's been hanging in Granny's house for years and years. There was a message written on the back of it in the same handwriting as the postcard. It said, "The summer of 1972".'

Sam's eyes shot up. 'My grandfather died the summer of 1972.'

'I've got a gut feeling about this, I think my granny and your grandfather knew each other. She went into so much detail about this cottage. She's been here.'

'Come on, let's get you inside.' Sam climbed out of the car then did the gentlemanly thing and opened the passenger side for Verity.

'You'd best come in and see if it lives up to your expectations.' Sam put the key in the lock and opened the door.

Verity stepped inside and was surprised to see Sam put his finger to his lips.

'Can you hear that?' he whispered.

'I can't hear anything,' Verity whispered back.

'That is the sound of the worst guard dog in the world. Not one bark!'

Verity stifled a giggle. 'Jimmy will be too busy dreaming about shoes.'

Hanging up her rucksack on the coat stand in the hallway, Sam led the way into the living room, pulled an armchair towards the open log fire and quickly lit the fire. 'I'm glad I got the fire ready yesterday. Take a seat and I'll get you a towel, a jumper and some tea. Then you can tell me all about this postcard.'

Verity was standing in the middle of the room, amazement no doubt written all over her face as she spun around taking in everything. 'This is surreal.'

As with the rest of Puffin Island, her granny had accurately described this room: the wood-framed window overlooking the garden, the oak beams running the length of the ceiling, the impressive open fire. On the wall hung a number of photographs. She took a closer look and one immediately caught her eye. Standing in front of a boat was a handsome young man holding up the largest fish she'd ever seen in her life. This had to be Sam's grandfather.

'What was your grandfather's name?' Verity asked, hearing Sam walk back into the room.

'Joe,' he replied.

'There was a Joe in my grandmother's stories. I remember now.' Verity couldn't hide the excitement in her voice. 'Let me think…' She was quiet for a second. 'Joe, that's right, he was destined for greater things, and…oh my…yes, a musician…' Verity was tripping over her words. 'She told me a story that he was in a band and was signed to a record label and was about to go on tour with none other than Bowie.' Verity laughed. 'Of course, I do know some of the stories had to be fictional.'

Sam looked amazed. 'You've got to be kidding me?' He narrowed his eyes at her. 'Because that's all true.'

Now it was Verity's turn to look amazed.

Sam placed two mugs on the table before passing Verity a towel. 'Here, drink that. At least your lips are a little less blue and you've stopped shivering.'

'I think amazement has taken over the shock.'

Draping the towel around her shoulders, Verity pointed to the photograph. 'That has to be your grandfather. You look just like him.'

Sam stood beside her. 'It is. That was the biggest catch of the day.'

'If I'd known there were fish as big as that in the bay you would never have got me in that water.' She turned and looked around the room. 'I have to say, I wouldn't have put you down as a cosy cottage kind of guy.'

'And what would you have put me down as?'

'Modern apartment, minimal things, large TV and the latest technology.' Verity sat back on the chair and hugged the mug of tea.

'That sounds like complete hell to me. Let me go and get you some warm clothes. I'm afraid it'll have to be a pair of my joggers, a T-shirt and a sweatshirt. I don't have many dresses in my wardrobe.' He smiled at her as he walked out of the door. Returning in five minutes, he handed her a pile of clothes. 'There's a bathroom just—'

'Down the hall to the left,' Verity finished off his sentence.

Sam cocked an eyebrow. 'Your granny was very thorough with her descriptions.'

'Do you, or did you, have a rope swing that hangs from an old oak tree at the side of the garden, and a gate that takes you straight down to a cove?'

'I do. And you have…a postcard?'

Verity nodded. 'What's your gut feeling? Do you think the postcard could be from your grandfather?'

'I'm not sure.'

'Wait there.'

Sam watched as Verity hurried back down the hallway and grabbed her rucksack from the coat stand. Returning to the living room she plonked herself on the green velvet sofa next to him and rummaged in her bag. 'Here, take a look at this.' She handed him the postcard. 'It's from your grandfather, isn't it? Have you got anything from that summer? Did your grandfather have any photographs from that time? Anything that would link them?'

Sam shook his head, and walked over to the dresser. He took out a small notebook then sat on the couch next to Verity. He opened the book and laid the postcard next to the first page.

'What's that?'

'This was my grandfather's wages book. He used to log his work hours, the days and times, and in this column the weight of the fish, as he got paid by the weight of the fish he caught. As you can see, some days were better than others.' Sam pointed to the writing on the page and then at the postcard. 'I don't want to burst your bubble, Verity, but I think you're barking up the wrong tree. The handwriting in this book and the postcard are different. Look at the letters.'

Verity examined both carefully.

'I do believe they knew each other, because how would you know about this place unless you're some sort of stalker or psychic? But as for the postcard, I don't think it was from him,' he said gently.

Verity felt disappointed. She so badly wanted the postcard to be from Joe as it would solve some of the mystery. 'Do you find it fascinating that they were probably sat here together back then and now here we are? I do.'

'It is a little surreal, I must admit. Even harder to believe, given that our paths crossed because of a chance meeting outside a greasy spoon.'

'It was fate. The universe brought us together for a reason.'

Sam smiled at her. 'Maybe it's going to take teamwork to discover what this secret is.'

'Teamwork, I like the sound of that.' Verity looked around. 'I still can't get over the fact that she's been here. In her stories this cottage was beautiful and so was Cliff Top Cottage. I have to admit that I was quite surprised by the real Cliff Top Cottage, as it wasn't how Granny described it at all.'

'Yeah, Pete has really let it go.'

'Do you know why?'

'I wouldn't like to guess at the reasons for anything that man does.'

The words were said with hostility. 'It sounds like you aren't a fan of Pete's?' she probed.

'Let's just say I'm still waiting for the truth to come out.'

'About?'

Sam lay the book and postcard on the coffee table and picked up his mug of tea. He clearly wasn't about to share any more of his thoughts on the matter. An awkward silence filled the room.

'Well, at least this cottage lived up to my expectations,' she babbled. 'I can't believe I'm sitting here.'

'You're very lucky to be sitting here after your latest escapade.'

Just at that moment Sam's phone rang.

'That was Nathan,' he said a moment later, after hanging up. 'He's already towed Hetty up to the garage, and will assess the damage later on this afternoon. For now, I need to get back to the coastguard's hut. Even though it's safe to cross the causeway, you still get the odd swimmer stranded when they decide to brave the cold water and get cramp. It's usually to impress a woman, and the swimmers are usually naked.'

'Is that what you tried to do yesterday?'

'I had my boxers on,' he replied with a wicked glint in his eye.

'But I do think you were trying to impress me.' She gave him a tiny smirk.

Sam stood up and pointed towards the kitchen. 'Jimmy's asleep in his crate. Help yourself to a shower. I'm sure you know where that is.'

She pointed through the door to the stairs.

'If you decide to make the ferry to Amsterdam, there's a taxi number on the corkboard in the kitchen, and if you decide you're staying and want to catch up on sleep, the bedroom is—'

'Through there.' Verity pointed. 'Or there's two upstairs. I should have pretended I was psychic, shouldn't I?' She laughed.

Sam shook his head in jest. 'If you do decide you're off on your travels'—he took a key off his keyring—'lock the door behind you and leave the key under the mat. If you don't go, I'll see you later.'

They looked at each other for a moment.

'Thanks for rescuing me.'

'You're welcome but I really have to go.' Sam edged backwards towards the door. He gave her one last smile before he shut the door behind him. Two seconds later it opened again. 'And if you go you'd better leave me some contact details. You'll need an update on the van and we can discuss the mystery of the postcard.'

'And here was me thinking you wanted my phone number, just because.'

'Goodbye, Verity Callaway.' The front shut again but this

time it didn't reopen. Verity heard the car engine start and the gravel crunched under the tyres as it pulled away from the cottage.

With Ava very much on her mind, she located the bathroom and was relieved to strip off her wet clothes. Climbing into the shower, she welcomed the warm water. She knew she wasn't going to make the ferry to Amsterdam and a tiny part of her was quite happy about that, despite the disastrous consequences of her actions. But there was also a part of her that wasn't looking forward to telling Ava, because she didn't yet know whether the garage could fix the van, and there was a strong likelihood that they couldn't – which would mean they had no travelling van to live and sleep in for their adventure together.

Ten minutes later, feeling clean and refreshed, Verity dried herself whilst taking a nosey around the bathroom. Sam had impeccable taste in grooming products and aftershaves, which were all lined up on a bathroom shelf. Squirting a tiny amount of aftershave into the air, Verity briefly closed her eyes and took in the aroma. That one was definitely Sam Wilson's signature scent; she recognised it immediately.

Verity got changed into the T-shirt and joggers, and the oversized sweatshirt was cosy as she pulled the sleeves down over her arms. She wandered back into the living room, eager to explore the rest of the cottage.

Slowly opening the kitchen door, she peered in. Jimmy was still fast asleep in his crate with a blanket draped over the top of it. There was the racing-green Aga that Granny had talked about and the inglenook with the wood burner.

The farmhouse table was positioned in the middle of the room. Everywhere was spick and span.

Verity opened another door and stepped down into a tiny hallway where a wrought-iron staircase spiralled upwards. Opposite was the snug, which was just as homely as the first room. The walls were covered with framed pictures, and there was another beautiful open fire with an oak beam mantel, and gorgeous wall lights in antique brass with shades that matched the curtains. The small chesterfield was covered in throws and the plushest velvet cushions she had ever seen. Two cosy fabric chairs, a huge rug and a small table with a computer had been placed in front of the window. At the back of the room was an impressive bookcase that stretched from floor to ceiling, filled with books.

Verity wandered towards it and ran her finger along the spines of the books. She was impressed. Sam had all the classics as well as fiction in different genres and numerous books on Puffin Island, which she assumed were written by local authors. She pulled one out. It was all about the history of puffins and included details of the puffin census that went back years. There was another book on the history of the island and its local trades. Taking it from the shelf, Verity sat down on the settee and flicked through the pages. There before her eyes was a photo of Joe Wilson, branded the youngest yet most competent fisherman on the island. His resemblance to Sam was uncanny; there could be no doubt he was his grandson. Their facial features were very similar, and they had the same wild hair and rugged good looks. She thought about what Sam had told her about his grandparents. It must have been difficult back in those days. Not only were they very young but for the relationship to fall apart and the two to go their separate ways when there was a child involved… Even in her own generation Verity knew numerous couples that were far from happy but stayed together for the sake of their children, and because splitting up would mean financial ruin. Fortunately, when she split up with Richard there were no children involved and the house belonged to her. And, as he never made any financial contribution to the upkeep, he had no claim on it whatsoever.

Closing the book, she stood up and slipped it back on the shelf.

'Oh my gosh,' she said out loud. She took a step back and scanned the bookcase from top to bottom. Her granny's stories had been so magical that she'd even convinced Verity that this cottage had a secret door leading to a secret sitting room, and that door was opened by a book in the bookcase. Very Harry Potter. Maybe her granny should have written children's books for a living. Verity remembered it very clearly. Her granny had told her that the book was on the second shelf from the top, third from the right, and apparently when you pulled it out a switch caused the bookcase to swing open. She chuckled to herself as her eyes skimmed the bookshelves. 'I mean, who has secret rooms behind bookshelves?'

There it was, the second shelf from the top, third book on the right. 'Surely not,' she said with a smile, knowing that secret doors only happened in the movies. But something made Verity look at the book in question. She was amazed to see it was the same book she'd bought from the bookshop only yesterday – *Pride and Prejudice*. Reaching up she took the book off the shelf, disappointed for a moment when the bookcase didn't swing open as her granny had told her.

This *Pride and Prejudice* was an earlier edition than hers, but in immaculate condition. Opening it, she read the inscription.

> *To Joe,*
> *A little something to mark the summer we'll never forget.*
> *Love always,*
> *Hetty x*

Verity's mouth fell wide open, recognising the familiar handwriting before she'd even read the signature.

'Granny,' she murmured with instant excitement. 'Wow!' She couldn't take her eyes off it. This was proof! This book connected her grandmother to Joe, and so the postcard *had* to be from him. With a pounding heart she carefully flicked through the pages hoping for more clues. She couldn't wait to show Sam, and willed him to hurry back from his shift, wondering if he knew about the writing inside the book.

And what is your secret? Verity knew if her granny had kept that picture hanging on her wall for years, the bond between her and Joe must have been a special one, though she couldn't help wondering how her grandfather fitted into the equation. But the main thought that was running through her mind was whether her granny might have told her those stories in so much detail – especially the part about the bookcase – because she wanted her to come to Puffin Island and discover something else? Was it just a coincidence that the book she'd inscribed to Joe was in the exact place she had described? Verity wasn't sure, but she felt sure there was more to discover about her granny's visit to Puffin Island. At that moment she made the decision to stay longer on the island. Having been close to Joe, Betty was Verity's best hope to shed more light on the situation. If she had anything to share, Verity wanted to hear it first-hand.

Laying the book on the settee, Verity stood on tiptoe and groped around for a switch. Finding one, feeling a thrill, she pressed it. There was an instant whirling sound and the bookcase began to move.

'No way!'

As she watched in amazement, the bookcase revealed a normal doorway. She stepped into the room and took in her surroundings. It was a comfy office space with a small desk, a computer and a comfy-looking sofa covered in a soft woollen throw. On the wall was a map of the island, showing every building, and to the side a list of all the residents. There was a photograph of The Sea Glass Restaurant on opening night with Sam cutting a ribbon. He hadn't changed much at all, his hair maybe a little shorter and less wild. On the far wall hung a number of guitars, along with photos of Sam sitting behind a microphone with a guitar on his knee. A number of them showed Amelia and Clemmie standing alongside him.

Verity wondered what it would be like to live within such a small community where everyone knew everyone. She'd barely ever spoken to her neighbours and though she made a point of saying a cheerful hello if she passed someone on the street, she generally didn't receive more than a grunt back, if she wasn't ignored completely. She'd often wished she had a local pub where she could wander in on her own, feeling comfortable chatting to all and sundry. The friendship she'd witnessed between Clemmie and Amelia was something she'd often wished for, a friendship close to home, a place where you could share all your news and go for walks and grab a coffee.

The window of the office looked out on to Lighthouse Lane and right outside was an old-fashioned-looking lamppost that resembled something from a Disney movie. The stream was bubbling away towards the harbour and the sun was beginning to shine down on the day. Feeling exhausted, Verity pulled back the throw and climbed underneath it. Resting her head on the cushion, before she knew it, she'd fallen asleep.

What seemed like only seconds later was in fact quite a few hours. Woken by a loud clang, Verity opened her eyes to find she was being watched by another pair of eyes, huge ones that were firmly fixed on her. 'Good morning, Jimmy!' As soon as Jimmy heard her voice his tail wagged furiously, then he sat back on his hind legs with his front paws stretched out and woofed playfully.

'No, Jimmy!' But it was too late. Jimmy launched himself at her and began licking her face. Quickly bringing the throw up to shield herself, Verity managed to wrestle him and push him off before he woofed again and bounded out of the room, soon returning shaking a toy in his mouth.

Smiling, Sam walked into the room behind the pup and

handed her a mug of coffee. 'I see Jimmy's found you and you've discovered the secret room.'

Verity shot up right. 'I can't believe it. The switch was exactly where Granny said it was.' Her voice was full of excitement. 'And there's more…' Verity threw back the throw and hurried to retrieve the book that was still lying on the sofa in the next room. She bounded back, as excitable as Jimmy, and thrust the book into Sam's hand.

Sam pointed. 'You know you can just push the door open?'

'And where's the fun in that when you have secret switches to open doors? And never mind that. Look! *Pride and Prejudice*!'

'*Pride and Prejudice*, arguably one of the greatest romance novels of all time. The opinionated heroine, Elizabeth Bennet, frequently finding herself at odds with her beau, the uptight Mr Darcy.'

'A man in touch with the classics, very impressive.'

'You look like you're about to combust.'

'This book was in the place of the secret switch. Now open it! That's definitely my granny's writing. Have you seen this before?'

'These classics were all boxed up in the attic. I stumbled across them about ten years ago and dusted them down. I didn't even check inside them.'

'You do know what this means though, don't you?'

'That they liked classics?'

Verity rolled her eyes. 'This confirms they knew each other. I'm convinced W is your grandfather! He has to be; it all fits. I wonder how long my granny was here for. Did they have a relationship? Did they keep in touch after she left the island?'

Sam shook his head. 'They didn't.'

'But you don't know that.'

'I do. The postcard was dated 1972, and this inscription mentions the summer they'll never forget. If it was the same summer, my grandfather passed away at the end of it.'

'That's so sad.' Verity stared at the book with her hand on her heart, suddenly feeling teary. 'Do you think she knew?'

Sam shrugged. 'Your guess is as good as mine.'

'We know she was here for the summer so she must have given him the book before she went home.'

Sam nodded. 'I do know that summer was the best of his life.'

'I'd like to think that had something to do with my grandmother.' She smiled.

'That was the summer his music began to take off. Betty told me everything. The crowds of girls flocking to the pub when the band was playing. That was the summer they got offered the record deal and it was confirmed they would support Bowie...and then everything changed.' Sam finished his tea and Verity realised it was because of Joe's death that the band didn't tour.

'I'd love to have heard him play. I have all the songs that he'd written kept in that cupboard over there. He had a songbook where he used to scribble down lyrics and music.'

'What a fantastic keepsake.'

'I didn't think much to their band name though.' Sam chuckled. 'The Men from Puffin Island.'

'My granny loved music, too. She was an amazing singer but she didn't seem to pass that gene on to me. Apparently she'd get up at any opportunity and belt out a song. I think we have our answer. I do think the postcard is from your grandfather.' Verity smiled. 'And I don't know where my grandfather fits into all this but if Joe couldn't live without her, I think they had a summer fling. She was a good catch, my granny, just like her granddaughter.' She playfully nudged Sam's arm and he gave her a heart-warming smile. 'I'm glad it's your grandfather, I think it's so romantic. Maybe when I get home there will be a postcard waiting on the mat telling me you can't live without me.' Verity was teasing but secretly she really wanted to see his reaction.

Sam shook his head in jest. 'I've no time for writing a postcard today, I have a meeting at one p.m., but I can make you some food before I go. I'm assuming you decided against catching the ferry today?'

Startled, Verity sat up straight. 'I still haven't messaged Ava! And I should be on the boat to Amsterdam right now.'

'Yeah, you've long missed that ferry ride.'

Verity exhaled. 'I'm not looking forward to this phone call. Ava isn't going to be happy. I need to charge my phone.' She disappeared into the other room, pulled out her phone and charger from her rucksack and plugged them in a socket at the side of the settee.

'I'll go and make you some food whilst you apologise and sort out your travel plans. Oh, and before I forget, there's a pile of clothes here from Clemmie. I picked them up from the tearoom on my way home.'

'Thank you, that's so kind.'

Sam headed towards the kitchen with Jimmy hot on his

heels. Verity looked at the screen of her phone, willing it to light up. As soon as a tiny bit of charge kicked in, it burst into life. From the continuous beep Verity could see there were at least nine missed calls from Ava and a voicemail. Damn. Her heart was racing as she checked her messages, her eyes closing as Ava's voice sounded out.

'I've tried to ring you umpteen times. Where are you? You shouldn't be on the ferry just yet.' Verity knew this message had probably been left hours ago when she was stranded on the causeway. Ava continued, 'I know you've always thought I'm a bit of a flaky friend and I'm so sorry but I'm going to live up to that reputation. Please don't kill me but I'm not on the ferry.' There was a long pause and Verity knew that Ava was trying to work out how to soften the blow. 'I applied for a job with a TV company, had the interview and never really thought much more of it. But I got the job and it starts in London on Monday. I'm so sorry, Verity, but it's an opportunity I can't give up. You can still go to Amsterdam without me though! You can do this by yourself. Ring me when you get a minute.'

Verity put the phone down with a huge smile on her face. She blew out a breath as Sam walked back into the room holding a tray. 'She didn't kill you then?'

'I've not actually spoken to her yet.'

'Verity!'

'No, it's okay, she's left me a voicemail. Ava's not on the ferry. She's not going to Amsterdam. She's been offered a job in London and is starting on Monday, but she's insisting I still go and find myself. She thinks it'll be good for me.'

'And what do you think about that?'

Her smile grew wider. 'I'm secretly chuffed. I wanted to

spend more time on the island and this gives me the perfect opportunity.'

'Well, that makes sense, but I have to say, at this time of year it'll be difficult to get a room at the hotel, and the B&B is usually booked up far in advance.'

'Even if my van can't go anywhere, once everything has dried out, I can still sleep in it, if Nathan can tow it to a safe spot for me. This was meant to be.' Verity could already picture herself sleeping on top of the cliffs and waking up to the sunrise overlooking the puffins and the harbour. That type of adventure was more on her level than fighting for her life dodging the thousands of bicycles on the busy streets of Amsterdam.

'There's always a spare room here in the meantime, until you get yourself sorted – and I don't mean the sofa in my office.'

'That's very kind of you. Thank you.'

'And anyway, I'm invested now.'

'Invested?'

'I want to know more about our grandparents, but in the meantime'—he pointed to the tray— 'sandwich, chocolate flapjack and crisps.'

'That looks amazing.'

'You can thank Beachcomber Bakery. I took the chance you'd still be here and grabbed it all on my way back. I always think a sandwich tastes better when it's made by someone else. I've got to head out now to a meeting but feel free to stay here. Keep the key in case you want to go out.' Sam called Jimmy and clipped on his lead. 'Make yourself at home.'

Verity was still smiling as the front door shut behind

them. She stood by the window and watched them walk down the lane. Not quite believing the turn of events in the last twenty-four hours, she looked up to the sky. A day of sunshine was not to be missed. She thought about last night as well, the same sky but dark with twinkling stars. When the shooting star whizzed across the night sky, she'd closed her eyes and made a wish, and that wish had just come true. She was staying on Puffin Island for a while longer, which gave her time to try to uncover more about her granny's time here – but, more importantly, it gave her an opportunity to hang around with Sam, which brought a huge smile to her face.

Chapter Nine

An hour later, Verity had eaten and changed into the clothes donated by Clemmie. She'd included a pair of trainers, luckily the same size as Verity's, which would do until her own were dry. She'd noticed that Sam had already placed her trainers on top of the Aga to dry out, which made her smile. She was soon walking down Lighthouse Lane, planning to call in to see Amelia in the bookshop and surprise her with the fact she was still here. Afterwards, she would pop into the tearoom to thank Clemmie (who obviously knew she was still here). Then she was going to make her way back up the cliffs to locate Nathan in the garage and assess the damage of the van, though she wasn't holding out much hope. Even if she was lucky and the insurance company paid out for the van, it wouldn't bring much money. The van was old, and the new fixtures and fittings were probably worth more than the vehicle.

Surprisingly, there wasn't a soul in sight on Lighthouse Lane. The whole place seemed deserted. Puffin Island had suddenly become a ghost town. Verity wondered where everyone was, considering it was early afternoon.

Strange, she thought, pushing on the door of The Story Shop, but it didn't open. Verity tried again but it was firmly shut. Then she noticed the note pinned to the front door.

The Story Shop is closed for the next two hours and will reopen at two-thirty p.m. Sorry for the inconvenience.

Maybe Amelia was taking a long lunch hour, possibly in the pub? Verity decided to head that way after calling in on Clemmie, but the tearoom had exactly the same note pinned to the front door. Finding the pub closed, and with a similar note outside, Verity carried on walking down Anchor Way, perplexed. She passed the hotel and headed towards Quaint Quarters, a small square filled with antique shops and an art gallery. She loved a good antique shop, with its distinct smell, where every item told its own story. But all the shops there were closed too. Just at that moment Verity noticed a woman hurrying out of the nearest antique shop. She locked the door and slapped a note on it.

'Excuse me?' said Verity, catching the woman's attention. 'Why is everywhere shut?'

'Island meeting. The usual clash of the titans.'

Verity had no clue what she meant and didn't have time to ask as the woman's heels were navigating the cobblestones at speed, heading towards the harbour. Verity decided to follow her, intrigued to know what the meeting was about. Once she reached the harbour, the woman headed past the jetty that led to The Sea Glass Restaurant and pushed open the door of a quaint black and white building nearby.

Above the door was a small wooden sign reading THE ISLAND HALL. Verity assumed it was equivalent to a village hall. She could hear voices echoing inside, as though someone was speaking through a microphone. Pinned to the door was a notice.

Puffin Island Meeting, one p.m., all residents welcome.

Curious to know what was going on inside, Verity took her chance and slipped into the building when she heard the sound of rapturous applause. Quickly taking a spare seat at the back of the room, she immediately spotted Amelia and Clemmie sitting in the front row. She recognised Cora and Dan from the pub, and Pete, too, who was sitting at the side of the stage. She slid down in her seat as Sam took to the stage and stood behind the microphone. Verity noticed that one side of the room began to grumble and didn't sound very welcoming at all.

'We all know why we're here.'

The room fell silent.

'With the vote very much upon us, we're here one last time to air what we think is right. The island is divided. Half of you can sit there telling yourself what I'm proposing is nonsense, but yet another idiot cost us time and money this morning.'

Verity had no clue what Sam was talking about but he wasn't beating around the bush. The way he was speaking, it sounded as though he was on a mission about something. He seemed rattled.

'Automatic barriers are the *only* way forward.'

'Nonsense,' shouted out a voice from the front.

'As an island we need to come together on this one. Automatic barriers that come down when the tide is rising will stop reckless drivers getting stuck on the causeway and having to be rescued.'

Sam had Verity's full attention now. Her eyes widened, her heart began to pound, and she couldn't believe what she was hearing. That idiot he was talking about…was her. How dare he! Who did he think he was? It had been a genuine mistake! She felt the urge to defend herself but she had to do everything in her power not to make her presence known. She wanted to see how this would play out.

'Drivers must take more responsibility and read the tide times. Oh, and stop ignoring the signs that it's not safe to cross. They don't take it seriously, and lives are at risk. Not forgetting the fact that the cost of rescues is increasing every year,' added Sam.

'Barriers would make no difference.'

Verity realised the voice coming from the front of the hall was Pete.

'You're always going to get people who think they know better.'

'I second Pete. Automatic barriers on the causeway will disrupt lives and cause potential problems in emergency situations,' stated Cora.

'Hear hear,' said Pete and everyone sitting on the right side of the room voiced their agreement.

'It's a risk living on the island,' Sam replied, 'because ambulances can't get through when the tide is high, making it difficult getting people to hospital in an emergency. We all know that, and accept it. The fact of the matter is that barriers will help to save lives.'

Pete stood up and pointed towards Sam. 'We all know what happened many years ago. The tide was high when that tourist suffered a heart attack and the ambulance couldn't get across the causeway, and neither the rescue helicopters nor the inshore lifeboat was available. That man was saved because the coastguard Land Rover was able to drive through three-feet-deep water on the causeway to the waiting ambulance on the mainland. If there were automatic barriers it wouldn't have been able to get through and that man would have probably died.'

The argument was beginning to get heated.

'It sounded like you cared there for a moment, Pete. It's a shame people died on *your* coastguard watch.'

The crowd fell quiet and Verity could hear sharply indrawn breaths all around the room. She wasn't sure what was going on here but it was obvious this had nothing to do with automatic barriers anymore.

'There's no need to get personal, Sam,' said the woman Verity had followed from the antique shop. 'That was a bit below the belt.'

There was a murmur of agreement around the room.

Red-faced, Pete stood up. 'I can't listen to any more of this.' Clutching his flat cap, he walked straight out of the hall, catching Verity's eye as he passed. There were tears in his eyes and she could see that he was genuinely upset. She cast a glance back towards Sam, who raked his hand through his hair.

'Automatic barriers will help to save more lives than not. If it wasn't for me seeing yet another tourist without any common sense driving along the causeway this morning, then they would have been stranded with no means of communication. Their own stupidity could have resulted in their death.'

Verity didn't want to hear any more. She stood up and immediately caught Sam's eye. She stared at him with a cold expression. She wasn't stupid; the clock had stopped. He knew it had been a genuine mistake and yet he'd made her out to be a complete idiot. She was fuming. People were inevitably going to find out it was her, because no doubt word would get round the island very quickly. From the look of surprise that quickly registered on Sam's face, she knew he was shocked to see her there. They continued to stare at each other for a brief second before she haughtily turned and walked out of the hall. He had no right to talk about her in that way, and it was unkind to talk to Pete that way in front of everyone, no matter what was going on between them. Pete was entitled to his opinion, just like everyone else.

Already striding across the bay, Pete was heading towards the cliff path when he stopped, wiped his handkerchief across his brow and sat down on a nearby bench. Verity was a little unsure what she had witnessed but she knew that was a side to Sam she didn't like at all, and she felt bad for Pete. She walked towards the bench.

'Pete, are you okay?'

He turned and looked towards her. 'Do I know you?' he said, stuffing his handkerchief back in his pocket.

'I was up on the cliff top yesterday and you asked me to leave. I shouldn't have been on your property and I want to apologise. And…I'm not sure what was going on in there but I don't like to see anyone upset.'

'You're not a resident; you shouldn't have been in there.'

'I'm this morning's idiot.' She hoped admitting to it would soften Pete a little, but unfortunately that didn't seem to be the case.

'It's people like you that help his cause to get those barriers installed. It's not difficult to understand that you shouldn't drive on the causeway at certain times. If there's water over the road, stay clear.' He stood abruptly and walked off, leaving Verity standing there in silence, watching him head towards the coastal path. She perched on the bench wondering what the hell Sam and Pete's argument was really about. She really didn't like the way Sam had spoken about her, or spoken to Pete.

Being a professional businessman, Sam should know there were ways of getting your point across without making personal attacks on others. Hearing voices behind her she turned to find that the islanders were beginning to spill out of the building and disperse. She spotted Sam immediately but he quickly turned away. She didn't mind; he was the last person she wanted to get into conversation with at the minute.

'Here she is, the village idiot Sam has just been talking about. There's always one, you know.' Clemmie gave a chuckle. 'Nice outfit, by the way. I used to wear something similar.'

Verity's two new friends were grinning as they plonked themselves either side of her on the bench.

'You're not funny! And don't try and make me smile. I'm livid. Who does he think he is, calling me an idiot in front of the whole island? It was a genuine mistake.'

Amelia nudged her elbow. 'It's a little funny. Fancy

driving over the causeway when you could actually see water on the road.'

'Hindsight is a wonderful thing. I honestly just thought it must be really shallow as I had checked the tide times but...'

'Ahh, don't worry about Sam, he's just very passionate about saving lives. Though sometimes he expresses it a little *too* passionately. It doesn't help that the island is completely divided about what to do.'

'This family feud has been going on a few months,' admitted Clemmie.

'And which side of the camp are you two on?'

'Don't ask,' replied Amelia with a smile.

'Different camps,' confirmed Clemmie. 'But we aren't going to fall out over it.'

'Is that why Sam and Pete don't like each other? You could have cut the tension between them with a knife.'

'Let's just say their dislike for each other runs a lot deeper than the causeway.' Clemmie gave Amelia a pointed look, which Verity noticed, but neither woman elaborated. Verity took it to mean that that was island business and if you didn't know, you didn't need to know.

'My point is that if there were automatic barriers and they were down you wouldn't have been able to cross the causeway and your lovely travelling van wouldn't be fighting for its life up at Nathan's garage,' added Clemmie, leaving Verity in no doubt what camp she belonged to.

'Have you been hanging out in the rescue hut all this time?' asked Amelia.

'Sam rescued me then he took me back to Cosy Nook Cottage.' Clemmie already knew where she'd been, so

Verity sat back on the bench to watch Amelia's reaction. It didn't disappoint. Her eyes widened and her jaw dropped.

'Really? Why would he do that? There's a cabin at the coastguard hut for stranded idiots.'

'Hey, less of the idiot,' protested Verity, rolling her eyes.

'Sorry I couldn't resist.'

'Yesterday, settling your bill and today…there's something going on here.' She waggled her finger in Verity's direction.

'There's nothing going on – and after he's just stood up in front of everyone and called me an idiot, there definitely won't be anything going on in the future. I've got a few choice words of my own I'd quite like to say to him.' Verity didn't share that only last night butterflies had taken flight in her stomach when they'd taken a moonlit dip together and shared a drink before she tucked herself up inside Hetty.

'Mmm, I'm not convinced. I saw those looks between you both when he was singing in the pub. The electricity sparking between you could have powered the whole of Puffin Island for a week.'

'You have a wonderful imagination, which is good, considering you're a writer,' Verity remarked good-humouredly, but her mind was fixed firmly on Amelia's words. If she'd noticed the spark between them, it surely had to be real.

'What's your plan now?' asked Clemmie.

'That's what I'm just contemplating. I need to find out what's happening to my van and how bad the damage is. Then I'll make a decision.'

'I need to go and open the bookshop.'

'And I need to open the tearoom, but let us know your next move.'

'I will. I'll go now and check up on the van so I can consider my options.'

Verity watched as Clemmie and Amelia headed towards Lighthouse Lane, passing Sam, who was standing on the corner of the lane chatting with Dan and Cora. As she stood up she caught his eye. They stared at each other for a moment before she turned and headed towards the cliff top, knowing she needed to let her anger subside before she said anything to him.

As she reached the cliff top path, the view of the puffins in the distance put a smile on her face. They were all huddled together in their pairs and Verity thought it was comical that each of them knew who their partner puffin was, despite all looking the same. Reaching the top of the cliff, she spotted Pete standing with a group of people outside his cottage. They had an official look about them and were huddled over what looked like a huge map spread out on top of the patio table. Pete was pointing to the map with a long stick but they all looked up as she walked past. Verity gave them a wave without hesitation and carried on walking towards the garage.

Cliff Top Garage was exactly that, a garage on the cliff top. There were a couple of open bays with vehicles on ramps. In one corner was a stack of tyres, a workbench piled with tools, safety signs and oily rags. A small waiting area housed a couple of plastic chairs, and a radio was blaring out. In one of the bays, a man was working under the bonnet of a car.

'Excuse me,' she said.

The man looked up, then moved away from the bonnet. At a guess he was in his early thirties, approximately six feet tall and with a chiselled jawline that was just about visible through the grease on his face.

He smiled. 'Can I help you?'

'Nathan?'

'Yes.'

'Hi, I'm Verity, I believe you're undertaking a post mortem on my van.'

'Ah, so you're the—'

'Please don't call me an idiot,' she cut in, smiling.

'I was going to say the woman who can't tell the time. You tourists do like to do whatever you can to keep me in a job, don't you?'

'I don't like the label, but I have to admit I *am* feeling a bit of an idiot.'

'There are some idiots who attempt to drive the causeway for fun but there are some genuine mistakes.'

'And are you for or against automatic barriers?'

'I keep out of the island's politics.' He grinned.

'Probably the best way.' Verity noticed the sign at the entrance of the garage and laughed. 'Is that the garage's motto – "Wheel be all right!"? But the question is, will my van?'

'There she is.' Nathan pointed. Hetty was parked at the side of the garage. All of her doors were wide open and the bonnet was propped open too.

'It's going to be a sunny day, so I suggest you take out the mattress and so on and any belongings that could dry out in the sun. There's even a washing line there to hang up any clothes or duvets.'

'A garage with a washing line. I've never seen that before.'

'It's an essential piece of kit, believe me. It comes in handy in situations like yours.'

They walked over to the van.

'Have you got the results of the post mortem? I'm assuming it's not going to be good with water in the engine?' Verity crossed her fingers. 'I've put so much work into this van. It should have been my travelling home for the next six months.'

'A small amount of water in the intake cylinders won't harm anything as long as it isn't enough to hydrolock the engine.'

'Which means?'

Nathan smiled. 'That means the water can't take up more space than is left when the piston gets to the top.'

Verity knew she had a look of confusion on her face. She had no clue what any of that meant. 'And again, in idiot's language that means?'

'Water won't compress, so the result is physical damage. But if the damage is minor, I can restore the engine with a new set of spark plugs and a change of fluids and oils. There is a possibility, if the engine has suffered from severe hydrolocking, it will require more in-depth repairs. You're next on my list so it shouldn't be too long before I have answers. I'll just finish off the car I'm working on. Feel free to hang up anything you wish. There's cleaning products and clean cloths on that shelf over there.'

'Thank you.'

Nathan soon had his head back under the bonnet of the car inside the workshop. Verity stepped inside the van and looked around. She was pleasantly surprised to see it wasn't as bad as she'd thought it would be. The water hadn't reached the height of the bed and the mattress was still dry. Water had seeped in through the doors and some food items in the bottom cupboards had been ruined but everything else didn't seem that bad. She just prayed the engine wasn't badly damaged.

Taking a mop and bucket, Verity began to mop up the excess water on the van's floor then moved on to the lower cupboards, throwing away the spoiled food.

An hour later, she sat down on one of the chairs. 'Have you always lived on the island?' she asked Nathan, who still had his head under the car's bonnet.

'Ten years now. My grandparents used to bring me on day trips from Sea's End and I was obsessed with all the boats in the harbour. I was always a tinkerer. Taking things apart and putting them back together. One summer I took apart my dad's lawn mower and couldn't put it back together so he got me a job in the local boathouse to keep me from destroying anything else, and I worked there until an opportunity came up at this place. I took an apprenticeship and when the gaffer retired ten years ago, I bought him out and moved into his place on the island while he retired to the South of France.'

'Very nice,' replied Verity. 'This place is so beautiful and working up here... I mean, look at that view.'

Nathan stood up and looked out across the sea. 'I couldn't think of working or living anywhere else.'

'You're very lucky. It must feel like you're constantly on holiday.'

'It did when I first moved onto the island, even though I had been working here for years and the islanders had already adopted me as one of their own.'

'That's lovely,' replied Verity. 'What's that building next to you?'

'That's puffin headquarters.'

'And that is?'

'It used to be Pete's veterinary practice before he retired. He still uses it from time to time to rescue injured puffins and still cares for any injured domestic animals on the island if the tide is in.'

Watching the group of people standing on the cliff top outside Pete's cottage, Verity asked, 'What exactly are they doing? It all looks very official.'

'It is. They take their puffin counting very seriously. The puffin census starts tomorrow but they're a ranger down. I noticed this morning they've appealed for someone to step in and help out, but most of the islanders have their own businesses, which would mean closing for a few days.'

'And what does the ranger do?'

'Counts the puffins.' He grinned.

'I suppose that was a stupid question.'

'Not at all,' Nathan said kindly. 'Now, I should probably crack on under this bonnet.' He wiped his hands on an oily rag. 'Then we can see if I'm writing a death certificate for that van of yours.'

Still watching the rangers, Verity found her thoughts tumbling over in her mind, and before she could stop herself, she began walking towards them. Pete was towering over the map, which was held down at the corners by four stones.

'Hi,' said Verity, wondering what sort of welcome she was going to get this time.

'You again. You keep popping up everywhere,' he said, nodding goodbye to the rest of the rangers, who were just leaving. They both watched as the small group headed down the path.

'Sorry, I didn't mean to interrupt.'

'You didn't.' Pete rolled up the map and secured it with an elastic band. 'We'd just finished.'

'I might be able to help you. I'm Verity.' She extended her hand and Pete hesitated before shaking it. 'And you're Puffin Pete, though obviously that's not your real name,' she prattled. 'And I meant what I said, I could help you.'

Pete didn't answer, just watched her carefully. Verity was on a mission to at least make him crack a smile, but she didn't like her chances.

'I hear you're a ranger down for the puffin census.'

Pete tilted his head to one side.

'I'm your girl, I can be your ranger.' Verity smiled. 'What do you think?'

'And what do you know about puffins?'

Verity grinned. 'I don't know where to start.'

'At the beginning,' came his reply.

She nodded. This was her opportunity to dazzle him with her knowledge. 'They're about this high.' She lowered her hand to the ground.

Pete raised both eyebrows.

'A puffin's beak changes colour during the year. In the winter the beak is a dull, greyish colour but in spring it blossoms to an outrageous orange.' She pointed to the puffins standing on the cliffs, but Pete continued staring at her. 'That bright colour helps puffins assess potential mates. I've often thought about wearing an orange lipstick to increase my chances of attracting a decent male, as I usually attract losers,' she joked, watching Pete closely. She was sure she'd seen a tiny twitch of his mouth. He might just be about to crack a smile.

'They're carnivores, live off small fish, herring, hake and sand eels. And they're fab flyers; I believe a puffin can flap their wings up to four hundred times a minute and can speed through the air up to eighty-eight kilometres an hour. So, they're pretty fast. Not only fab flyers, but swimmers, too. They use their webbed feet as a rudder and can dive below sixty metres. They usually pair up with the same partner as in previous years. It's amazing, isn't it, how they actually know who their puffin partner is? I mean, they all look the same. Anyway, some puffins have had the same partner for over twenty years. Unlike me, I didn't even get him up the aisle, though I know now that was a blessing in disguise. Once a cheat, always a cheat. Hence why I'm here. I'm on a journey to find myself and become a strong, independent woman. To be fair, it's been a hell of a start.'

Pete smiled.

Job done.

Verity was secretly pleased.

'Oh! And when starting a puffin family, they dig out a burrow using their sharp claws and beak, then build nests lined with feathers and grass, and that's where the female lays her eggs. Thirty-six to forty-five days later the baby puffling hatches.'

'I'm impressed. How do you know so much about puffins?'

'My granny was obsessed with puffins and I'm a veterinary assistant. Not that there's many puffins where I live.'

'Do you have references?'

'I do. I have paper copies in the van'—she pointed behind her—'or I can email them across.'

Pete nodded. 'Paper copies work. I'm not one for technology.'

'I'll go now then and bring them straight back.' Verity nearly tripped up as she walked backwards. 'Don't go anywhere! And by the way, I'm sure you smiled then, just a little.'

His smile widened. 'Don't go counting your pufflings before they've hatched. I want to see your references first. And where are you staying? On the island?'

Verity had to think fast on her feet as she didn't want to mention Sam after witnessing this afternoon's incident in the village hall. 'In my travelling van.' She pointed towards the garage but passed it and hurried back to Cosy Nook Cottage, where the references were tucked safely inside her rucksack. Even though she was on a high, there was a possibility Sam would be there. As she practically ran down the coastal path, she wondered exactly what he was going to say to her, knowing that she'd heard exactly what he'd said about her.

Chapter Ten

Standing on the step outside Cosy Nook Cottage, Verity didn't know whether to knock or let herself in with the key. But before she could make a decision the front door opened and Sam was standing there. 'You can come in, you know.'

It felt like he'd been waiting for her. Sam stepped aside and she walked past him. He'd changed his clothes since this morning and Verity tried not to give him a once-over as she walked past, even though his delicious aroma got her every time. Determined not to let him off the hook lightly, or make this easy for him, she stood in the middle of the living room. As soon as Jimmy got wind the front door had been opened, he bounded in and launched himself at her. She ruffled his head and smiled at the adorable dog before he ran off through the kitchen into the garden.

'He likes to sit at the back gate, watching the world go by.'

You couldn't mistake the tension in the air but Verity wasn't going to be the one to address it first. She waited.

'You're mad at me, I can tell.' Sam looked rather sheepish.

'Why would I possibly be mad at you? Oh wait, perhaps it could be the fact you called me an idiot quite a few times in front of the whole island?' she said pointedly.

'I wasn't really calling you'—he held out his hands towards her—'an idiot, as such…'

'As such?' She cocked an eyebrow. 'It sounded very clear to me exactly what you were calling me.'

'I was just making a point that people don't take enough notice of the tide times, and it costs money. If there were barriers—'

'I've already heard your speech. The way you spoke to Pete in front of everyone was unforgivable.'

'You don't know the whole situation so who are you to judge?'

Verity could see the mention of Pete had instantly maddened him.

'What's the situation?'

Sam didn't answer.

'Sometimes it's good to talk to someone who isn't involved in said situation.'

For a second Sam looked as if he might say something but then he changed his mind.

'Whatever has gone on between you two, there are ways of talking to people and that wasn't kind, especially in front of everyone. You don't know what battles he's fighting; no one knows what's going on in anyone's life.'

'Unbelievable. You've only been here two minutes and

without knowing all the facts have decided I'm in the wrong.'

'So tell me the facts.' Verity thought she saw a look of sadness flash across his face.

'It's private business but what he did was unforgivable and I have to live with the consequences every day.' He paused. 'But I'm sorry if you thought I made you out to be an—'

'Idiot,' she interrupted. 'You know it was a genuine mistake and you could have used me as a positive example.' She projected her voice. '"Only this morning, Verity, who is visiting the island, got stuck on the causeway and had to be rescued. Unfortunately, the clock had stopped in her van and she thought it was safe to cross. If the barriers had been there, it would have stopped her driving on to the causeway." Instead, you made me out to be some sort of halfwit.'

Sam held her gaze. 'You're right. I'm sorry. I'm just passionate about keeping everyone as safe as possible and we've been butting heads on this matter for quite a while now.'

'I'm assuming there's more to your dislike of Pete than his opposition to the barriers?'

From Sam's silence, Verity knew that was exactly the case but she didn't push it. It was clear that whatever it was ran deep. 'You know what my granny once told me? We all only have one time on this earth so be nice to each other. We may have a difference of opinion but the fact we aren't all the same is wonderful and is what makes the world go around.'

'Sometimes things happen that can't be put right.'

Once again, they stared at each other for some time before Verity broke the silence. 'Thank you for the apology. I've been up to see Nathan and he's looking at the van. I just need to get my rucksack, I need my references.'

'References?'

'I may have just landed myself a job for a few days as a volunteer ranger, counting puffins!'

'The puffin census? Pete's in charge of that, how's that come about?'

'I followed him out of the hall because he looked upset. I wanted to make sure he was okay so I checked on him again after I visited the garage.'

Sam's eyes widened. His mouth opened but no words came out.

'Look, I'm not taking sides here, and it's obviously none of my business, but I don't like to see anyone upset and he looked distressed, like he had the weight of the world on his shoulders. It might just be that he needs a friend, living up there on his own.'

'And you're suggesting that you're going to be that friend?'

Verity was quiet. She could see by the look on Sam's face he was not enjoying this conversation. 'Whatever it is between you both, it's not my argument. I take people as I find them and treat them how they treat me.'

'This is unbelievable. He's got the weight of the world on his shoulders all right.'

'I'm going to go.' She pointed to the door.

Sam stepped aside and didn't say any more. The door closed behind her, leaving Verity wondering what the hell had gone on between them.

Chapter Eleven

Verity walked back towards Cliff Top Cottage, the conversation with Sam very much on her mind. From the short time she'd spent in his company she thought of him as ambitious yet laid back, enjoying life and living for the moment without many cares; but he definitely had a problem with Pete. What could be so bad as to cause so much resentment between the two men? As she ambled up the cliff path towards the cottage she saw Pete sitting outside on a rickety old chair, with a newspaper spread across his lap. He looked up when he heard the crunch of gravel under her feet.

He closed the newspaper. 'You came back then?'

'I did. You didn't doubt me, did you?' She smiled, placing her rucksack on the table and rummaging inside. 'Here we go. They were sorry to see me go and didn't expect it, if I'm honest.'

'Why did you resign?' He nodded towards the wicker rocking chair beside him. Verity sat down and immediately rocked backward, taking her feet clean off the ground. She tried to steady herself.

Pete tried to hide his smile. 'That chair gets me every time.'

'I needed a change of scenery. I'm fast approaching thirty and needed to sort out my life.'

'And you had your heart broken.'

She eyed him carefully. 'And that, too. But since I've been here, I'm lucky the thought of him has barely crossed my mind.'

Pete nodded. 'Counting puffins will keep you busy.'

'Does that mean I've got the job?'

'Judging by these references I'd be silly not to take you on. It's clear they would take you back in a heartbeat.'

'That was the plan for after my travels, but I'm beginning to think there's more to life than the same street that I've lived in for a very long time, going through the same routine, with the new added nuisance of constantly trying to avoid my ex, who has moved in across the street.'

'That can't be easy.'

'What about you? How long have you been here?'

Pete looked towards the cottage. 'A lifetime.'

'Have you ever thought about moving?'

'No, I couldn't. I'm waiting.'

'Waiting for what?

'Just waiting,' he replied, taking out his handkerchief and mopping his brow. 'Would you like a drink?

'Tea would be good. If you have time.'

'I have a lot of time on my hands now I'm retired. I used to be in the same game as you.'

'I think you were higher up the game than me. I believe

that used to be your vet's practice,' she said, pointing to the building.

'It did. I do miss the everyday routine.'

Verity watched Pete disappear inside the cottage. Even though at first he appeared to be a little rough around the edges, he'd really started to soften and Verity liked him. She didn't find him difficult to talk to at all.

He soon returned and handed her a mug of tea. 'You'll need old clothes for the puffin count as you're mainly going to be wriggling on the ground with your arm stuffed down a hole. Bare hands, too, as you have to detect the presence of monogamous pairs and whether they're sitting on an egg. I can guarantee after a while you'll be sick of it.' Pete held out his hand. It was covered with tiny scars. 'Puffin bites. I suppose it's only natural they're unsettled when they see a hand coming into the burrow.'

Verity looked down at her own hands.

'There's still time to change your mind.'

'Absolutely not, I'm up for the challenge.'

Pete nodded. 'So, why a veterinary assistant? Why not carry on with your learning, become the boss?'

Verity knew exactly why and saying it out loud she could kick herself now. 'Because my partner at the time didn't like me to grow. He kind of sucked the life out of me a little, and it's only in looking back now that I can see how he suppressed my personality to fit in with him, and his friends, and the life *he* wanted…'

'But now? There's nothing stopping you if you have the drive and ambition.'

Verity considered what Pete was saying. 'You're absolutely right but that'll mean a lot more studying.'

'But it would be worth it in the long run.'

'You've certainly given me something to think about.' Verity looked over towards the building by the garage that used to be Pete's veterinary surgery. 'It's a shame it's closed.'

'It won't be for long. I know there aren't many residents on the island but the vet from Sea's End is looking to open a second surgery and we're in the middle of negotiations. It might only be a part-time surgery at first but my guess is those hours will increase as time goes on.'

They both looked up as a shadow was cast over them. Nathan was standing there with a smile on his face. 'You're one lucky lady.'

Verity gave a tiny gasp and put her hand on her heart. 'Are you saying what I think you're saying?'

Nathan nodded. 'You can pick up the van tomorrow lunchtime.'

'Thank you!'

'I've even fixed the clock for you, so you don't have any more causeway accidents in the future.'

'What's this?' asked Pete as they watched Nathan walk back towards the garage.

'I'm the idiot that drove onto the causeway this morning and got stranded.' She put up her hands. 'But in my defence it was a genuine accident. My phone was flat and the clock in my van wasn't working.'

'And where do you sit on the barrier discussion?'

'I can actually see both sides and I do hope you can work it out soon between you all. It can't be much fun butting heads all the time.'

'It's never fun butting heads when each side is

passionate. Where are you going to stay tonight, the hotel or B&B?'

'I'll be sleeping in my van once it's ready, but tonight I'm staying with Sam.'

At least, she hoped that invitation was open for one more night, despite their disagreement.

'It's a lovely cottage he has.'

'Yes, but I think you're in one of the best spots on the island.'

Pete looked towards his cottage but didn't say anything, just nodded.

'I'd best be going,' she said, not wanting to outstay her welcome. 'What time do you want me reporting for duty?'

'Eight a.m. sharp. Meeting here.'

'I'll see you in the morning then. Thank you for my tea.'

Taking back her references, Verity headed down the cliff path and across the bay. The tearoom was heaving when she passed and Clemmie waved in her direction as Verity weaved through the tourists wandering up and down Lighthouse Lane. Cosy Nook Cottage was up ahead and Verity was hoping everything was okay between her and Sam. As she approached the rainbow cottages, she spotted Sam standing on the doorstep talking to a woman. Verity recognised her immediately from the photographs on the internet – it was Betty! She was back from her trip.

Stopping a few feet away so as not to interrupt, Verity caught the tail-end of their conversation.

'The vigil is coming up, Sam. You know I loved your grandfather and you know I love you, but I honestly think you have to let it lie. I don't want to fall out with you, but no one knows what happened that night and you're scuppering your chances of ever finding out by acting like this, especially with this feud still ongoing. You know I can't take sides.'

'Betty, I can't let this lie. My gut feeling has always told me there's more to this then it seems, and I can't shake that feeling. I think there's something we don't know.'

'Or it could have just been the tragic accident it appeared to be at the time.'

'That logbook tells us they were on shift together so where was he? Why wasn't he there?'

'Over the years we've had the same conversation and I know it's always especially raw for you around the time of the anniversary, but you know he'll turn up at the remembrance vigil and you need to make peace with that. He deserves to be able to pay his respects too.' Betty touched his arm briefly before she walked away.

Verity wanted to meet Betty and share what she'd discovered about Joe and the book, hoping that the woman could shed a little more light on the situation, but now didn't seem the right moment to introduce herself, so she kept her head down until Betty had passed.

Knocking on the cottage door a moment later, Verity stood and waited, feeling a little apprehensive. She didn't like any sort of conflict and there appeared to be a wealth of it between Sam and Pete. Jimmy barked and could be heard frantically sniffing on the other side of the door, and when Sam opened it Verity was relieved to be greeted with a smile.

'You came back. I wasn't sure if you would.'

'For one night only, if you'll have me?' She gave him a hopeful smile and crossed her fingers.

'Only one night?'

'Hetty has survived and I can get her back tomorrow!'

'Wow! How lucky are you?'

'Very lucky.'

'Are you hungry?'

'I'm ravenous and that smell is making me even hungrier.' Verity stepped into the living room then popped her head into the kitchen.

'Homemade lasagne and garlic bread.'

'A man of many talents.'

'A glass of wine?'

'You're spoiling me.'

Sam went to the fridge and took out a chilled bottle of wine. After pouring them both a glass he gestured towards the open back door. Jimmy had already run outside ahead of them.

'It's a beautiful evening and I can't stay indoors on an evening like this.'

Verity followed him outside. 'Look at that view. The sea and the horizon line are such a pretty colour today.'

'It's gorgeous, isn't it?'

Verity liked the way his eyes shone at her as he said that. She was sure he didn't just mean the view.

Just beyond the gate was a beautiful small cove with unspoiled shallow blue waters. Verity walked towards the gate and stood next to Jimmy.

'I couldn't imagine having this at the bottom of my garden. You have a beautiful cove, whereas out of my bedroom window I have a wonderful view of a coffee factory.' She chuckled. 'But not for the next six months. Aww, look at that.' In the middle of the cove's tiny beach was a bistro table and chairs, the table covered in a white tablecloth with a couple of plates and glasses on top. 'What a pretty setting. Are you expecting company?' She nudged his elbow playfully.

'I was hoping.' Sam opened the gate. 'Come on.'

Jimmy ran out of the gate straight to the water's edge, and charged through the shallow waves. Sam walked onto the sand and pulled out a chair. 'Welcome to Cosy Nook Cove.'

'Your own cove! It's like something a millionaire would have.'

'It's always been part of the cottage.'

Verity sat down and looked out across the water. Sam sat down opposite her and took a sip of wine. 'Are we friends again?' he asked. 'I don't like the thought of us not talking.'

She nodded then smiled. 'We're friends, and for the record, I don't either.'

'I wasn't sure whether you'd come back after this morning.'

'I'm not one for holding grudges, and I could smell that lasagne all the way from the cliff top. I'm not an idiot, I wasn't going to miss out on that, now, was I?' She grinned.

'I'm sorry again about that. I should have used a different word.'

'You're forgiven. Even more so when you feed me.'

Suddenly, Sam looked alarmed. 'Oh my…the lasagne!' he exclaimed, standing up quickly. 'It was ready ten minutes ago.'

Verity watched Sam hurry through the gate back into the kitchen before he reappeared holding a tray loaded with lasagne, garlic bread and a fresh green salad.

'Dinner is served.'

With Jimmy now lying in the shade by the rocks, Sam served up the food.

'I think I may come again, if I get this kind of treatment.'

'You're welcome anytime. What are your plans once the van is fixed?'

Verity picked up her knife and fork. 'I'm going to stay for a few days while I help with the puffin census, then see how I feel. As you know, Ava, my friend, isn't going to make it to Amsterdam and I was only going so as to escape heartache and find myself.'

'And how's that going?'

'Very well,' she replied. 'A week ago I'd have never envisaged I'd be sitting here with a handsome man, having dinner in a private cove. My old life already seems a distant memory. It's funny, actually, I've come to realise I never really knew my ex at all. You watch documentaries about people leading double lives but you never expect it from someone you actually know. And if he can lie that easily all the time, I can't see him ever changing his ways. Good luck to both of them, I say. And what about you? Have you ever had someone special in your life?'

'Once,' he admitted. 'An experience never to be repeated.'

Sam looked out across the water, avoiding Verity's eyes.

'You may feel different when a new someone special walks into your life.'

He shook his head. 'I'm single through choice. It's the best way for me.'

'Why would you think that?'

'Because it's true.'

'If my opinion matters, that's a waste. You have a lot to offer.'

He raised his eyebrow. 'Such as?'

'A dog, which is always a bonus, a beautiful cove and, to be honest, on a scale of one to ten you aren't that bad looking.'

Sam laughed. 'And where would I be on that scale?'

'I'd say around a nine point five. There's always room for improvement.' She winked then grinned. 'And it's not cool to go fishing for compliments, you know,' she added, knowing she had a glint in her eye.

'And what about you? Do you think you'll ever go looking for love again?'

'Absolutely!' she replied without hesitation. 'I want a family, though preferably not with a lying, cheating bastard. I have a lot to share with the right person and they're definitely missing out right at this moment because, look at me, I'm a good catch. I'm sitting here in clothes belonging to someone else, I've got no job – though that could change at any moment because I'm sure I'll get something when I start looking – and I'm sleeping in the back of a van.'

'You're definitely a good catch for someone.' He gave her a warm, lopsided grin.

Verity noted the 'for someone'. 'I'm glad you think so.'

They held eye contact for a second as they picked up their drinks. Every time Verity looked into his eyes her heart leapt and she got an all-over jittery feeling. She was attracted to him and could feel the electricity sparking between them, and, despite what he was claiming, she suspected he could feel it too.

'I have to say, you aren't a half bad cook. I think this is

possibly the best lasagne I've ever tasted. It's definitely up there with the best. It's nice of you to cook for me. I usually go through the ready meals in the frozen counter in the local supermarket. They're so bland that sometimes I question exactly what I've eaten.'

'I do have a confession to make. I know it said it was homemade, and that's not a lie…it's just not homemade by me!'

'Sam!'

'Betty makes meals to order at the tearoom and I put in an order this morning.'

'So you knew you were going to wine and dine me then, did you?'

'I hoped…and if not, it would freeze!'

'Sam Wilson, is this a date?' She was teasing him yet secretly wanted to see his reaction.

'I'd prefer to stay single, but that doesn't stop me having dinner with an attractive woman and enjoying myself, does it?'

She smiled, liking the way he called her attractive. 'I just don't understand why you're single by choice. Has something happened for you to think that way?' She knew she was being nosey, but she really wanted to know what had happened between him and Alice.

'It's just the way it is, but it doesn't mean that I don't like female company. I'm having a wonderful evening.' He picked up his glass, his eyes not leaving hers as he sipped his wine. As he put the glass down, her gaze dropped to his lips and she wondered exactly what it would it be like to kiss him.

'I know, you're one of these commitment-phobes.' Verity

didn't want to drop the conversation so presented her question in a joking manner.

'I'm committed to my dog, my restaurant, the upkeep of my cottage and memories of my family.'

'You know exactly what I meant. I think it's very sad that you don't want to find your special person to share all that with.'

'Maybe I'm enough. Maybe I like my own company. Maybe I'm happy because my life is full of peace and calm.'

'But are you happy with life?'

'What do you mean by that?'

Without thinking, she said, 'I overheard part of your conversation with Betty earlier, when I arrived. Fighting with Pete can't make you happy; this ongoing feud between you two must be draining.'

As soon as she said Pete's name the smile dropped from Sam's face and she instantly wished she'd never said a word.

'Let's not have this conversation and spoil the evening.' Sam slid back his chair and walked to the water's edge. Jimmy was soon by his side and Sam bent down and threw a stick into the water.

Verity quietly exhaled. She could kick herself. She didn't mean to upset Sam or the evening. Knowing she'd overstepped the mark, she picked up both of their glasses and walked to the water's edge. She handed one glass to Sam.

'I'm sorry, I didn't mean to upset you.'

'It's difficult to talk about.'

'It's okay, I shouldn't have pushed the conversation. I suppose I'm just finding it difficult to understand the issue now that I've spent some time in your company and in Pete's. You both seem like decent people to me. Whatever is going on, wouldn't a simple conversation between you both be the way forward? You could talk it out, agree to disagree, and as for the barriers on the island, I'm no rocket scientist but even I could come up with a simple solution that would satisfy both sides.'

'Don't you think I've tried with Pete? I've tried to have that conversation on more than one occasion but…'

'But? What can be that bad?'

Sam looked her straight in the eyes. 'I think Pete was responsible for my grandfather's death and he's the only one that knows the truth.'

Verity let the long pause that followed Sam's shocking declaration hang in the air for as long as she dared.

'Why do you think that?'

'Sorry, Verity, I just need a little space. Can you give me a minute?'

She nodded and watched as Sam turned and headed towards the gate, Jimmy close on his heels as they disappeared into the kitchen. Standing on the sand, she wasn't quite sure what to do. Should she follow him or not? He said he needed space but to her it looked like he was battling some sort of trauma. Not wanting to see him upset, she decided to follow, but as soon as she stepped into the kitchen, she heard the front door shut behind him. She could kick herself. He'd gone to all this trouble to spend some time with her and now she'd driven him away. Making her way back to the cove, Verity cleared away the dishes and washed them up before heading back outside. After pouring herself some more wine she sat back, thinking about the death of Joe Wilson. She Googled him from her phone and browsed through a selection of images. One caught her eye as she immediately recognised the makeshift stage in the corner of The Olde Ship Inn, in exactly the same spot where Sam had performed only last night. The next photo showed the group standing on a jetty, a crowd stretching all along Blue Water Bay. Verity knew it was Puffin Island from the lighthouse towering in the distance. Scrolling further down she was shocked to read the next headline.

Multi-talented Joe Wilson, singer-songwriter, loses his life in the same spot he performed only hours earlier to a packed-out bay.

There was a photo of Joe with his hands clutching a microphone, looking very rock 'n' roll with a guitar slung across his body. Verity read the article and felt her eyes brimming with tears as she learned the way his life was taken.

'Playing detective?'

Sam was back and standing behind her, looking down at her phone screen.

'You're back.'

'I'm sorry. I just needed a breather and I used the time to pick up another bottle.' He held up the wine.

'You don't need to be sorry. I honestly wasn't prying as such. I was just trying to understand why you were so upset. Sam, this is awful, such a tragic accident.'

'It's okay, it's not a secret; it's there in black and white.'

'I don't recognise that pier, is it no longer there?'

Sam sat back down opposite her. 'The pier was demolished after there had been numerous deaths. Never mind the causeway putting lives at risk, that pier was the worst danger on the island.'

'How?' asked Verity, not quite understanding.

'The pier was on stilts and tourists loved to jump off it, thinking it was safe, despite numerous signs telling them not to enter the water under the pier. The rip currents that flow through there are well known to everyone on the island, as they can quickly drag people and debris away from the shallows and out into the deeper water, but tourists didn't always read the safety warnings.'

'But your grandfather would know about the rip currents, surely?'

'He did because he was also one of the volunteer coastguards.'

'So how was he dragged out to sea?'

'According to the coastguard logbook he was on duty that night along with...'

'Pete?'

Sam nodded. 'His so-called best friend. But something just doesn't stack up. I know it was before my time, but I believe there's more to my grandfather's death.'

'It says here it was an accident.'

'It could have been, but, as I said, my grandfather was a volunteer coastguard and knew about the rip currents. He wouldn't have just jumped in without backup.'

'What does Pete say?'

'This is where it gets interesting, because for whatever reason he was late for duty that day. The logbook shows he clocked in thirty minutes late. No one was ever late on duty.

You were there to save lives and if you couldn't attend your shift or were going to be late, you'd arrange for another coastguard to cover you.'

'What was Pete's excuse for being late?'

'It was never explained. All I know is that Pete was late and my grandfather died.'

'And you think he has something to do with it?'

'I think he knows more than he's letting on, but he won't speak to me about it. When I was younger, I tried to talk to him about it, but I admit I was a little hot-headed in my approach.'

'What happened?'

'He was up at Cliff Top Cottage and we actually ended up getting into an altercation.'

'You got into a fight?'

'I'm not proud about it, but yes. I think more out of frustration than anger. He couldn't or wouldn't give me any answers no matter how many times I asked him where he was that night. Why hadn't he arrived on time? Was he late because they'd had some sort of falling out? After I suggested that, Pete shook his head and went to walk away but I grabbed his shoulder, spun him around and went to land a punch clean on his jaw. But I missed. Lost my balance and fell to the ground. Before I knew it, he was holding out his hand to help me up. I refused, got up, brushed myself down and went in for a second punch. That time he defended himself and grabbed my hand. He pushed me backwards and I fell again. I decided to grab his legs and we were both grappling on the ground until I felt my legs being pulled. I looked around and it was Betty.' He paused whilst he filled the glasses with a little more wine.

'Sam Wilson, get up on your feet right this minute,' said Sam, mimicking her voice, and smiled. 'You don't mess with Betty Rose. If she says jump, you bloody jump.'

Verity smiled. 'My granny was a bit like that,' she shared. 'Heart of gold, would do anything for anyone, but if she was mad or you crossed her, you'd know about it.'

'Betty literally got me by the scruff of the neck and marched me down the cliff top path, along the bay and up Lighthouse Lane. Betty lives in Cobblestone Cottage near the tearoom. She didn't let go of the scruff of my neck until she sat me down on the chair in her kitchen.'

'I know I shouldn't laugh but…' A giggle escaped Verity. 'And what's Betty's take on it all?'

'She's never talked about it in much detail. She did admit that she knew for a fact Pete was nowhere near the pier at the time, but she said she would never divulge how she knew that. I just had to trust her.'

'And would she lie to you?'

Sam shook his head. 'What you see is what you get with Betty, but because she's never told me how she knows for sure, from time to time it still eats away at me. I just want answers and for some reason no one is giving them to me. It's like she's protecting something or someone.'

'I can see how difficult it must be for you, especially each year when the anniversary comes around.'

'And this year it's been fifty years. Pete has never had another conversation with me about it but that night, during the fight, I could see in his eyes he knew something. I've no evidence to back this up, but I think he's been living with the guilt of something for all these years.'

'And what makes you think that?'

'You yourself mentioned that Cliff Top Cottage was one of the most sought-after cottages on the island, just like mine, and you're right. I've received letters through the door on many occasions asking if I wanted to sell the property, and people have offered me more than the actual value of the cottage, but I'd never part with it. And it would have been the same for Cliff Top Cottage, except that soon after my grandfather's death, Pete started letting it fall apart. People say it was like he had no love for the cottage anymore. He kept himself to himself, concentrated on his job, and never played music again in public.'

'Played music?'

'Pete was in the band with my grandfather.'

'Wow! So he was offered the record contract and had the chance to go on tour too?'

Sam nodded. 'My grandfather and Pete were like Lennon and McCartney. Girls flocked at their feet. They wrote songs together, they performed together and, according to Betty and the magazine articles, you barely ever saw one without the other. Which makes me wonder yet again where Pete was that night, and why he wasn't there to help my grandfather when he needed it.'

Verity unlocked her phone and glanced at the photos of the band. 'Which one is Pete?' she asked.

Sam pointed. 'That's my grandfather – he was the lead singer and guitarist – and that's Pete, who was also a singer and guitarist. On the drums was Betty's late husband Eric, and John, another local resident, was the keyboard player. John is now a retired fisherman and lives in one of the cottages by the harbour.'

'And what's his relationship like with Pete?'

'Very much the same as Betty's. They're still friends.'

'Don't be annoyed with me when I say this…' She paused, knowing that Sam was incredibly vulnerable and that she needed to word this very carefully. 'Have you ever considered that Pete may just have been grieving like everyone else? It must have been a shock to him if he lost his best friend, and grief affects people in many different ways. I know that, even now, when I think of my granny, I can get very emotional.' She reached across and placed her hand on top of his, and noticed the tears filling his eyes before he quickly blinked them away.

'I get all that, I really do, but there's just one question I want answered, and I don't think that's too much to ask. But apparently it's a question no one is prepared to answer, and when Pete passes away, he'll take it with him to the grave.'

'And what is that question?'

'Like I've said, where was Pete the night my grandfather died? What made him late for his shift?'

'With the fiftieth anniversary coming up, maybe this is your chance to try again. Maybe you could attempt to put the feud behind you? Build some bridges. There's one thing that should be uniting you both at this time and that's the love you both have for your grandfather.'

'I wish it was that easy.'

'Make it that easy. Only you can do this. You never know, if you open up to Pete like you have to me, you might just get the answers you need. It must be worth thinking about, surely?'

Sam looked at her. 'Are you always this wise?'

'I have my moments.'

'Thank you.'

'For?'

'Listening. I've never really talked about it before; only to Betty, and she must be sick of hearing about it by now.' Sam stood up and held his arms open. Verity placed her glass down before stepping into them. He hugged her tight, a proper hug. Resting her head against his chest, she took in his scent, the fragrance of the aftershave she'd squirted in his bathroom. She briefly closed her eyes, not wanting to step out from his arms.

Sam pulled away slowly and handed her back her glass as they walked side by side to the water's edge.

They watched Jimmy chase a seagull along the waterline for a while before Sam asked, 'Have you got any plans for tonight or would you like to watch a film on Netflix?'

'No plans and that'll be lovely as long as it's not some action-packed boys' film.'

He grinned. 'I don't mind getting in touch with my feminine side. I'll be right back.'

She looked at him, confused. 'Where are you going? Are we not watching the film inside?'

'Wait and see. I'll be back!'

'Never mind quoting Arnold Schwarzenegger, we agreed no action films!'

Sam grinned as he disappeared back inside the cottage. Jimmy raced after him, giving a playful bark, leaving Verity wondering what Sam was up to. A couple of minutes later he reappeared carrying a mountain of cushions and dropped them on the sand in front of the bistro table. He laid out a large blanket then arranged the cushions in a long line. Without saying another word, he disappeared inside again. When he reappeared this time, he was juggling candles and a lighter.

'Are you sure I can't help you with anything?'

'No, you relax. Two more trips and we'll be good to go.' His eyes sparkled as he caught Verity's gaze. Walking around the blanket and cushions he began to space the tealight candles out evenly. On the second walk around he lit them all.

'Candles, very romantic,' she murmured.

'Keeps the midges away.' He gave her a lopsided grin.

After returning to the cottage again, he brought out a picnic basket and placed it at one end of the blanket. 'I'm going to get Jimmy settled in the kitchen then I'll be back out.'

'Are we really staying out here? Where's the TV?'

'Wait and see.' He wasn't giving anything away.

Five minutes later, Sam shut the cottage door and walked towards Verity carrying a cardboard box and a small fabric stool. 'I'm hoping this will work.'

'What is it?'

'This is a smartphone projector. A great way to watch movies. Just place your smartphone inside the box, face it forward, and the lens at the front of the box enlarges the image up to eight times and projects the image onto any surface. It's perfect as it requires no set-up.'

'I've never seen one of those.'

'It's like magic. The whole thing is made from cardboard and glass, totally wireless, and uses no additional power. Sometimes in The Sea Glass Restaurant we project images of the fish swimming in the sea onto the wall. But first, let's get ourselves comfy.' With the most gorgeous smile, Sam sat up for a moment and reached inside the picnic basket. 'Something to celebrate your time on Puffin Island.' He held up a bottle and two flutes.

'Champagne! Wow, you're pulling out all the stops. I thought you'd just bought more wine.'

'That can keep.' Sam popped the cork, which launched into the air and landed on the sand right at the edge of the water. Verity giggled and got up to race after it.

'What are you doing?' he asked, watching her in amusement.

'Keeping the cork. It's going in my memory box to commemorate my time on Puffin Island,' she replied, flopping back down on the cushions and placing it on the blanket next to her before sitting cross-legged. She felt extremely relaxed and comfortable in Sam's company, enjoying every moment of the evening. Today had gotten off to a shaky start with him, but she liked how he'd opened up to her this evening, especially as she knew it must have been difficult, given he didn't have full closure over his grandfather's death. Sitting next to him now, she felt like she'd known him for years.

Sam poured the champagne and handed her a glass. 'Just for you.' After filling his own he clinked his glass against hers. 'Here's to great company, and a fabulous film night.'

'But how do we watch the film?'

Sam reached inside the box, pressed the screen on his phone, then placed it back inside the projector and rested it on top of the fabric stool. He pointed it towards a smooth white rock that lay right in front of them. The image was projected onto the rock like a screen in the cinema.

'How cool is that?' Verity was amazed.

'Pretty cool,' he said, taking out a large bowl of popcorn and placing it at the edge of the blanket. He lay down on his stomach, and Verity mirrored his actions, their bodies touching.

'You never said which film we're watching.'

'I thought I'd keep the beach theme.'

She laughed. 'Please tell me we're not watching *Jaws*.'

'Not quite.'

Verity threw back her head and laughed as *The Little Mermaid* began to play.

'It's personally one of my faves,' he said, grinning and taking a handful of popcorn out of the bowl. He popped a couple of pieces into his mouth then held some towards Verity. His hand brushed against hers, sending shivers through her entire body as he gave her an adorable smile.

Verity was unsure exactly what was happening here. Despite his earlier protestation that he wasn't looking for a relationship, this felt very much like a date to her – possibly the most romantic date she'd ever been on. When she'd set off from home on her journey, the last thing on her mind was getting involved in any sort of relationship, but she knew the second she'd spotted Sam queuing at the greasy spoon there was something special about him.

The best thing to do was sit back and enjoy this night and his company without overthinking it, which was already becoming extremely difficult, because if Verity was to be honest with herself, the red-hot desire she felt for Sam was beginning to consume her. He was quickly becoming the reason she wanted to stay on Puffin Island a little longer.

Chapter Twelve

'Verity! Why are you whispering?'

Verity was lying in bed in the spare room of Cosy Nook Cottage with the duvet pulled over her head. She'd rung Ava to wish her good luck with her move to London.

'Because he might hear me.'

'Who might hear you? Where are you?'

'Sam Wilson, the gorgeous guy from the greasy spoon that I followed onto the ferry and after I tried to drown Hetty. He's taken me in.'

'You're in some random guy's house?'

'It's not just a house, it's a gorgeous cottage with stunning views, a secret bookcase and, would you believe, its own cove.'

'He might be a mass murderer. You don't even know this guy.'

'He's not a mass murderer. He's a normal guy with a dog, which is good as animal people are always the best. And he owns and manages The Sea Glass Restaurant, which is a floating restaurant on the harbour. I'm having a blast, we've been swimming in the sea close to midnight under the starlit sky. He sings, too, and performed in the pub – he was amazing – and last night, you're not going to believe this, but—'

'Did you sleep with him?'

'Don't be ridiculous,' came Verity's instant reply. Even though she'd wondered many times last night what it would be like to spend the night with Sam. When the movie finished, they'd packed up all the stuff from the cove and ventured back inside. Then Sam did the gentlemanly thing and showed her to her room, closing the door behind her and leaving her feeling a twinge of disappointment that there wasn't even a goodnight kiss on offer, especially after they'd been flirting with each other all night.

'That's a little disappointing.'

'Ava! I've only just come out of a relationship.'

'He never bowled you off your feet like this Sam character though. If we're being honest, he bored you most of the time. I can remember you asking me, Is this it? Is this what getting into a serious relationship is like? It's just cleaning and tidying up after someone and watching what he wants on TV? You'd checked out a long time ago, you just didn't want to admit it.'

The more Verity thought about that, the more she knew Ava was speaking the truth. Richard had never excited her. In fact, it was just like Ava had said; she was often bored and, to be honest with herself, felt lonelier in that relationship than when she was single. Even though she barely knew Sam, he created an excitement in the pit of her stomach she'd never felt with Richard.

'You're right. Last night he organised a cinema in his private cove, with champagne, candles and the sound of the sea lapping at the shore.'

'It sounds like something that only happens in the movies. Did he at least kiss you?'

'No!'

'What's wrong with him? There has to be something wrong with him!'

'We just had fun. He's not looking for a relationship.'

'That's what's wrong with him. There's some underlying issue there. Commitment issues. What's happened in his past for him not to want a relationship? Broken heart?'

'You're allowed to be happy on your own, you know.'

'Mmm, I'm not sure who you're trying to convince here. Sounds to me that you already like this guy, and if he's telling you he's happy single, you'll end up with your heart broken – especially given that you'll have to leave the island eventually.'

Verity's head was telling her exactly the same thing but last night her heart had not stopped leaping.

'What if I don't leave the island? I'm just throwing it out there.'

'You've only been there a couple of days. Everyone loves a holiday, but after a couple of weeks they always want to get back to the comfort of their own home.'

Verity wasn't sure about that. 'That might be so if your ex hasn't moved into the street with the woman he'd been having an affair with.'

'Fair point. But what I'm saying is that right now it's a novelty…'

'I've already made friends. Clemmie owns the tearoom and Amelia works in the bookshop and the pub.'

'It sounds like you're having a good time.'

'I am, so I'm going to keep enjoying myself. Oh! Guess what I'm going to be doing? I'm counting puffins!'

'You're doing what?'

'Today, I'm a Puffin Ranger. I've got myself a volunteer job helping with the puffin census.'

'You're living the dream, Verity Callaway!'

Verity laughed as she said goodbye and hung up. Usually, it was Ava who was the impulsive one, but this time it was Verity who felt free and ready to embrace the unexpected by throwing herself into island life.

Hearing a soft knock on her bedroom door, she jumped out of bed and pulled on Sam's sweatshirt.

Standing on the other side of the door was Sam, holding out a cup of tea. 'Coffee for the ranger. I've made breakfast, if you want to join me?'

'Coffee and breakfast! This bed and breakfast will be getting a five-star review on TripAdvisor from me,' she joked, padding down the stairs after him.

Stepping into the kitchen, Verity was immediately welcomed by Jimmy who circled around her, his tail wagging. 'Good morning, Jimmy!' She patted the top of his head and sat down at the table, which was draped with a pristine white tablecloth, and set for two places. Sam put toast in a rack in the middle of the table, followed by two plates of a full English breakfast.

'Gosh, I need to stay here more often. This will keep me going until this evening. Thank you, this looks amazing.'

'I've heard counting puffins is difficult work so this

might help you get through the day. You'll need to leave soon?'

'I'll grab a quick shower after this and then head up to the cliffs.' Verity glanced towards the window. 'Not a cloud in the sky. It'll be a beautiful day.'

Sam nodded towards the kitchen counter. 'I've left you some sun cream. You'll need it as you won't feel the burn up on the cliffs with the breeze from the sea. You should also cover up your shoulders, and there's a cap there, too, if you need to borrow one.'

'Aww, you do look after me, don't you?' His kindness gave her a warm, fuzzy feeling and she smiled as she tucked into her breakfast. Within ten minutes Verity had devoured the lot and whilst Sam loaded the dishwasher she grabbed a quick shower. As soon as she was ready, she found Sam with his coat on, waiting for her at the bottom of the stairs. 'I've got a delivery at the restaurant so I need to get going but this is for you.' He handed her a flask and a carrier bag.

Verity peeped inside the bag. 'You've made me lunch?'

'It's just a sandwich, crisps and fruit to keep you going.'

'You, Sam Wilson, are a keeper! You've thought of everything.' Without thinking she leaned across and kissed him on his cheek, then lingered for a second looking at his lips. 'One day you'll make someone a good husband.'

As soon as she said the words, she noticed his smile slip slightly.

'Sorry, did I say something wrong? I was just joking. No one has ever done anything like this for me before...' It was true – in all the time she had lived with Richard he'd never made her lunch or worried she'd get sunburnt.

'No, honestly. It's okay. You have a good day and I'll see you later. I can't wait to hear all about it. You still have your key?' She nodded and watched him leave the cottage and disappear at the end of the drive with Jimmy at his heels.

Verity realised her words had instantly and completely changed Sam's mood. He'd opened up about his family and his grandfather's death but he'd never opened up about his past love, Alice. Verity was left wondering what exactly had gone on there.

Chapter Thirteen

A short while later, Verity walked down the lane. In the tearoom garden Clemmie was setting out the tables ready for the day ahead.

'You're going to be busy with such a glorious day forecast,' trilled Verity, leaning on the wooden gate and getting Clemmie's attention.

Clemmie spun around. 'Aren't we just. Afternoon tea is already fully booked! Thankfully, Grandmother is back and helping today. Which reminds me, I was going to catch you today—'

'She remembers my granny, doesn't she?' asked Verity, hopefully.

'She does and she can't wait to meet you. Come round after we close.'

'We know who sent the postcard.'

Clemmie stopped what she was doing and walked over towards her. 'You do?'

'It was Joe Wilson. The W is for Wilson. We—'

'You keep saying "we". Who is this "we"?'

'Sam and I…'

'So, you've forgiven him for calling you an idiot?' teased Clemmie.

Verity rolled her eyes. 'I found a signed book my granny gave to Joe – in Sam's cottage.'

'And what about the secret?'

'That I'm not sure of yet, but maybe your grandmother can shed some light on it for us. I'll be back later to find out. In other good news, I can pick up the van today.'

'That's fantastic news! Did you stay at Sam's last night?' Clemmie wanted all the gossip.

'Don't look at me like that. My travelling van is back up on her wheels today so I'll have a roof over my head again…though I have to say, there's nothing wrong with Sam's roof.'

'You're smiling and there's a glow about you. Is that the first flush of love I'm detecting?' Clemmie narrowed her eyes.

'I'm just enjoying spending time with him,' Verity replied, but she knew it was more than that. Already Sam was constantly on her mind and every time she set eyes on him every inch of her body began tingling.

'Mmm. I've known a lot of women stranded on that causeway over the years but he's never taken any of them in.'

'What can I say?' She grinned. 'But…can I ask you something in confidence?'

'Of course.' Clemmie took a step closer and leaned in.

'What happened between Sam and Alice?'

'It's no secret that Sam was engaged to Alice. Sam could

have the pick of any girl, and many tourists had tried, but when she walked on to this island, she managed to get his attention. They were in the same line of business – they both had restaurants – and it seemed she fell in love with Sam, but Puffin Island wasn't enough for her. They had a very public proposal but their engagement fell apart when she chose her career over him.'

'Could she not have had both?'

'You need to ask Sam that. Anyway, since Alice there's been no one. He's thrown himself into work, become part of the Puffin Island committee, which is all about doing what's best for the people that live here, and stayed away from women…until you.'

'He's not interested in me. He's quite clearly stated he's better off on his own.'

'And you believe that? I saw the way he was looking at you in the pub.'

'Any type of heartbreak is difficult to get over,' replied Verity. The past six months had been difficult for her, but Puffin Island had started to put her heart back together so quickly. She was excited about the future for the first time in ages. 'I'd best get going. I'm off counting puffins!'

'I wouldn't like to be in your shoes if you're late. Pete is a stickler for timekeeping. I'll let my grandmother know you'll pop in later.'

'Perfect.' Verity couldn't wait to hear what Betty remembered about the past and she couldn't wait to ask her about the postcard's secret.

It took a little over ten minutes to reach the top of the cliff. Surrounded by such stunning views, the walk was very therapeutic. Verity could hear nothing except the slapping of the waves against the rocks and the shore below, and the calls of the gulls circling above the whitewashed cliffs. She took in the magnificent view and thought about her conversation with Ava. She'd joked about staying on the island, which prompted a host of other questions. Where would she live? What would she do for a living? And what did she have to go back to Staffordshire for? Yes, she had a house, but she didn't have to live in it for the rest of her life. Home was where your heart is, after all, and she was coming to realise that her heart was no longer in that place. Twelve months ago, if anyone had told her she would be single, giving up her job and renting out her house, she would have thought them deluded. But now here she was, and the street she'd left behind couldn't compare in excitement with this island. Ava had convinced her to be brave and embark on this journey, and now being here seemed like the most natural thing in the world.

Hearing voices carried by the breeze, Verity looked ahead to see the group of rangers standing outside Cliff Top Cottage, each holding a clipboard. As soon as Pete spotted her he smiled. 'Here she is, I told you she wouldn't let us down. Everyone, this is Verity, a fully qualified veterinary assistant who will be helping us over the next few days.'

After all the introductions were made, the rangers began walking slowly towards the cliff top. 'We're going to be working together,' Pete informed her as he handed her a clipboard and a pen. 'Have you got a drink? And you may need sun cream.'

Verity held up her bag. 'Drinks and snacks are in here and I smothered myself in sun cream just before I left.' She pulled on Sam's hat and they followed the other rangers. 'Have you always been involved in the census?' she asked.

'Yes,' Pete replied, looking out over the cliffs. 'And always been obsessed with puffins. I can sit and watch them for hours and most days that's exactly what I do.' He pointed. 'We're heading that way. We have the same routine each year: we split off into the different areas and each take a section. We start at the lowest point and work our way up to the highest.' Verity noticed that the rangers had scattered in different directions. 'Watch your footing as we descend – sometimes the gravel can cause you to slip.'

He pointed to the route they were taking and they began to follow the narrow path.

Suddenly Verity stopped in her tracks and grabbed Pete's arm. She swung a glance around the cliff top, petrified.

'What is it?' Pete's eyes widened in concern.

'Cows, I can't do cows. I'm terrified of cows.'

'Cows?'

'There it is again! That loud mooing. Pete, I really can't do cows. Why are they up here on a cliff?' Verity was still clutching Pete's arm for dear life. 'They chased me once through a field and I honestly thought I was going to die. Like they say in the movies, my life flashed before my eyes. I ended up scrabbling through a pile of nettles to escape.'

'What are you going on about? When was the last time you saw cows up on the cliffs?'

'It's not that unusual, surely? You get sheep and goats all the time.'

'Usually in the mountains, not on the cliffs on Puffin Island, otherwise we would have had to rename this place Cow Island.' He smiled at her. 'And you can let go of my arm. It's about to be bitten to death by puffins, never mind you squeezing the life out of it first.'

'Sorry, sorry… Woah! There it is again.'

Pete was still smiling.

'It's not funny. Look.' Verity held out her hand. She was visibly shaking.

'That's not cows. That loud mooing noise you can hear is the puffins! They sound a lot like cows but I promise you the only cows are on the farm on the other side of the island. There may also be a painting of one in the art gallery, but I promise that's as far as it goes.'

'Puffins? That's the puffins?'

'That noise is definitely the puffins,' he confirmed. 'Some people actually think they sound like a muffled chainsaw. Come on.' Pete carried on walking. 'You're safe.'

Relieved, Verity exhaled then threw back her head and let out a peal of laughter. 'I can't believe I thought it was cows.'

This time Pete stopped in his tracks and turned back towards her. He stared at her closely.

Verity had her hand on her chest. 'Sorry, I've been told on many occasions that my laugh is a little loud.'

'Never apologise for laughing.' He was still looking at her oddly.

'To be honest, I can't remember the last time I properly laughed. Laughter has been knocked out of me for a quite a while… Is there a reason you're still staring at me?' she asked, starting to worry.

Pete's face was suddenly pallid.

'You look like you've seen a ghost.'

'Sorry, sorry, you just took me by surprise.' He took a handkerchief out of his pocket and wiped his brow. 'I didn't mean to stare, you just reminded me of someone I used to know.'

He carried on walking and the path widened. Verity walked beside him.

'Was she someone special?'

Suddenly Pete looked a little tearful.

'I'm sorry, I didn't mean to be nosey.'

'You're not. And yes, extremely special. I think about her every day.'

'Where is this special person of yours now?'

'She's out there somewhere. Hopefully one day I'll see her walking back up that cliff top so my life can restart. I have every faith.'

There was sadness in Pete's voice and Verity began to realise the reason Pete had never married or had children. He was waiting for the love of his life to return.

'Was she a groupie? I've heard all about your famous band,' she said, trying to lighten the sombre mood.

'You know about the band?'

'The Men from Puffin Island!'

Pete smiled again. 'Such an imaginative name. Do you know it took us nearly three months to come up with it?' He gave a little chuckle. 'We'd been performing together for at least six months and called ourselves "the band with no name" as we couldn't decide on a name between us. We could write songs but coming up with a name was the hardest thing ever. Our following—'

'Your groupies,' Verity interrupted.

'Groupies – were increasing every day. There were even girls trying to swim across the causeway because they knew we lived on the island. All of a sudden everywhere we went became manic. Girls would hide on the cliffs, camp out on the bay and hire boats just to try and get a glimpse of us. This one night we were due to play a gig at The Olde Ship Inn but the pub was that packed we couldn't even get to the stage so we ended up performing on the beach, just down there. I think that's when it hit the news and word started to spread. That night Joe introduced us as The Men from Puffin Island and the name seemed to stick. I wasn't sure I was keen on it as first, thought it was a little daft ...'

'The Beatles called themselves The Beatles, so it's not as daft as that.'

'That's very true...and it did what it said on the tin. We *were* the men from Puffin Island and each one of us was proud of where we came from. We were young, early twenties, and we all had the biggest egos you could ever imagine and dreams of being a global band, bigger than The Beatles. We could play as good as them, too. Joe and I wrote all the songs together.'

'There's nothing wrong with having big dreams.'

'But it wasn't meant to be.' Pete stopped on the edge of the cliff and looked over towards the bay, lost in his own thoughts. Verity knew he was probably thinking about Joe. 'And what are your dreams, Verity?'

'To experience more in life. I'm nearly thirty and on my own in this world.'

'No parents?'

'A mother, but she's never championed me. The only

time I was flavour of the month was when I found a man who she thought was successful and could show off to her friends. The funny thing was, he didn't like her one bit. When I found out about his infidelity, that was the time I needed someone the most. I was so alone, and even though she was living across the Channel, I reached out to her, hoping she would be there for me. Maybe she'd invite me to France, maybe build some bridges.' Verity's voice faltered. 'But no. I should have known better. She was cold towards me, said it must have been my fault, claiming he would never do that and I'd never be anything without him. That was the last time we spoke. I didn't make the decision lightly to cut her out of my life – it was a build-up of things over the years'

'That must have been difficult. I can't imagine a mother not putting their own child first.'

'I've learned from all this – it's okay to cut off toxic family members. She was never good for my mental health but I let her affect me for years because she was my mother. She'd rather go to her grave than take responsibility for how she treated me, but I'm happy to say I've largely made peace with it. I'm certainly getting over all the heartbreak of Richard's infidelity.'

'And your father?'

'My mother always kept his identity hidden. For what reason, I'm really not sure.'

They carried on walking down a steep part of the cliff. 'You must have had some good influences in your life, I hope?' said Pete.

'Yes, my granny and granddad. They took over my upbringing from an early age. We were so close. My granny is the reason I became a veterinary assistant, as she was obsessed with animals. But going back to your question, my dream is to be happy and live my life the best I can. I'd like children one day.'

'From what I've seen of you so far, I think you'll make a wonderful mother.'

'Thank you, that's a lovely thing to say.' Verity took a sip of her water and pointed towards the bay. 'What are they doing over there?'

'It'll soon be fifty years since we lost Joe and they're setting up for his remembrance service.' Pete took off his hat for a moment and clutched it in his hand.

'You miss him, don't you?'

'Every day I wish I could talk to him one last time,' he admitted.

'You're going to the remembrance service, aren't you?' Verity could see by the sadness in his eyes how much he was still hurting. Maybe she could talk to Sam again and encourage him to chat to Pete before the service. It was possible that if they spoke to each other and let each other know exactly how they were feeling, they could move on and help each other through the undoubtedly emotional service.

'Even though I know I probably won't be welcomed by certain members of Joe's family, I'll stand at the back and pay my respects.'

'Everyone has the right to pay respects to someone they loved dearly.'

Pete nodded and pointed to the burrow in the ground. 'This is your first burrow. Let's start counting those puffins.'

Verity looked at the hole in the ground. 'Have I got to stick my hand in there?'

'You do, but first put this on.' Pete handed her what looked like a sleeve of a jumper. 'They may nip your hand or scratch your arm. This is just a little bit of added protection.'

Verity slipped it on then knelt on the ground.

'You'll need to lie on your stomach and slide your hand in slowly. Try not to panic.'

'It's the fear of the unknown that worries me,' she replied, wriggling onto her stomach.

'You'll be fine. You're just feeling for puffins and eggs.'

Slowly and nervously, Verity slipped her hand into the burrow, biting her lip in anticipation of being nipped at any moment. 'I can feel an egg,' she said excitedly. 'Oooh, and another.'

Pete smiled. 'I can remember the first time I felt an egg in a burrow. It's like when the chickens lay for the first time, you feel like a proud parent.'

'Two eggs, two puffins. OUCH! And one nip of the beak,' she exclaimed, quickly retracting her hand. 'Gosh, that really does hurt.' She rubbed the back of the hand.

'The top of your hand will soon be that numb from the all the nips that you won't feel a thing by the time you finish today.'

'And I volunteered for this job because...'

'Of your love of puffins.'

'I'm beginning to wonder,' she said, sliding her hand into the next burrow. 'Ouch!'

Pete chuckled. 'I can remember the very first time I was bitten by a puffin. It was the same day I was bitten at work by a chihuahua. I've come across some big dogs in my time, and ones that looked as if they weren't very friendly, but they were a walk in the park compared to this tiny creature. It was brought in in a designer handbag because it didn't like walking on wet ground when it was raining.'

'What a diva!'

'"Twinkle", she was called, "because she was a little star".' Pete rolled his eyes.

'Aww, she sounds adorable.'

'There was nothing adorable about her or the owner. She would make any excuse to visit the surgery with that dog. Every time I saw her name on the list for the day it filled me with dread.'

'And the reason why the owner brought her in was...'

'She thought Twinkle had a cold as she'd sneezed a couple of times. I was going to suggest maybe it was the perfume the owner was wearing. It was that strong it made me sneeze the second she walked into the surgery. Anyway, there was absolutely nothing wrong with the dog but as usual I went through the motions, giving her the once-over as the owner gave me the once-over. I turned towards the computer to write up the notes and something took a huge bite out of my backside. I wondered for years whether it was the dog or the owner.'

Verity laughed. 'I know who my money would be on.'

Pete stopped at the next burrow.

'I thought I'd miss the routine of my job but I have to say, at the minute I'm not missing it at all,' she said.

'That's probably because it feels like you're on holiday.'

'You're not the first person to say that and it's probably

true, but being in such a beautiful place, I have begun to question where I really want to be.'

'You and every other tourist want to live here once they've visited, but unfortunately – or fortunately, if you're a curmudgeon like me – it's not very often a property comes up for sale.' He looked up towards his cottage, now high above them on top of the cliff. 'I've been offered ridiculous amounts of money for that place.'

'Ever tempted?'

'Never.' He pointed to the next burrow.

Verity got down on her stomach again. 'How come it's me that's constantly getting bitten?'

'Because I'm chief supervisor, and if I'm honest with you, if I get down, I'm not sure I'd get back up at my age,' said Pete with a laugh.

For the next few hours they continued to count the burrows and record their findings. Verity soon forgot the number of times she'd been bitten. Pete was right, after a while you became immune to it. In the early afternoon Pete called time on the count.

'We'll be burnt to a crisp and will be suffering from sunstroke if we carry on. Let's reconvene early tomorrow morning.' He blew a whistle and waved at the other rangers as a signal to quit.

'I've really enjoyed myself today,' said Verity. 'Thanks for letting me tag along.'

'It's my pleasure.'

Back at the cliff top, they headed towards the cottage.

Nathan was walking towards them, holding up the keys to Hetty.

'She's all yours, along with the bill,' he said apologetically. 'I wasn't sure where to send it.'

Verity smiled. 'Thank you, It's great to have her back. I'll sort out the payment and get it to you.'

'Much appreciated. Oh, and Pete, I've just noticed Cooper up at the old surgery. He was asking if you were around.'

'Who's Cooper?' asked Verity.

'Remember I told you the vet from Sea's End was looking to open a second surgery? That's Cooper, he's come to do some measuring up.'

'The new surgery is going ahead then?'

'It looks that way. It will be good for the island to have its own practice again.'

'Do you think it would be something that's happening soon?'

Pete nodded. 'Yes, as soon as the contracts are signed. I'll have to go now but I'll see you same time tomorrow morning.'

'See you tomorrow.'

Ambling back down the path towards the bay, Verity noticed that flowers were already beginning to be laid down near where the old pier used to stand. There was also a photograph of Joe, propped on an easel, with candles scattered about. It must be comforting to Sam to know that the residents of Puffin Island had never forgotten his grandfather. Sitting down on a nearby bench and reaching into her bag for her sandwich, Verity thought about Pete. She'd enjoyed every minute of the morning and their easy-flowing conversation. He was a knowledgeable and interesting man. She admired how, even though the popularity of the band had been growing back in the day, he'd continued with his studies to qualify as a vet. She gazed at the photo of Joe. He was as deviously handsome as Sam. Tucking into her sandwich, she stretched out her legs and admired the blue sky and the water glistening in the sunshine. A gang of hikers was heading towards the path along the cliff. Children clutching fishing nets were dangling them from the small rocks at the side of the bay.

'Penny for them?'

She spun around to see Amelia standing behind her.

'Just grabbing some food, what are you up to?'

'On a break. The bookshop has been heaving this morning. I've never known so many customers, which is amazing, but they've all interrupted my proper job of writing.'

Verity laughed. 'It's a genius move to get paid for one job whilst furthering your career in another field.'

'I'm not just a pretty face,' said Amelia with a grin. 'I'll have to get back, but before I go, how was counting puffins?'

'Puffin good! I really enjoyed it.' Verity held out her arm to show Amelia her counting wounds.

'Are they bites? They looked like they enjoyed you too!'

'Pete was right: after a few nibbles you become immune to it.'

Amelia nodded to the photo of Joe. 'How is Pete? This time of year must hit him hard.'

'I think he had a moment up on the cliff top when he saw that Joe's photo was down here.'

'I know Betty is struggling at the minute too.'

'I don't know the ins and outs of everything, but I do think Sam and Pete could help each other at a time like this. Wouldn't Joe want them to unite and put their differences to one side, at least for one day?'

'Who knows? Even after all this time Sam is still convinced there was more to that night than what has been reported.'

'But surely if nothing has come out after fifty years there's nothing *to* come out.'

Amelia gave a little shrug. 'Or people are good at keeping secrets,' she ventured. She held up her coffee and pointed towards Lighthouse Lane. 'I'll catch up with you later.'

At Amelia's mention of secrets, Verity thought of the postcard and the message written on it. She had had ample opportunity to chat about it with Pete this morning but she'd decided to wait and speak to Betty first and see what her take was on potential secrets from the past. But Amelia was right. People were good at keeping secrets. Her granny had never mentioned 'W' or Puffin Island except in her stories, yet she had still kept the picture of the puffins hanging on the wall in her favourite room in the house for all those years.

As she finished her lunch, she noticed a well-dressed man walking down the path from the cliff top and assumed that it must be Cooper. He headed towards a Range Rover parked at the edge of the bay and pressed the fob on a bunch of keys to unlock it. Taking a punt, Verity Googled 'vets practice in Sea's End' on her phone and clicked through to the website, navigating to the list of staff members, looking for Cooper's photo to confirm it was him – and it was. The website had all the usual general information about the surgery and its opening times, but at the top of the web page something caught Verity's eye – a heading reading 'Current Vacancies'.

So there would be vacancies at the new practice opening very soon on Puffin Island. Verity's heart began to race when she noticed there was one for a veterinary assistant. She doubled-ticked every box of what they were looking for. Now all she needed to do was send a CV with a covering letter. Looking up from the screen and staring out over the water, she wondered, could she actually apply? What was stopping her? Well, there was the matter of a place to live. Her van would be fun to live in for a little while but there was no way she would survive the cold winter months without proper heat or a shower. In her head she'd already moved to Puffin Island, but in reality was it even possible? Looking for houses to rent, she found there was nothing on the island; the nearest vacant property was in a village on the other side of Sea's End. It wasn't a million miles away though, so it certainly gave her food for thought.

Throwing her phone into her bag she headed back towards Cosy Nook Cottage. Her plan was to have a shower and then catch up with Betty. She couldn't wait to hear what she had to say.

———

Ten minutes later, she was standing in the shower at Cosy Nook Cottage, taking advantage of the gorgeous-smelling body wash and expensive shampoo, not knowing when her next shower would be, if she moved back into the van tonight. Singing at the top of her lungs, she enjoyed every second of the shower. As she switched the water off, she heard someone banging around downstairs. Sam must be home. Quickly, she dried herself, pulled on clean clothes and headed downstairs.

Sam was in the kitchen and Jimmy was wolfing down the food in his bowl.

'I was hoping that was you upstairs and not a burglar but when I heard the singing…'

'Firstly, I've never known a burglar to have a shower, and secondly, tone-deaf I may be, but if you can't sing in the shower what's the point of living?' she said boldly, trying not to let her embarrassment show.

He grinned and looked at her arm. 'Woah, you look like you've been eaten alive.'

'Yes, those puffins quite liked the taste of me.'

'You can't blame them though, can you?' He grinned.

'What can I say, the puffins have good taste.'

'They do,' he replied, catching her eye and giving her a warm smile. 'I'm just back to feed Jimmy and escape from the restaurant for half an hour before heading back. We've got a busy night ahead; all the tables are booked and there's a fresh delivery of fish.'

'Business is booming.'

'And that's something I can't complain about. How was your morning? Did you enjoy counting puffins?'

'I did – and it was great to spend the time with Pete. He's such an interesting character and very knowledgeable, not to mention intelligent. He told me all about the band

and his work at the surgery. He didn't give too much away about his love life but my reckoning is that he had his heart broken when he was young and is still hoping she may walk back up that cliff top and into his arms one day.' Verity knew she was babbling but the words just kept coming out, because Sam's face wasn't as smiley as it was two seconds ago. She recognised the look well; it was nearly the same look her ex used to give her whenever she said something he didn't like. He was clearly disturbed at what she was saying, but Verity didn't want to walk on eggshells – she'd had years of that with her ex.

'I can tell that you don't like me speaking well about Pete, but he's actually been lovely to me today and I honestly don't have a bad word to say about him. He was professional, good company, funny, informative and completely easy to be around.' She watched Sam bristle. 'But I'll tell you this, when he noticed the photo of Joe down by the bay, he became very emotional. Your grandfather's death still has a massive effect on him.'

'Probably because of a guilty conscience eating away at him,' said Sam, coldly.

'But you have no concrete evidence. What if – and just hear me out because I've got nothing to lose by throwing this out there, but – what if nothing went on that night? What if it was truly just an accident and you're making Pete's life a misery for no reason? It's a little immature, don't you think?' Verity really wished she hadn't added the last sentence as Sam's eyebrows shot up and his intense stare as he processed her words unnerved her for a second.

'This has nothing to do with you. You've been on this island for a matter of hours—'

'Days,' she interrupted, holding her own.

'Hours,' he repeated. 'And you're giving an opinion on something you know nothing about. I've shared my thoughts with you, which was difficult enough, and now you're attacking me.' Sam was defensive and the dark look on his face didn't go away.

'I'm not attacking you. I'm just trying to present a different side.' Verity kept her voice soft, hoping to calm the situation a little.

'Something doesn't stack up. We all know as coastguards about the rip currents and there was no way my grandfather would willingly enter the water without backup.'

'Maybe he slipped off the pier into the water and just couldn't get out.'

'If that's the case then why has Pete never explained where he was that night or why he was late for his shift? Because he's hiding something.'

'Or maybe he doesn't need to explain anything to anyone as there's nothing to explain. He's devastated to this day. He lost his best friend and has never got over it.'

'So I should just get over it?' asked Sam, coldly.

'I know you want justice for your grandfather, but Pete was his actual friend, his best friend. They were inseparable. They'd just landed a huge music contract and were about to conquer the world together.'

'But they didn't, did they? Because somehow my grandfather ended up being taking by a rip current.'

Verity took a deep breath. She knew what she about to say was not going to go down well at all. 'Forgive me when I say this, but you never met your grandfather—'

'What are you implying, that it hurts less?' Sam cut in, his voice raised. 'I was robbed of a relationship with my grandfather.'

'That's not what I'm saying, but Pete was there at the time. Just from today I can see he's genuinely cut up about it. Wouldn't your energy be better spent uniting and coming together in memory of your grandfather? I bet Pete has lots of stories about their friendship and growing up that you've never even heard. You might find it comforting. I really don't think Pete wants any sort of animosity with the grandson of his best friend. You'd be like the grandson he never had. Today, despite everything, he didn't have a bad word to say about you.'

Sam shook his head. 'I'm really not sure why you think you can come in here and give your opinion on something that doesn't even involve you.'

They stared at each other.

Stalemate.

Even though Verity knew she had overstepped the mark, she still thought that this argument that had been going on for years was a waste of energy, and that some good could actually come of it if Sam wasn't so stubborn and learned to let go and move on.

'I think you should go,' Sam said at last.

Tension hung in the air. Even Jimmy must have sensed something was wrong as he'd climbed into his crate and was lying down staring at them, his head resting on his paws.

'Fine. I'll get my things.'

Sam didn't say anything, just turned his back and switched on the kettle. Whether she was right or wrong,

Verity still thought he needed to stop and think about what he was losing from this ongoing feud.

She packed her belongings and came back downstairs. The back door was open and Sam was standing in the garden, hugging a mug of tea and looking out towards the cove.

She placed the front door key on the table. 'The thing is, Sam, if you keep pushing Pete away, you're going to lose the chance to gain valuable information and first-hand stories about your grandfather. Stories that could be passed down to your own children one day. I'm sure they would be proud of their rockstar great-grandfather and happy to hear stories you learned from someone who was actually there.'

Sam remained silent and didn't look at her.

Verity ruffled the top of Jimmy's head, walked to the front door and closed it behind her. She exhaled and was hit by a wave of emotion. With one last look at the cottage, she saw that Sam was now standing in the window. Their eyes met, and he moved away. Fighting back tears and with her head bent low, she headed down Lighthouse Lane. From what she'd seen so far, Sam was very good at holding grudges, which probably meant for the rest of her time on the island they were going to have to avoid each other.

Chapter Fourteen

A rriving at the garage, Verity found Hetty gleaming. She'd been washed and was ready and waiting. With his head buried under another bonnet, Nathan was singing along to the radio.

'Hi.'

Nathan jumped, banging his head.

'Oh gosh, I'm so sorry. I didn't mean to sneak up on you.'

'Don't worry. You wouldn't believe the number of times I've done that over the years.' He wiped his hands on an oily rag and smiled at Verity. 'I've actually lost count and I probably need to apologise to you.'

'What for?'

'My singing!' He grinned. 'I wouldn't wish it on anyone.'

Verity smiled, her thoughts immediately turning to Sam and the beautiful song he'd sung in the pub, which had melted her heart. 'Luckily your head was buried in the bonnet so it wasn't too traumatic.' Pointing to Hetty, she said, 'She's so clean. Thank you.'

'And dry. And she'll stay that way as long as you keep away from the causeway.' Nathan grinned.

'I'll do my best. I know this is a bit cheeky but would it be possible for me to park her over there and sleep in her?' Verity pointed to a grassy area in front of the garage.

'Are you sure you want to sleep up here where you're away from everything and everyone?'

'I think it will be perfect and peaceful, and waking up to that view will be something I'll never forget.'

Nathan looked out across the sea. 'I still think it's spectacular after all these years. Be my guest, but don't park her too near the edge. You do know the puffins moo like cows, right? The noise can be very eerie up here when it echoes around the cliffs in the dead of the night.'

'I know exactly what the puffins sound like. Frightened the life out of me, they did.'

'And me. The first time I heard them I thought the cliff top was full of cows.'

They both laughed.

Sitting behind the wheel of Hetty again, she was thankful that her beloved van was back in full working order and that her dip in the sea hadn't been her final chapter. She turned the key, the engine started the first time, and she reversed onto the grassy spot she'd pointed out to Nathan. She positioned the van so that the sliding side door overlooked the cliff edge. When she was enjoying a morning brew in bed, she could open the door and take in the beauty of her surroundings.

The van was parked, Verity set up her windbreaker and

deckchair and placed a small table outside with her camping stove. Her plan for the rest of the day was to head back down to the harbour, call in and see Betty and, on the way back, pop in to Puffin Pantry to pick up some sausages for her tea.

Excited at the possibility of uncovering her granny and Joe's secret, Verity set off towards the tearoom, with the postcard tucked away in her bag. She was feeling a little nervous about meeting Betty, but in a good way. She arrived five minutes before closing time to find Clemmie outside, wiping down the tables.

'Here she is!' Clemmie cried. 'You have to tell me what you've done to the local heartthrob, because he stormed past here earlier with a thunderous look on his face.'

Verity followed Clemmie into the tearoom. 'I'm trying to push that from my mind.'

'What, you've actually had an argument?'

'I suppose you could say that. I'm back to sleeping in the van tonight. I've parked it up on the cliff top.'

'What happened?'

'He didn't like me saying good things about Pete. But I think it was my saying that he was acting immaturely that sent him over the edge.'

Clemmie's eyes widened. 'Ouch. That may have dented his ego a little.'

'I was a teeny bit out of order but I also think Sam's being stubborn. Pete is a really interesting character, easy to get on with, and his stories are entertaining.'

'Pete, easy to get on with? Are you casting magic spells over all the men on Puffin Island?'

Verity laughed.

'I've never known Pete to speak to a tourist, never mind give them a temporary job as a ranger. I'm thinking you may have drugged him.'

Verity grinned. 'Only with my infectious personality.'

'If it's any consolation, we've also said the same to Sam, but again that resulted in us not speaking for a while. The best way is to keep out of it. He needs to work this out for himself. We've lived with this feud on the island for many years and it's only going to get worse. With the vigil and the vote coming up in the next couple of weeks, I can't see them putting their differences aside.'

'Vote?'

'The safety barriers on the causeway. Do we have them or not. That's the only way to settle it.'

'Tensions will be running high then.'

Just at that moment the door at the back of the tearoom opened and Betty stepped through it and gasped. 'I don't believe this. Hetty's granddaughter.' With her arms open wide she hurried towards Verity and enveloped her in a huge hug.

'Betty, Verity, Verity, Betty.' Clemmie introduced them with a smile.

'I was so worried you wouldn't remember my granny after all these years.'

'Remember her? Hetty was my best friend for the summer, and even worked here in the tearoom. She rented a room upstairs.'

'No way! She was here for a whole summer?'

'Yes, and I was so sad when she went home. There are times in life when you just click with someone and I clicked instantly

with your granny. The adventures we shared that summer…'
Betty gave a little chuckle. 'I bet she's told you all about what
we got up to. How is she? Does she know you're here?'

Clemmie looked towards Verity. Apparently she hadn't
shared the news of Hetty's death.

'I'm sorry to have to tell you that my grandmother has
passed away. It was over twelve years ago now.'

The smile slipped from Betty's face. 'Oh no, I'm so sorry
to hear that.' She swallowed. 'Come on through to the back
room. Are you okay to carry on tidying up?' she asked
Clemmie.

'Of course. I'll bring you through a pot of tea, and there
are a couple of slices of Victoria sponge left.'

Betty nodded her thanks and led the way to the living
quarters of the cottage. 'I can see your granny standing
behind that counter. She turned up that summer and
wanted a job.'

'This looks just like a normal cottage back here.'

'It is a normal cottage, except that the front room was
turned into a tearoom many moons ago.'

It actually wasn't too dissimilar to Sam's cottage, old-
fashioned as it was, with its oak-beamed ceiling. Blue velvet
settees were positioned in an L shape in front of the open
fireplace along with an oversized rug and a coffee table. A
floor-to-ceiling bookcase was rammed with books, and a
sage-coloured dresser was covered with framed
photographs.

'Take a seat. So, are you following in your granny's
footsteps? Are you staying for the summer?'

'This time last week I didn't even know Puffin Island

was a real place, even though I'd visited it many times as a child.'

'I'm confused,' said Betty.

'My granny used to tell me bedtime stories about this place, including your teashop, but I always thought it was fictional. She described it exactly how it is,' Verity said, looking around, 'which amazed me when I arrived – and is still amazing me, to be honest.'

Clemmie walked in just then with a tray and placed it on the coffee table in front of them.

'Look at that vintage teapot! It's so pretty,' said Verity admiringly.

'Vintage like my grandma and pretty like me,' teased Clemmie, missing a playful swipe from Betty as she walked past. Grinning, she shut the door behind her.

Betty poured the tea and handed Verity a slice of cake. 'How did you realise we all existed in real life?'

Verity shared how she'd found the postcard.

'What an amazing story. How much do you know about your granny's time here?'

'Absolutely nothing. All I know is she spoke very fondly about this place, but the postcard suggests that there was some sort of secret between Joe and Granny. And I know my granny never forgot him because there's been a picture of puffins hanging on the wall in her living room for years, which is signed at the back in the same handwriting as the postcard by "W", which must have been Joe.'

Betty was quiet for a moment and Verity knew she was unsure how much she should share with her.

'I feel like I'm breaking a confidence,' admitted Betty.

'I understand, really I do, but you're the only person

who can answer my questions about my granny's time here.'

Betty took a sip of tea and smiled. 'I can still remember her laugh. It was a very distinctive laugh, a proper laugh right from her belly. And that smile of hers had all the boys falling over her. She arrived here for the summer after an argument with her boyfriend at the time – Alf.'

'Alf was my granddad. Can you remember what their argument was about?'

Betty was quiet for a second.

'Please, Betty, I need to know.'

'Alf had proposed to your grandmother, but Hetty wasn't a hundred per cent sure. They'd been together since the age of eleven and his proposal made her wonder if there was more to life than what she knew. From what she told me, the pressure from both families was immense, and she didn't want to let anyone down. She just wanted to make the right decision.

'The proposal took place in front of both families. I remembered she told me Alf had gathered everyone together, and Hetty felt like she couldn't say no in front of them all. So she said yes and everyone danced the night away at the local church hall. The next morning, she told Alf she'd felt pressured and wanted more than settling down straightaway, she wanted to visit places and see things. Alf was hurt, and didn't understand. He said that wasn't what you do in life and told Hetty to stop daydreaming. The row escalated and then Hetty spotted an advert in a newspaper for a singer at a club in Sea's End. Before she knew it, she'd taken flight and ended up here, trying to work out exactly what she wanted. I can still remember the day she walked into the tearoom, which was owned by my mother at the time. She had this funny little accent, quite posh, and was wearing a fur coat and denim shorts and had legs like a giraffe. Her hair was curled and bounced above the shoulders and her crimson lips could be seen from the other side of the harbour. She stood in the doorway smoking a cigarette. You should have seen my mother's face when she clocked Hetty. I thought she was about to have a heart attack!' Betty laughed. 'You'd never guess how my mother greeted her.'

'Tell me.'

'"Movie star or hooker?"'

Verity gasped. 'Your mother never said that.'

'Oh, she did. My mother never held back. She was well known on the island for her straight talking. Your grandmother replied, "Movie star" but said she was out of work and needed a job.'

'What happened to the singing job?'

'By the time she'd arrived at Sea's End the job had been filled, so Hetty hitched a lift across the causeway to see what the island was all about. Once here, she decided to stay. She took a trial shift, my mother hired her for the summer, she rented a room here and we became the best of friends. There was never a dull moment with Hetty. I thought we'd be friends for ever and was completely heartbroken when she left and disappeared from my life as quickly as she came into it. But I never forgot her.'

'Where did she disappear to?'

'I'm assuming she'd got whatever she needed to out of her system and went back home to marry Alf. In fact, she never said goodbye. I remember that day so clearly. It was early evening and I went up to her room to see what she was going to wear on our night out, but she was gone. Her bed was made, her suitcase and belongings no longer there. I was hoping she'd simply gone to stay with Joe, who was besotted with her.'

'Tell me all about my granny and Joe,' insisted Verity.

'Your granny sang her way into his heart. We were at The Olde Ship Inn and The Men from Puffin Island were performing that night.'

'Sam told me your husband Eric was part of the band.'

Betty nodded. 'He was the drummer, but we weren't married at that time. That came a few years later. There was also John, who played keyboard, and Pete. After the band had played, we got a lock-in at the pub. Of course, I was allowed to stay as Eric was my boyfriend, and that's when I introduced Hetty to everyone. They all began messing around with their instruments and Hetty took to the microphone. Your granny had a set of lungs on her, let me tell you. She belted out a song and blew everyone's socks off. The whole band was mesmerised. If I could pinpoint the moment Joe fell completely in love with her, that would be it. But Hetty was in a quandary, as she was still trying to figure out how she was feeling about everything back home. She knew Alf wouldn't wait around for ever and if she stayed away too long there was a possibility her family would disown her. Hetty left me a letter saying goodbye and thanking me and my mum for everything we'd done for her that summer—'

'And the secret mentioned in the postcard message? What do you think that was about?' Verity blurted, unable to stop herself.

'I think it may have just been the fact they had a summer romance. Hetty may also have confided in Joe about Alf and the situation back home.' Betty swallowed, her eyes suddenly glistening with tears. 'I really missed her after she'd left, and she honestly couldn't have picked a worse time to leave. I could have really done with her friendship because…' Betty paused. 'It was the same evening that Joe passed away.'

Verity gave a tiny gasp. 'Oh Betty, that must have been awful for you.'

Betty nodded. 'It was awful for everyone. I lost two people I really loved on the same day. I was never sure if your granny knew about Joe's death. I'm assuming she would have found out as it was reported in the newspapers, but she didn't get in touch, so I was never certain. Hetty was someone special, and a breath of fresh air around this place.' Betty reached for a tissue from the box on the table and dabbed her eyes. 'Look at me, a daft old woman getting emotional. I honestly thought one day she would breeze back through the tearoom door…and now she's gone…and we'll never have the chance to speak again. Still, at least I got to meet you.'

'It sounds like when she chose to go back to my grandfather, she had to try and put that summer behind her and throw herself into married life, but I can tell you she never forgot this place. That summer meant a lot to her.' Verity rummaged in her bag. 'Here, have a look at the postcard.'

Betty took the postcard, and smiled at the puffins. 'Hetty was obsessed with the puffins. She would wander up to the cliff top and sit on the bench, watching them for hours.'

Betty turned the postcard over. For a second, Verity thought she noticed a flicker of uncertainty flash across Betty's eyes.

'Who else knows about this postcard?' asked Betty.

'Clemmie, Amelia and Sam…and now you.'

Betty nodded. 'Can we keep it that way for now?'

'Any particular reason why?' probed Verity.

'I'm just thinking with Joe's vigil coming up… I think it's best for now. Trust me.' Betty gave Verity a strange look. Verity was convinced that Betty was holding something back.

Chapter Fifteen

Verity was sitting outside her van, the sausages sizzling on the camping stove giving off the most wonderful aroma. They would be delicious with the crusty bread Verity had picked up from Beachcomber Bakery and she couldn't wait to tuck into her evening meal. After turning the sausages over in the pan, she sat in the camping chair staring out over the sea while thinking about everything that Betty had shared with her. Maybe there was nothing more to her granny's visit than a young, confused woman who wasn't sure what she wanted from her future. Verity was certain that her granny would have known about Joe's death if it had made the newspapers. Betty had told her that Joe had received an SOS call saying a man had been taken by the rip current, and he had dived straight in to rescue him without a thought for his own safety. She felt for her granny, who may well have grieved over Joe's loss in silence, though at the same time relieved that her secret summer romance would never be revealed.

Verity had concluded that the summer romance was indeed the secret referred to in the postcard and that her granny had probably confided in Joe about her situation at home. Verity was also convinced that her granny must have broken Joe's heart when she told him she was heading back home, and Joe must have sent the postcard just before his accident.

Suddenly hearing the sound of music on the light breeze, Verity sat up and listened. Someone on the cliff top was strumming a guitar and singing softly. Verity followed the sound, which led her to the back garden of Cliff Top Cottage, where Pete was sitting on a chair overlooking the sea. Verity perched on a nearby rock and listened. After he finished, he gave the guitar one last strum and then balanced it against his chair and tilted his face towards the sky.

'No wonder you were offered a record contract. That was absolutely breathtaking. Your voice is unique.' She held out her arm. 'You've given me goosebumps.'

Pete spun around, his eyes full of tears.

'Sorry, I didn't mean to sneak up on you but when I heard you singing and playing I had to come over. I'm sure I've heard that song before, but I can't for the life of me remember what it's called.'

'You won't know the song. I wrote it many years ago and I've never sung it in public.'

'It was beautiful, so heartfelt.' Verity came over and sat next to him. 'I think you should sing more. I could sit and listen to you all night.'

'These days I only sing for me.'

'Why? You're so talented! People are missing out. You've still got what it takes.'

'That's kind of you to say so, but I'm not sure at my age I do anymore. I think I'm a little long in the tooth and my sex appeal disappeared a long time ago.' Pete gave a little chuckle.

'Women swoon over a man with a guitar who can sing, no matter how old he is,' Verity rushed to reassure him, though her words immediately made her think of Sam. The night he'd sung in the pub she'd been in awe, unable to take her eyes off him.

'Maybe,' he smiled, 'but I've never sung in public since...'

'Joe,' Verity finished off his sentence.

He nodded. 'It just didn't feel right. The rest of the band talked about what we should do at the time. The record company didn't retract the contract – in fact, we could have still gone on tour – but it just didn't feel right and I didn't want to leave Puffin Island. It would never have been the same without Joe. I was always used to having him at our side. It was fun and we were a gang. I wasn't born to be a solo artist.' There was a sadness in his voice. 'But let's not be maudlin. There were times when we had *too* much fun,' he admitted, a wicked glint in his eye.

'I can imagine!'

Pete laughed. 'When we first started out, we played to no one. We'd turn up to a working men's club or a pub and the room was empty, or the pub would be packed but they weren't there for us and people took no notice of us. We'd finish the set without even a clap or a cheer. But as they say, it's character-building.'

'When did you start to get noticed?'

Pete smiled and pointed over to the lighthouse. 'The lighthouse became famous before we did. The number of lives it saved was phenomenal. A company over in Sea's End decided to organise one of those sexy calendars to raise money for lifeboats, and needed models. Joe saw the advert in the local newspaper and signed us up because he got wind that the national newspapers would be turning up to report on the story. We got the gig along with some other applicants and we got allocated a month of the year.'

'Let me guess, The Men from Puffin Island were either February…or possibly December?'

'February for Valentines, but there was a method to Joe's madness. He'd decided what we needed was publicity and his plan was to hijack the shoot and play a couple of songs outside the lighthouse when the national newspapers arrived. What Joe failed to tell the rest of the band was that they wanted the calendar models to pose naked. We were stripped off and given items to cover our modesty. When Joe gave the signal we picked up our guitars and before we knew it we were playing naked outside the lighthouse. The news coverage we got…' Pete whistled. 'Believe me when I say that the next gig we played was packed to the rafters and that's no exaggeration.'

Verity threw her head back and laughed. 'Joe had good business acumen.'

'We forgave him, even though the photographs for the calendar were taken in the middle of November. It was minus four, the wind from the sea was icy and we all nearly froze to death!'

'But it got you noticed.'

'It got us noticed all right and the ferry company couldn't thank us enough. Their tickets went through the roof from teenage girls trying to get to Puffin Island, and all the B&Bs in Sea's End and on the island were constantly full.'

'Win, win. It sounds like you all had a blast and I bet you broke some hearts.'

Pete was thoughtful for a second, and by the look on his face he'd been transported somewhere else entirely. 'Possibly,' he replied, looking over his shoulder. 'Can you smell that? Someone is cooking.'

Verity sprung to her feet. 'Damn, I forgot my sausages! Got to go,' she called over her shoulder, practically sprinting back to her van. 'Lovely talking to you!' she shouted. Swiftly lifting the pan off the camping stove she stared disappointedly at the charcoaled sausages.

'You'll be okay with some ketchup. Maybe a lot of ketchup,' she murmured, cutting the bread and attempting to slice the cremated sausages in half with a blunt knife.

Sitting down on the chair with the plate balanced on her knee, she dug in. The sausages were just about bearable when swilled down with a glass of wine.

Ten minutes later she noticed an outside water tap at the garage, filled the kettle and placed it on the stove. She squirted washing-up liquid in the sausage pan, knowing it was going to take some cleaning. She was definitely glamping with no glamour now. As she scrubbed, she could still hear Pete strumming his guitar. She smiled at the story of the calendar and briefly wondered if the picture of the band in the buff was still floating around somewhere. From the other images she'd seen on the internet, they had been a group of very handsome men.

Pete was singing the same song and, even though he had been adamant that he'd never sung it in public, Verity knew she'd heard it before. She just couldn't place where.

Chapter Sixteen

The evening coastal breeze was getting a little chilly and Verity was sitting outside her van with a blanket wrapped around her shoulders and a book resting on her lap. She couldn't concentrate on the words though, and had read the same paragraph over and over again. She was thinking about Sam, and then the conversation with Betty. Even though she'd promised Betty she wouldn't say anything about the postcard, she'd been tempted to ask Pete if he remembered her granny. Surely, if she'd spent time with Joe and sung with them, he wasn't likely to forget her? And maybe he'd have stories about her granny he could share. But Betty had lived on the island a long time and she probably knew best, especially with the vigil coming up.

Feeling tired, she checked her watch and found it was a little after nine p.m. With an early start for the puffin count tomorrow she decided she might as well tuck herself up in bed. As she stood up, she saw a familiar figure walking on the far side of the cliff. Jimmy was running ahead of Sam, his nose to the ground as he ran in zigzag lines. There was no doubt that Sam would have noticed the van and possibly clocked Verity sitting outside but to her disappointment he didn't head over. Packing up her things she looked towards Cliff Top Cottage. The bedroom light was on and the curtains open. She spotted Pete for a moment as he stood in the window before closing the curtains, no doubt checking all was quiet on the cliff top before heading to bed.

Going to sleep without clearing the air with Sam wasn't sitting right with Verity. She didn't want to fall out with him and certainly didn't want them ignoring each other. She thought about calling across to him but he'd walked further on. He probably wouldn't hear her now, anyway. Knowing she would put it right tomorrow and apologise, she closed the van door when she heard an almighty shout. For a second, she wasn't sure if she'd imagined it. Staying silent, she listened. There it was again. Quickly sliding back the door she saw Sam in the distance pacing up and down at the top of the cliff screaming 'Jimmy' at the top of his lungs. The panic in his voice was obvious. Something was very wrong.

Verity pulled on her trainers and began to run towards Sam, who was now hurrying down the narrow path at the cliff edge. By the time she'd reached the top, Sam had nearly disappeared out of sight.

'Sam,' she yelled.

He looked up.

'What is it? What's going on?'

'It's Jimmy, he's chased a seagull over the cliff edge. Get help. I can see him, he's lying on a ledge a few feet down, but he's not moving.'

Without hesitation, Verity ran towards Cliff Top Cottage, hammered on the door and began shouting Pete's name. There was no movement. She banged continuously until, with relief, she saw the curtain move. The window was flung open and Pete looked down at her. 'Are you okay?'

'Pete, we need your help. A dog is injured and trapped on a ledge just below the cliff edge.'

Immediately the window slammed shut and within seconds the front door was flung open. Pete slipped on his shoes and pulled on his jumper. 'We need the stretcher, a couple of blankets and my emergency bag from the surgery. Do we know if the animal is still breathing?'

'I'm not sure.'

Speedily they headed to the old vet's surgery next to the garage. Pete opened up and thrust his medical bag into Verity's hand. 'You take that, I'm just going to get the stretcher. How big is the dog?'

'It's Jimmy, Sam's dog.'

That bit of information didn't faze Pete. He grabbed a foldaway stretcher from the back of the surgery, along with a couple of blankets. Soon they were back at the top of the cliff.

'Whereabouts are they? I can't see anyone.'

Verity pointed below them. 'Just there. What do you think his chances are?' she asked.

'Difficult to say. He's lucky he landed on a ledge. Follow me, and mind your footing.'

With his bag in one hand and using the stretcher to help him, Pete carefully climbed down the cliff path towards Sam. Verity was right behind him carrying the blankets. When they reached the ledge Sam was bent over Jimmy. His jumper was lying over the dog and he was frantically searching on his phone.

'You aren't going to get a signal down here,' Verity said gently.

Sam looked up. Verity noticed how pale he looked. 'Can you help him? he's still breathing but very slowly.' There was urgency in his voice.

Verity laid a hand on Sam's arm. 'We're going to do our very best.'

'Thank you.' His voice faltered as he stepped to the side. 'The daft bugger chased a seagull to the edge and the ground gave way beneath him.'

'Just try and keep calm. He's still with us.' Pete looked back to the top of the cliff. 'We need to get him back up top but first we need to get him onto the stretcher.'

Verity nodded and unfolded the stretcher. Thankfully there was enough space to lay it down flat. Pete crouched by Jimmy's shoulders. 'Verity, on a count of three, can you carefully lift his legs?'

She nodded.

Pete slipped his arms under Jimmy then looked towards her. 'One…two…three…'

In one movement they lifted Jimmy onto the stretcher. Pete fastened the top strap whilst Verity secured the bottom one.

'He's not just a dog. He's my life.'

'I know,' replied Pete. 'I understand. Now, are you able to lift the bottom end of the stretcher?'

Sam nodded and they were soon on the move, Verity bringing up the rear.

As the evening wind pushed lightly against them, their

steps were in sync and they moved briskly towards the surgery.

'There are some electric fires scattered around. Put them on low, we need to keep Jimmy warm. You'll also need to disinfect the table and set up one of the large crates with blankets,' Pete instructed as he and Sam carried the stretcher through the door and placed it on the table. Jimmy's eyes were droopy and the rise and fall of his chest extremely slow. Before removing the stretcher from underneath him. Pete pointed to the white scrubs hanging on the back of the door. 'Get those on then sterilise your hands.'

Verity did exactly what Pete said and he did the same. Sam was standing at the side of the table clutching Jimmy's lead in one hand and slowly stroking his head with the other. 'I knew I shouldn't have let him off the lead up there.'

'He wouldn't be the first to chase a seagull near the edge of the cliff and he won't be the last,' said Pete, kindly.

Verity pointed to the table in the waiting room. 'There's strong sweet tea in that mug and a whisky in that glass. You're likely in shock and it'll take the edge off it.'

'You found my whisky then?' asked Pete.

'You vets are all the same. Always a bottle of whisky stashed in the cupboard in the main desk.'

'That's because the veterinary assistants usually drive us to drink... But you never know when someone might need it and this is definitely one of those times.'

Sam's eyes didn't leave Jimmy. 'Come on, buddy, you can't leave me. Everyone leaves me,' he murmured.

Verity touched Sam's shoulder. 'We're going to do our very best.'

Pete looked towards Jimmy then at Sam. 'I'm sorry, Sam, I'm going to have to ask you to take a seat in the waiting room.'

With tears in his eyes, Sam kissed the top of Jimmy's head. 'Do not leave me, I love you.'

They watched Sam leave the room and swig back the whisky. Verity closed the door.

'What are our chances here?' she asked in a whisper.

'We can only do our best and hope it's enough. But he's lucky that ledge broke his fall. My guess is that he's landed on his back end and that leg is definitely broken. It just depends how broken. Let's get him some pain relief and sedation and get him X-rayed.'

'Do we need fluids?'

Pete nodded. 'Yes, initiate an intravenous. Do you know how to?'

Verity smiled. 'Of course.'

'Along with a urinary catheter. We don't want him feeling the need to stand and urinate. We need to keep his stress levels to a minimum. I'm going to check for organ injury and signs of trauma then take bloods. I'll get him sedated then we can take radiographs, check the leg for breaks, get abdominal and chest views and verify the heart and lungs are without complications.'

It was soon clear the back leg was broken. With the help of Verity, Pete aligned it to the best position for healing and placed metal implants around the bone to support it and keep the broken parts together.

'Do we need another metal pin just there?' asked Verity.

Pete nodded. 'We do.'

They worked mainly in silence, doing everything they could to help Jimmy.

'We need to keep him here tonight for observation,' Pete said once they were done. 'Let's move him into the large crate. There's plenty of soft padding and he won't be able to move too much. We can provide water in a clip-on bowl.' He pointed to the corner of the room. 'I've got observation cameras still linked up to my phone so I can keep an eye on him throughout the night. It's warm in here and we can keep the lights low.'

They moved Jimmy together and watched him for a moment before cleaning up and sterilising all the equipment and the table.

'It's going to be around twelve weeks recovery, which is going to be difficult for Jimmy as I've seen the way he races across those cliff tops.' Pete smiled affectionately at the dog. 'He's going to be okay though, I'm glad to say. I have to admit I wasn't sure there for a minute.' He turned towards Verity. 'You were very calm and efficient. Anyone would be lucky to have you as part of their team.'

'Thank you, that means a lot.' She hesitated for a moment. 'Can I ask you something?'

Pete nodded as he washed his hands at the sink in the corner of the room.

'Cooper, have you ever worked with him?'

Drying his hands before stepping out of his scrubs, he smiled. 'I taught him everything he knows. He was my apprentice for many years. He works hard and is a bloody good vet. I offered to make him a partner in this surgery but he was hungry to go it alone and I don't blame him. It was probably for the best as I think we might have butted heads and I'd have got on his nerves.'

'Why do you say that?'

'Because I'm stuck in my ways. I like routine and at my time of life I'm not open to change, whereas I know you youngsters like to come in with all your new ideas. But my motto is, if it's not broken, don't try to fix it. Still, Cooper has done very well for himself and even if we were never partners as such, I can't think of anyone better to take over this place. Why do you ask?'

'Because I've been thinking…but it may just be a pipe dream and I probably can't…' Verity knew she was trying to talk herself out of it while also wanting someone to tell her she should definitely do it.

'Probably can't what?'

'I saw Cooper is advertising for staff, for this place.'

'He is.' Pete narrowed his eyes. 'He's going to modernise it a little first but he's hoping to open this surgery in the next month. Are you thinking of staying?'

Verity blew out a breath. 'This is going to sound…' She paused and then tried again. 'I feel a little daft saying this…'

'Never feel daft, it's better to get stuff off your chest than keep it in. Just say it.'

'Am I good enough?'

'Good enough for…'

'To apply for one of Cooper's jobs?'

A huge smile spread across Pete's face.

'You're more than good enough.'

'But could I stay? Could I leave everything behind?'

'Exactly what are you leaving behind?' asked Pete as he listened to Jimmy's heartbeat one last time before shutting the door to the dog crate. 'Because from what you've told me about what brought you to this island in the first place, there's nothing to go back for.'

Verity thought for a moment. 'You have a point. There's just my house, which was where my grandparents lived.'

'You shouldn't feel loyalty to live in a house just because your grandparents lived there. Houses are just bricks and mortar. You still have your memories. This is your time now. Do what you want to do. And the answer is yes. You should apply for a job with Cooper. After this evening I'll definitely be recommending you.'

'I'm seriously thinking about it. It's just my living arrangements that worry me.'

'Apply for the job and see what happens. Things always have a way of working themselves out if they're meant to be.' Pete pointed to Jimmy. 'He's comfortable, and the cameras are on. Let's go and chat to Sam.'

Despite the animosity between them, Pete was being so kind to Sam. Verity figured that must have been difficult, knowing how Sam had reacted towards him over the years. She followed Pete out of the surgery into the waiting room.

It looked like Sam hadn't moved a muscle for the past hour. He was sitting in the plastic chair leaning backwards with his arms crossed, his head against the wall. As soon as he realised the door had opened, he sat up.

'Thank God. I thought you were never going to come out of that room.'

Instantly, Pete put his mind at ease. 'Jimmy is

comfortable and sedated. He has a broken leg but he's going to make a full recovery. He's a very lucky dog.'

Verity smiled as Sam looked at the two of them, the relief evident on his face. Knowing that Jimmy was going to be okay, he pressed his hands to his eyes to try and control the tears. Pete passed him a tissue.

'Do you want to see him?' Pete gestured towards the open door and Verity led the way.

'He's heavily sedated but stable. His leg has been pinned. The implants are hidden under the skin and they're going to be left in place after the bone has healed. The hardest thing for you both will be the next twelve weeks until he makes a full recovery. We can't move him tonight but if everything is okay in the morning and after I check him over again, he can go home. He'll need lots of rest and I'd suggest you keep him crated to limit movement.'

Sam was bent over the side of the crate. He stroked Jimmy gently. 'I thought I'd lost you there for a minute.' His voice was full of emotion.

'We have the camera on him and any movement at all will alert my phone. I'll be able to see and check in on him at any time through the night but I don't think he'll be making any further moves for now. I'll come across first thing before the puffin count and we can sort out any medication for pain relief, et cetera, before he goes home.'

Sam stood up and Verity was delighted to see him extend his hand to Pete. Pete shook it without hesitation.

'Thank you,' said Sam sincerely. 'I can't thank you enough.'

Pete nodded his head in acknowledgement. 'It's all down to this one, too.' He gestured towards Verity.

'Thank you,' said Sam, turning towards Verity.

'Now if it's okay with you, I'd like to go home and have a cup of tea,' said Pete.

'Thank you both again. You went above and beyond tonight.'

'Always happy to do so when animals are concerned.' Pete now extended his hand towards Verity. 'Thank you for being my wing woman. You were impressive in there and I couldn't have done it without you.'

'Team work makes the dream work,' trilled Verity.

With one last look at Jimmy, who was still fast asleep, they headed outside and Pete locked up the surgery. 'I'll see you both in the morning.'

Verity and Sam watched him walk the short distance to Cliff Top Cottage. 'How are you feeling?' asked Verity.

'Mixed emotions. An hour ago, I felt like the bottom had fallen out of my world. He chases birds all the time but I never thought he'd be stupid enough to launch himself off the cliff. I'm so relieved he's still here.'

'Thank God Pete was about.'

Sam looked towards the cottage and nodded. 'Yes, I'm extremely grateful, and thank you, too. I don't know what I'd have done if you hadn't heard me shout.'

'Let's not think about that now. Would you like to come back for a drink? I have wine.'

Sam glanced towards the van and nodded. 'You're all settled in then? Not a bad view.'

'Definitely not a bad view.' She nudged his arm playfully. 'Let's get you a drink and we could even throw a few coals on the firepit.'

They stared at each other for a second. 'I'm surprised you're even speaking to me after earlier.'

'Luckily for you, I'm not one for holding grudges.'

'Which makes my life a lot easier. If it's okay with you, I think I need a hug. I thought I'd be pushing my luck if I asked Pete for one.' He stretched his arms wide.

Verity chuckled, stepping into his arms and squeezing him tight. 'Jimmy will be okay, but you'll have your work cut out keeping him off that leg.'

Pulling away slowly, she opened the van. 'Here, grab these.' She passed him a couple of chairs then brought out a small firepit along with a bag of coal.

Sam popped his head into the van. 'It's like the Tardis in here. Did you convert this? It's like a proper home.'

'I did. There was blood, sweat, tears and a few war wounds but not as many as those sustained today from the puffins.' Verity opened the fridge, took out a bottle of wine and passed it to him. 'It has all the mod cons. This is my shower.' She held up the pet shower system.

'Wow, you're spoiling yourself.'

'And my camping toilet.' She pointed.

'I don't think I need to see that.' He grinned. 'But I'm impressed with this pet shower. How does it work?' He pushed in the pump.

'Woah! Don't do that!'

But it was too late; water had squirted out all over Sam's socks. Verity quickly thrust the hose outside.

'It's actually quite powerful,' said Sam, thoughtfully.

'And now your socks are soaked. You get the fire going and I'll find you a new pair of socks.'

With a smile Sam stepped outside and collected nearby

twigs to put in the bottom of the firepit before adding the coals. 'Any matches?'

'Yes, I'll be right there,' she replied, rummaging through one of the drawers. There they were, exactly what she was looking for. 'Here, catch,' she said, standing in the doorway and throwing Sam a box of matches and a pair of long pink fluffy socks, followed by a towel.

Sam cocked an eyebrow. 'You expect me to wear these? Have you not got anything less...neon?'

'No one is going to see you, and those are good socks. Better than the wet ones you're wearing.'

Playfully Sam shook his head and by the time Verity had mopped up the water and joined him outside, his trainers were on a box next to the firepit and his socks draped on a nearby bush. His legs were stretched out and the fluffy pink socks stretched up his calves.

'They suit you.' She smiled.

'They're pretty good socks, to be fair.'

Verity poured the wine and handed Sam a glass. Sitting watching the sea lapping against the rocks in the distance, Verity chanced a glance at him. 'You shook Pete's hand. It was good to see you both being amicable.'

'He took care of Jimmy, you both did. I would never have got him over to Sea's End in time. If it wasn't for the two of you he might not have made it.'

'But he did.'

Sam paused and took a sideward glance towards Verity. 'I've been thinking about what you said.'

'What is it I said?'

'About talking to Pete before the vigil. When you said,

surely if something had happened back then, it would have come out by now.'

Verity didn't interrupt. The islanders had tried to put an end to this feud for years with no breakthrough. Could it actually be possible that Sam was beginning to move on?

'I know you're right. Pete will have stories about my grandfather I don't know, and by not moving on, all those stories and memories will be lost.'

'What did I do or say that was different compared to Betty or others on the island?'

'I suppose you put me in my place, told me exactly how I am. I like how you said it's sometimes better to talk to someone who is not directly involved in the situation. So thank you.' Without warning, Sam took Verity's hand and rested it on his knee. 'I saw a very caring side to Pete this evening. He was patient, professional, wasn't fazed that it was my dog and didn't treat me as an enemy, which I wouldn't have blamed him for after the way I've treated him over the years.'

'Are you going to have a chat with him before the vigil?'

Sam nodded. 'I'm going to go and speak to him tomorrow. I think this is a good time to bury the hatchet.'

Verity smiled. This was good news for everyone. 'I'm glad you've made that decision and I do think, if something did go on that night, fifty years is long enough for a secret like that to be buried. Talking of secrets, I've seen Betty. Isn't she just wonderful! She agrees the postcard is from your grandfather. My granny and your grandpa Joe had a summer romance.'

'What are the chances of that? Did Betty divulge what their secret was?'

'I think it was more about my granny's secret. She arrived here after my grandfather's marriage proposal. I think she was rather scared about her future and decided to take some time to figure out some things while she was here. Then she met Joe and, though she obviously cared for him, in the end she was more scared about her family disowning her if she didn't go back. I can't quite wrap my head around the fact that they knew each other and we've come across each other by chance.'

'Life has a funny way of working.'

'It really does.' Slowly pulling her hand away from Sam's, she held up her glass. 'To past friendships, and current ones, too.'

Sam touched his glass to hers before taking a sip. 'And what are your plans? When will you be leaving?'

Cooper's advert popped into her mind. 'I'm actually not sure. I've enjoyed my time here, despite having been pecked alive by puffins. Tell me what it's like living here. Have you ever been tempted to move?'

'Absolutely not. Why would I?' He gestured towards the sea view in front of them.

'You're lucky. It's very different from where I live.'

'In what way?'

'I live in a built-up area where everything's squashed together, there's constant traffic, litter in the parks, and no one speaks when you pass them in the street. In fact, they would do anything not to make eye contact. It's such a different vibe here. I feel comfortable, and I even have friends already, as Clemmie and Amelia immediately welcomed me with open arms. Everyone knows everyone. This is a proper community and you're like one big family.

Here people actually do care. You can feel a part of something.'

'A change from the norm does us good sometimes. Humans are creatures of habit and even though they could change their lives, they don't. They just dream. I know that first-hand. They don't change anything because they fear failure and wonder. What if it doesn't work out? In my book, failure makes you grow, and that's a good thing.'

'How do you make that out?'

'It teaches us lessons, like how to do it different next time. Opening the restaurant, I started out thinking I was the boss so what I said should go, but I soon realised it's the whole team that makes the business successful. They have skills I don't have and vice versa and so I need to lean on them. I could not have made that restaurant as successful as it is today without them. I saw a similar bond tonight. You and Pete were a team in there.'

'We were,' replied Verity, thinking about what Sam had just said. 'It's funny really, this time last year I thought my future was one thing, but now it's something else entirely.'

'And what have you learned from that?'

'That I'm in charge of my own happiness. Sitting here, I think it's the best thing that's ever happened to me.'

'Why?'

'Because I'm growing. I was stuck in a relationship because society dictates you should be part of a couple, otherwise…what the hell is wrong with you? People stay when they aren't happy because they fear the unknown or they think they can't manage on their own financially. But the alternative is to stay and be unhappy, to waste your life and watch it tick by. I'd never have been allowed…'

'Never *allowed*?'

'Yep, I'd never have been allowed to go on holiday with my friend, or convert a van into a home. I'd never have been allowed to have a drink on Sunday afternoon or spend the day shopping with my girlfriend. Spending money on a new pair of shoes or a coat would have caused arguments.'

'And your thoughts now?'

'I'm free. I know the best thing to happen to me was his affair. I'm not trapped anymore. I'm in charge of my own financial affairs, I can travel the world, drink wine overlooking the sea... And you know what makes me smile? The thought of someone else waking up next to my ex thinking they've won the lottery. Whereas it's me who's won my life back. I actually feel happy and excited about the future, and I can't remember the last time I felt that way. What makes me a little disappointed with myself, he might have had an affair but why the hell did I stay in that relationship for so long?'

Sam smiled at her. 'I can hear the passion in your voice.'

'I'm beginning to realise that I've only stayed where I live for so long because the house I'm living in once belonged to my grandparents. But now, if I were to leave it behind, I could use it as a stepping stone into the rest of my life.'

'Your grandparents will still be with you wherever you land.'

Verity was mulling everything over. 'It is time for changes. I'm sorry I upset you this morning. It wasn't anything to do with me and you were right, I shouldn't judge a situation when I'm not in it myself.'

'I appreciate the apology and I'm sorry too.' He reached

across and took her hand. 'I'm not used to someone telling me exactly how it is.'

'I can be a little bossy sometimes. Maybe I need to work on that.'

'A *little* bossy?'

Verity playfully swiped him before standing up and wandering back to the van. She soon returned holding a blanket. 'It's getting a little chilly.' Moving her chair closer to his, she laid the blanket across both of them. She felt a tiny thrill when Sam unexpectedly slipped his hand under the blanket and rested it on her knee. He stretched out, his legs brushing against hers, and she felt a flush of warmth. Verity had never been swept off her feet before, but this was beginning to feel like the start of something significant.

They stared at each other in a contemplative silence, both smiling, until he leaned forward and hooked a stray strand of hair behind her ear like it was the most natural thing in the world. She knew the connection between them was strong in this moment and she took the chance to ask a question that had been bugging her.

'Just remind me again why you're choosing the single life? I saw everyone falling all over you in the pub. You could have your pick of any of those girls.'

'I just don't think you need to be in a relationship to be happy. I live in each moment, just like now, and enjoy things for what they are. Are you feeling happy now?'

'Yes.'

'That's my point. The beginning of the night wasn't the best but sitting here with you, I'm happy. What more do I need than that?'

Ava had said the same thing to her in the past. *Just enjoy the time you spend with someone without wondering what it will turn into or whether you'll see them again.* But Verity had never experienced such a carefree life before. Every time she found someone attractive, she knew where she stood right from the beginning and the other person always wanted what she did. To her, just going with the flow had always been like wasting time.

But given that her previous relationships had never worked out, although each one had been mapped out in the hope that they would be happy ever after, maybe it was time to adopt a different approach and live in the moment.

'And what is this?'

Sam looked at her. His gaze warmed her body all over, and anticipation of his answer ignited her hormones. She saw him swallow as lust pulsed through her veins. Their fingers were entwined. Sam studied her face, the gleam in his eyes telling her he liked her as much as she liked him.

He gave her a sultry smile and at last replied. 'Two people enjoying each other's company.'

His eyes didn't leave hers. The intensity between them was increasing and Verity's gaze dropped to his lips.

'What if the right girl came along and changed everything?'

Sam didn't answer so Verity did what she had wanted to do since the moment she first saw him outside the greasy spoon – she kissed him. She was torn: she wasn't sure that a one-night stand would be enough, but she wanted this moment with Sam all the same. She pulled away from the kiss slowly, but Sam cupped his hands around her face and pulled her back in.

His kiss was tender, leaving her wanting so much more,

and Verity suddenly realised that if this was going with the flow then it didn't feel too bad. Her whole body was electrified by his touch.

'I wasn't expecting that,' she murmured.

'Yes, you were,' he whispered.

Risking another future broken heart, Verity stood up, taking both of his hands in hers and pulling him towards her. The moon shining on them was the perfect romantic backdrop and she was ready to take control.

'I don't want to overstep the mark,' murmured Sam as Verity began slowly kissing him again.

'I'm an adult, I know what I'm doing,' she replied, her body alive to the thrill of never having done anything like this before. With her hands clasped around his neck, he put his hands around her waist, then slowly slid to her bare skin. His lips skimmed hers and then he deepened the kiss. Verity let out a small sigh as his tongue teased her, setting off every nerve ending in her body. Still kissing, they side-stepped to the van. Sliding the door open with her foot, she backed towards the bed.

'It's quite cosy in here.'

'Isn't it? Can I...say something?'

Sam stopped kissing her for a second and looked at her with adoration.

'I've never had sex with a man who is wearing fluffy pink socks.'

'Well, prepare yourself, because I'm keeping them on. It's cold in here!' He grinned foolishly at her.

She threw back her head and laughed as Sam lifted her off her feet, laid her down on the bed and lowered himself onto the mattress. Turning him on his back, Verity straddled him, all her worries about a future broken heart evaporating as her hands slid under his shirt. She gave a tiny groan as her hands traced the contours of his body. She began to unbutton his shirt slowly, already imagining the feel of his chest against her naked skin. Sam quickly whipped off the shirt as she lowered her lips to his chest and began kissing his body. Soon her hands were raking through his hair as he flipped her onto her back.

She gave another tiny gasp as Sam ran his fingers under her top then skimmed the waistband of her jeans, pulling her in close. She squirmed with pleasure as he raised her top, kissing her breasts through the soft fabric of her bra. With one swift move he unclasped it and lowered his mouth to her nipple. She shivered, her back arching as his kisses moved down her body, one hand still stroking her breast. He gently tugged at her jeans and without hesitation she wriggled out of them, leaving Sam skimming the top of her pants before she pressed herself against him, willing him to peel the knickers from her body.

In this moment Verity wanted him more than she'd ever wanted anyone, and despite the inevitability of heartbreak, she embraced the chance of having raw passionate sex with this man, something she'd never experienced in her life before.

Right on cue, Sam took her breath away.

Chapter Seventeen

Going with the flow didn't quite have the same feeling when Verity woke up the next morning to find Sam wasn't lying next to her. When she'd fallen asleep in his arms, she'd had a huge smile on her face – but not anymore. His clothes were gone and the pink fluffy socks were hanging on the back of the chair. Last night she was full of excitement and this morning she felt empty, like the two empty wine glasses on the small outdoor table – the only trace he'd been there. Why hadn't he woken her and when did he sneak out?

Sitting up in bed, she grabbed her dressing gown before swinging her legs to the floor, then pulled back the van door...and jumped out of her skin when she found Pete standing there.

'Woah! You frightened the life out of me.'

Pete tapped his watch. 'I won't be recommending you to Cooper if you can't even turn up for voluntary work on time.'

Verity wondered if he was joking and felt a sense of rising panic. 'What time is it?' She quickly grabbed her phone. 'I'm so sorry, Pete, I've overslept.' With the wine and the kissing and the...Sam...she'd forgotten to set her alarm.

'I'll wait five minutes...over there.' He pointed to the cottage, where Verity noticed the other rangers were already waiting.

Quickly closing the door, she brushed her teeth in bottled water from the fridge and pulled her brush through her hair. Stumbling, she pulled on clean clothes, slipped her feet into her trainers and lifted up her T-shirt to spray deodorant. It might have been just her imagination but she was sure she could smell sex all around her in the cramped space of her van. Hurrying towards the cottage and Pete, she noticed the other rangers making their way to their own sections of the cliff.

'I slept like a log,' she said, taking a clipboard from Pete.

'Would that be down to the coastal air or the company?'

Damn, he must have seen Sam sneak out. She took her chance to try and fill in some blanks. 'Do you know what time he left?'

'Just after six a.m., when I left the cottage to go and check on Jimmy.'

'And how is Jimmy?' She felt awful; she hadn't given Jimmy a second thought from the moment she'd woken up.

'Feeling sorry for himself but he's eating and drinking, which is a very good sign. Sam is coming to collect him at lunchtime.'

They walked in an awkward silence, Verity feeling a little embarrassed that Pete knew Sam had spent the night.

'I don't usually behave in that way,' she finally blurted.

Pete looked sideward at her. 'Don't feel the need to explain yourself to me. It's none of my business. My business is you turning up for work on time.'

'I'm sorry about that.'

Pete nodded, but Verity's mood had slumped. She knew last night had been completely her choice, she'd even felt empowered that she could make that choice, but now she was feeling regret, and it wasn't good for her emotional health. Never having been in this situation before, she had no clue what to say or how to act when she next saw Sam.

'Would you be free around two p.m.?' asked Pete.

'I'll need to check my busy schedule.' She smiled. 'Yes, I'm free.'

'I need to go over to the solicitors at Sea's End to sign the contract for the sale of the surgery.'

'Did you want me to come with you?' she asked, a bit confused.

He handed her a bunch of keys. 'No, Sam is coming to collect Jimmy and I need someone here to let him in. I've already administered the medication this morning so Jimmy just needs to be handed over, the cage cleaned down, and the surgery locked again.' Pete must have sensed Verity's hesitation. 'Or I can rearrange the solicitors? I just didn't schedule in a dog chasing a seagull over the cliff edge when I agreed to the appointment.'

'And why not? That would have been my very first thought.' She smiled, taking the keys from him. 'Of course I can do that for you.' She was intrigued to find out how Sam would act towards her and whether he would acknowledge what had happened last night. It was better to see him in the privacy of the surgery than to run into him in the street.

As they began to count the puffins, Verity realised she was quieter than yesterday. She couldn't get Sam off her mind. Even though he'd been honest with her and told her that he wasn't looking for a relationship, she couldn't help feeling down because he'd left without saying goodbye. She should be revelling in the fact that she had been wrapped in the arms of a gorgeous man and enjoyed great sex, but instead she was disappointed, because when she'd played the scenario out in her head, they'd woken up together and he'd told her what a great night he'd had, before asking to see her again. Instead, she'd woken alone and had no idea where they stood with one another.

'Have you thought any more about applying for the job with Cooper?' Pete interrupted her thoughts as he stuck his hand down one of the burrows.

'I'm thinking about it. It's just—'

'Houses are sellable, and life is what you make it,' interrupted Pete, as though he could read her thoughts.

He retracted his arm from the burrow and noted down the number of puffins on the sheet of paper.

'How is it they don't bite or scratch you?' she asked, jealous.

'They know me. I'm not called Puffin Pete for nothing, you know. Your turn.'

Verity lay down on her stomach and reached inside the next burrow. 'I was thinking about it but now I'm not so sure. I suppose it's the fear of the unknown.'

'If you get the job, just see how it goes. You've got your property rented out and you could use that income to rent somewhere around here.'

'It makes perfect sense but what if the novelty of the

island wears off once I'm no longer in holiday mode? What happens then?'

Pete pointed towards the sea. 'That's not a novelty. Waking up and seeing that sea every day is the thing that's kept me going all these years. Tell me the pros and cons.'

Verity pulled her arm out of the burrow. 'I think they're beginning to like me. No bites that time.' She smiled.

'Definitely a pro,' said Pete, drawing a line down the centre of another piece of paper. 'All the pros?' He wound his hand around in a circular motion to encourage her to start talking.

'Pros: I've made friends in Clemmie and Amelia. And I just love all of this.' She swept her arm towards the sea and the bay. 'It's miles away from my past and no one knows anything about me unless I tell them.'

'Fresh start,' Pete said as he noted it down.

'I don't already have a job so I could start work straightaway.'

'Noted.'

'I don't have any friends in Staffordshire anymore and it would be a relief to move away from my ex. And there's something about this place. I love that you have a proper community where everyone knows everyone and there's always someone you can talk to. I guess the bottom line is that I like it here.'

'And the cons?'

'I have a house in Staffordshire.'

'And...'

'I can't think of anything else.'

'Then it's a no-brainer. Apply for the job. See what happens.'

Verity sighed. 'Actually, there is another con, and I don't know what I'm going to do about it.'

'Why, has something happened?' asked Pete.

'Sam happened. I think I've been stupid.'

'Because of last night?'

Verity nodded. 'I feel an idiot. My gut feeling is unsettled. I think I made the wrong judgement.'

'Did you have all the facts to make the judgement?'

'Yes, but I went ahead anyway, even knowing it was never going to go any further. And now I have to face him.'

'It's difficult when feelings are involved.'

'But that's the thing, I don't understand how I can even have feelings so soon. They've crept up on me and now they're all I can think about.'

Last night she'd felt something she hadn't felt in a long time – sexy, desired – and there was no way Sam hadn't felt the same connection between them.

'I thought I was in control, but now I feel like I've let myself down.'

The swirling feelings of being sexy and desired had now turned into ones of shame and embarrassment.

'Why?'

'Because he made it pretty clear it was a one-off and he didn't want more. I suppose I got caught up in the moment, the romance of it all, and blurred my own boundaries. To be honest, I think I was hoping I could change his mind and he'd wake up this morning telling me he wanted me.'

'There's no point dwelling on it.' Pete hesitated. 'Sam is a good guy. We probably have far more in common than he'll ever know, which is why I can say with some confidence that he's likely just protecting his heart.'

'Anything you would like to share?'

Pete shook his head.

Verity knew that in Sam's case it probably had something to do with how things had ended with Alice. As for Pete, she decided against questioning him further. If he didn't want to talk about his past that was his right.

'Come on, next burrow.' Pete pointed.

Four hours later they called it a day. The sun was beating down and they'd covered a lot of ground.

'Not bad, only thirteen bites today,' Verity said as she looked down at her hand.

Pete smiled. 'Not one bite for me.' They walked back towards Cliff Top Cottage.

'Are you sure you're okay handing over Jimmy for me?'

'If I'm applying for the job with Cooper and sticking around, I'm going to have to face Sam often. I might as well get the first meeting over and done with sooner rather than later.'

'You've made up your mind then?'

'You've convinced me that I have nothing to lose. Do I really want to go back to a street where I look out of the window before I venture outside, and I constantly dread bumping into the ex? Absolutely not.' Verity rolled her eyes.

'You don't need to feel any dread here,' said Pete, kindly. 'You can stand here and look around you for as long as you like.'

Verity did exactly that, frustrated to find that that feeling of dread had transferred to Sam.

'Do you know what I see?'

'What?' asked Verity.

'Someone who has triumphed in difficult circumstances. You can now do what you want, when you want, and that includes moving halfway across the country. My guess is that nothing has changed in his life, other than the woman on his arm, but everything has changed in yours, and for the better. Don't look back, just look forward.'

'You're right, Pete. Whatever the consequences of last night's antics, I'm excited about the possibility of staying here. Someone up there has saved me from a mundane, boring life and delivered me new possibilities and choices that I'm actually eager to embrace.'

'Apply for the job. I think you've made the right decision.'

'I will, and when I hand over Jimmy, I'm going to hold my head up high and be professional.'

'You've got this.'

'In fact, I'll take my laptop and apply for the job whilst I'm there. Then, later this afternoon, I'm going to call in to the bookshop and see if Amelia would like to do something tonight if she's not working.'

Pete smiled. 'Don't let the buggers get you down.' He waved as he headed towards his cottage.

Talking to Pete had helped. He reminded Verity of her granddad, whose advice she had always valued. Hearing her phone ring in her pocket, she looked at the screen. It was Ava.

'Afternoon!' Verity answered as she unlocked the van and slid open the door.

'How's life on Puffin Island? Are you still there, heading

to your next destination or heading home? You've been quiet.'

'I'm still here.' She blew out a breath.

'Oooh, it sounds like you have gossip.'

Verity spilled the beans. 'A one-night stand has been ticked off the bucket list before I hit thirty.'

'Is this Verity Callaway I'm talking to? Miss Prim and Proper? You're a dark horse. Finally, you've become a modern woman!'

'Don't, I feel awful about it.'

'Why?'

'Because I suppose I've never done anything like that before. I'm usually in some sort of relationship before I've gone to that stage.'

'The sea air must have addled your brain.'

'It's not funny, I could cry.'

'And who was this guy?'

Verity hesitated. 'Sam.'

'Aww, gorgeous Sam whom you followed to Puffin Island after stalking him at the ferry port? Gorgeous Sam whose cottage you've been staying in?'

'I didn't stalk him!' she exclaimed, indignantly.

'Mmm, I'd say you got what you wanted, so why not embrace it for what it is? Why could you cry? Was it rubbish sex?'

'The best I've ever had. But he's made it clear he's not looking for a relationship.'

'So just sit back and enjoy the ride – literally.' Ava laughed. 'Have fun whilst you're on the island. It's a bit like a holiday romance, then you go home.'

For a moment Verity was quiet.

'The silence is telling me there may be more,' prompted Ava.

'Where *is* home?'

'The Midlands.'

'But what have I got there? Yes, I have a house, but it's rented out for the next six months so I can't go back just yet.'

'I know, and that's my fault, but you could always come and stay in my digs in London. We can still have our adventure. It just won't be exactly what we had planned.'

'Hmm…the fast-paced city or the soothing island with the perfect view?'

'Are we talking about the sea view or Sam?'

'The sea! There's an opportunity to apply for a job here on the island as a veterinary assistant. I've no idea where I'll live, but I could maybe book the hotel or the B&B until a house comes up for rent. What do you think?'

'Wow! I wasn't expecting that. I think, what have you got to lose? Go for it!'

'That's what Pete said.'

'Pete? Sam? Please tell me you aren't working your way around the island.'

'Don't be ridiculous! Pete is the main ranger in charge of the puffin count. He used to be a vet but is selling the surgery to Cooper, who already has a practice in Sea's End and wants to expand.'

'And this Cooper? You don't fancy him too, do you? Because it's never a good idea to mix work and pleasure.'

'I do not fancy Cooper,' insisted Verity. 'But what do you really think? Am I just dreaming? I only turned up here because of the postcard.'

'And how is the search for the long lost lover going?'

'The search is over. Mystery solved. Betty, who has lived here on the island all her life, remembers my granny. She came for the summer and stayed with her. It turns out Joe Wilson, aka "W", was Sam's granddad and he and Granny were close and possibly had a holiday romance. I think the secret mentioned in the postcard was the fact that my granny was engaged to my granddad while she was on the island, but never told anyone. She came to the island to sort out her feelings for him after he proposed suddenly.'

'Keeping it in the family…'

'Ava! She apparently returned home and chose my granddad over Joe. But I'm not sure of all the ins and outs.'

'And how has the grandfather aged? You'll be able to see how good Sam's gene pool is.'

'His grandfather was killed in a tragic accident at sea, just after my grandmother left the island.'

'Gosh, does that mean you have to stay to keep Sam safe? We certainly don't want history repeating itself.'

'Ava! It's not something to joke about. It's been fifty years since his death and there's a vigil being held in his memory soon.'

'I'm sorry, I didn't mean to offend.'

'You didn't. It's just all going on here. There's the vigil, plus the island's vote on safety barriers to stop idiots trying to drown themselves on the causeway, and we finish the puffin count tomorrow.'

'That all sounds…actually, it sounds like you're living your best life, just like me. Which reminds me, I'm due back at work in five. Anyway, tonight I'm off to a wine bar with my new work colleagues.'

'All glam and glitz.'

'And yours sounds...all very wholesome and community-minded.'

'Enjoy your evening.'

'Stay out of trouble.'

'Always.'

Verity sniffed her armpit and then her hair, and then checked the time. As she had forty minutes until Sam was due to pick up Jimmy, she decided to use the time taking a much-needed shower. After a night of passion and a morning of sliding along the ground she didn't smell pretty at all. Glancing towards the garage she saw it was shut for lunch, according to the sign swinging outside in the light breeze. She waved at Pete as he drove past her and realised that with Nathan and Pete gone for a while, she would have ample time to use her pet shower in privacy. She simply couldn't meet Sam smelling and looking like this.

As soon as the container was full of water, she propped the shower head over a branch of a nearby tree and pumped the container, before slipping into a white bikini and flip-flops. She switched on Spotify on her phone, and the first song on her playlist sounded out. Pressing the nozzle on the shower head, she stepped under the cold water.

'Brrr!' She shivered, wetting her hair and rubbing shampoo into it. She smiled as a Britney track finished and she immediately thought of Kev. Even though it was only a few days since she'd driven away from her street in the early hours, it felt like a lifetime ago. Standing there, letting the cold water fall over her body, she didn't feel any desire at all to go back. It was strange, knowing she'd outgrown the place where she was brought up.

The next song played out. 'Where you from, you sexy thing?' she sang at the top of her lungs, jiggling her backside as she lifted her arms above her head and twirled around. Still singing and jigging, she rinsed off the shampoo. As the song came to its end and the water ran out, she squeezed the water from her hair and spun around – only to meet an amused smile. Sam! She nearly jumped out of her skin.

'Woah! Where did you come from?'

'You like Hot Chocolate?'

'Massive fan!'

'You in a bikini singing along to my favourite song was not a sight I was expecting to see in my lunch hour, but it's very welcome.'

'I aim to please.' She pointed towards a towel draped over the camping chair.

As he turned to grab it for her, she admired his attire. He was dressed for work in a crisp white short-sleeved shirt that clung to his torso, and tailored navy trousers. And there it was again, that uncontrollable tingle, the goosebumps and flutters that gathered in her stomach every time she laid eyes on him. He made her nervous, but in a good way.

Sam handed her the towel. Verity was relieved; things didn't seem awkward between them at all. Maybe this morning she'd been overthinking the situation. Maybe Sam had started to see things differently.

'A welcome sight, did you say?' Verity knew she was

pushing it but she wanted to gauge his reaction. She pulled the towel around her body.

'It's the best sight I've seen all morning. But, saying that, I've spent that morning coming face to face with around two hundred seabass, a hundred lobsters and about the same number of oysters,' he replied playfully.

'Cheeky! What are you doing here on the cliff top? Have you come to apologise for sneaking out of the van and not waking me this morning?'

'I didn't sneak anywhere. How you slept through the noise of those puffins is beyond me.'

Verity smiled as she dried herself. 'Slept like a baby.' She pointed towards the van. 'I'm just going to get changed.' She stepped inside but didn't want to the let the conversation drop. 'Don't you miss cuddling up to someone at night?' The van door was slightly ajar and she could see Sam inspecting the shower, which was still hooked over the branch of the tree.

'I did last night.' She saw him smile.

'But wouldn't you want more of that?' She moved away from the crack in the door as he glanced in her direction.

'Like I've said, I just enjoy living in the moment. No ties, no commitments.'

Verity opened the door wide.

'Wow!' He was unashamedly staring at her.

She had slipped on an off-the-shoulder maxi dress and a pair of flat sandals, and the appreciative look in his glistening blue eyes was exactly the reaction she had hoped for. She gave him a beatific smile that lit up her face as she swept her wet hair over her shoulders.

'I'm not always in jeans or joggers. Well, actually, ninety per cent of the time I am.'

'You should wear a dress more often. It suits you.'

'I might just do that.' She pointed towards the surgery. 'I take it you're here to collect Jimmy? Even though you're early.'

'I was hoping Pete was around to hand him back to me as I've taken the rest of the day off. I want to get Jimmy settled at home.'

Verity jangled the keys. 'Pete's had to nip to Sea's End, and he's left me in charge of the handover. Let me just grab my laptop, as I want to pinch a bit of his power and WiFi this afternoon.'

They walked side by side towards the surgery. 'I have to say I was impressed with your singing,' Sam remarked. 'Not so sure about the dancing though.'

'I honestly think my singing is worse than my dancing.' She grinned as she opened the surgery, picked up the post from the floor and placed it on the counter along with her laptop. 'Jimmy won't be able to put weight on his leg but he'll try. It might take him a moment to get his balance, too.' Verity opened the door to the back room and immediately Jimmy let out a bark.

'There you are.' Sam was by his side in an instant and opened the crate door.

As predicted, Jimmy tried to get to his feet but his balance was off and as his bad leg touched the floor he let out a whimper. Sam steadied him. 'I'm afraid you're going to have to hop for a while, pal.'

'He'll soon get used to it,' said Verity, encouragingly.

Sam looked at her. 'I know I said thank you yesterday but I'm very grateful...to you both.'

'It's my job to assist,' she said. 'I believe Pete has already given you the medication?'

Sam nodded.

'And how are you going to get him home?'

'I'm going to carry him. And then we're going to curl up and have a boys' afternoon.'

'Which consists of?'

'Watching James Bond and having a few treats. Do you know what time Pete will be back?'

'In the next hour, I should imagine.'

'I was hoping to catch him for that chat. I'm sure Jimmy will be asleep at some point this afternoon so just I'll pop back to see him then.'

'You're doing the right thing, moving on.'

Sam nodded. 'Thanks to your straight talking. I'm not having anyone else call me immature.'

Verity laughed. 'I think you're being very mature speaking to Pete.'

Sam gathered Jimmy up in his arms, and they made their goodbyes.

Verity stood in the doorway and watched as Sam headed along the cliff path. As soon as he was out of sight, she texted Ava.

All very strange, I've seen Sam and it wasn't in the least bit awkward. That was not what I was expecting.

Ava's reply came instantly.

> He made his intentions clear, there's no need for it to be awkward.

Verity thought about Ava's reply and decided she was right.

> And in other news, I'm applying for the job!

> You'll definitely get it!

Verity hoped so. She opened her laptop, went to Cooper's website and pressed on the link to apply for the job. After reading through the job description, she uploaded her CV and her references. She paused when the application asked for her personal details. They needed her address, which was normal, but what *was* her address right now? She decided on:

Verity Callaway
The Travelling Van
Parked between Cliff Top Cottage and Cliff Top Garage
Puffin Island

She smiled. She would either stand out from the crowd or her application would be dismissed because she had no permanent address.

She hit send, and with a whoosh the message was on its way. It was now only a matter of time before she knew one way or the other.

She closed the laptop and spent the next hour cleaning. After sterilising Jimmy's crate, she disinfected all the worktops and gave the surgery a good mop round, then stood with her arms folded leaning against the operating table. She was really hoping that she would get an interview. This place had a good feel about it. Leaving everywhere spick and span and fully disinfected, she grabbed her laptop and the keys. She'd actually done it, applied for a job on the island, and she felt a spring in her step as she opened the surgery door.

'The post,' she muttered, grabbing the letters from the counter then locking the door behind her. Pete's car was back, and she was just about to head towards his cottage with the post when she heard raised voices and stopped in her tracks. The arguing was coming from the open front door of Pete's cottage. Unsure what to do, she hesitated. She didn't mean to listen but it was difficult not to because the woman's voice was getting louder.

'How have you kept this to yourself? I thought I was your friend. How many times have I put my neck on the line for you?' she screamed, presumably at Pete.

'And how have you kept that a secret from *me* for all these years?' Pete replied.

'Because it wasn't my secret to tell. I promised.'

Verity finally recognised the voice – it was Betty. Rooted to the spot, she watched as Pete stepped outside, visibly upset and dabbing his eyes with his handkerchief.

Damn. Whatever was going on between them, she didn't want to get in the middle of it. Juggling the letters, she dropped them on the ground and quickly bent to scoop them up. There were three of them, and Verity stared at the bold type on the top one before glancing at the other two. Each was addressed the same: to 'Mr W. P. Fenwick'. Verity's heart began thumping.

Fumbling with the keys, she turned and marched back to the surgery, quickly opened the door and threw open her laptop. 'Come on,' she murmured to herself, urging the internet to load and promising herself that as soon as she started earning a salary again, she would treat herself to a new laptop. Tapping 'Veterinary Surgery Puffin Island' into the search engine, she clinked on the link that popped up.

Clinical Director and Veterinary Surgeon of the Puffin Island Practice – Wallace Peter Fenwick.

All Verity could do was stare at the name. Her pulse was racing as well as her thoughts. She gazed at the photo of Pete. 'Wallace,' she murmured as the conversations with Pete began to click into place. Was it possible the postcard wasn't from Joe? Was it actually *Pete* who had written to her grandmother?

Verity picked up the letters again and turned towards the door. Whilst Betty and Pete were together, she was going to take her chance. Hurrying towards the cottage, she stepped through the front door and found Pete and Betty standing in the living room.

'I recognised the handwriting!' Betty was shouting. As she turned to Verity she breathed out slowly, clearly uncomfortable with the situation.

Verity switched her gaze to Pete, finding a look of pure shock and disbelief on his face.

Turmoil flushed through her body. She had an uneasy feeling that they'd been arguing about her.

'Wallace.' The name left Verity's mouth. 'Joe isn't "W", is he?' The look between Betty and Pete said it all. Neither needed to answer her question.

Verity glanced towards the letters in her hand. She

swallowed. 'It's you, isn't it? You sent the postcard from Puffin Island?'

Caught up in some romantic idea, she'd convinced herself the postcard was from Joe, but was that because it gave her a connection to Sam, gave them something in common? Had she been so determined to believe it simply because she was hoping for that connection to flourish?

Pete hesitated then nodded slowly. 'And you're Henrietta's granddaughter.' His voice broke.

Verity nodded. 'I am.'

Betty touched Pete's arm. 'I'll leave you both alone.'

'Stay.' Pete had lowered his voice to a whisper. 'It's time,' he said. 'It's time you knew the truth – or my version of events, at least, and I think it's time you tell me yours.'

Betty hesitated but then nodded.

'What's going on?' asked Verity.

Pete gestured to her to take a seat. She had no idea what she was about to discover, but judging by the looks on their faces, whatever Pete and Betty were about to say wasn't going to be easy for either of them.

Chapter Eighteen

O nce inside the cottage, Verity could see that the interior reflected the exterior. Minimal furniture, no warmth, threadbare curtains and worn carpets. Pete disappeared through the door. The clatter of china could be heard, followed by the whistle of a kettle. Verity's eyes were drawn to an old dresser in the corner of the room that was full of books and framed photographs. The majority were photos of the band but Verity's eyes were firmly fixed on one photograph, showing a very young woman whom she immediately recognised. Betty was watching her closely.

Verity rose and picked up the photograph. 'My granny looks so young.'

'And beautiful,' added Betty.

She felt the reassuring touch of Betty's hand on her arm. She sat back down as Pete reappeared and placed a tray on the table with three china cups and a pot of tea.

Verity had no idea what she was about to hear but her heart was beating so fast that she pressed a hand to her chest to calm it. Pete dabbed his eyes with his handkerchief and sat down in the armchair. He moved the cushion and let out a shuddering breath. Verity could see he was shaking and distraught.

'How is Hetty?'

A bolt of fear shot through Verity as his question registered with her and she realised Pete didn't know her granny had passed.

'My grandmother passed away twelve years ago.' Verity's voice was soft, knowing the news would likely be devastating.

Pete gave a sharp intake of breath and wiped his eyes again with his handkerchief. 'I'm so sorry to hear that.'

The room fell silent and in that moment Verity could see Pete's heart had snapped in two, possibly for the second time in his lifetime.

'I can see you're hurting, but believe me, my granny never forgot you. I grew up hearing stories about Puffin Island and its wonderful people. She loved this place.'

'I know, and then things all got messed up and when she didn't get in touch after the postcard—'

'My granny never received the postcard,' Verity interrupted.

'She didn't receive it? But then how did you get hold of it?'

'It had been trapped in an old postbox at the side of her house that had been sealed up for years. I removed the postbox as I was prepping the house before I left, and had a look to see if anything was inside. That's when I found your postcard.'

Pete's face crumpled. 'Day after day I waited for her to

walk back up that cliff path. I put my whole life on hold...'
He paused for a moment as he tried to gather himself. 'I
thought the postcard would prompt her to get in touch as I
told her I couldn't imagine my life without her. And that
was the truth, I couldn't. What we had was real, and now I
know she never knew how I really felt, and it's too late to
tell her.'

'I'm so sorry,' soothed Verity.

'Her silence left me wondering what had I done wrong.
The rejection was too much to bear and left me questioning
whether she had ever truly cared.'

'I'm certain she cared but can I ask, the postcard...what
was the secret you shared?'

Pete looked pained, and Verity could feel her heart
sinking.

'When Henrietta was here in the summer of 1972,
everyone fell in love with her. Joe, especially, wanted her to
be his girl, but Hetty and I couldn't deny how we felt for
one another. The secret was the affair we never told Joe
about.'

'I think you need to tell Verity what you just told me,'
added Betty.

'You played your part,' Pete said, harshly.

Betty held up her hands in agreement but remained
silent.

'My real name is Wallace, but only my very good friends
call me that, as it didn't fit in with the image of the band.
And because I lived in this cottage and looked after the
welfare of the puffins the islanders have just always called
me Puffin Pete, Pete being my middle name. Henrietta was
actually the last person to call me Wallace. She thought it

was very sophisticated but I wasn't convinced.' Pete gave a little smile. 'I can see your resemblance to her now; you look quite like her.'

Verity stayed quiet. She could see from Pete's face he was mulling over the past.

'The summer of 1972 was the best and worst summer of my life. The band was becoming famous, screaming girls were arriving across the causeway in their droves and camping out on the beach just to get a glimpse of us. We still had everyday jobs, though they were becoming more and more difficult to hold down. Joe, my best friend, he hadn't been lucky in love. He became a father at a young age and though his family sadly separated, he provided for them and was a brilliant father. One evening, he burst through the door of the cottage and announced that there was a new girl in town, and in the same breath declared that he was going to marry her one day. He said he could feel it in his bones.'

'Granny?'

Pete nodded. 'He was smitten, fell in love with her instantly. As they say, when you know, you just know.' Pete swallowed. 'I teased him rotten, telling him no one could fall in love that quickly, but Joe was adamant he'd never seen a girl so pretty. Hetty turned up in the pub that night with Betty.'

'I've already told Verity that she lived at the cottage. Neither of them knew why your granny was here...' she added, looking at Verity.

'Until today.' Pete gave Betty a stern look. 'I didn't know your grandfather had proposed.'

'Hetty confided in me that she was trying to figure out the future she wanted, and I couldn't break her confidence.'

'If Joe felt so strongly, Pete, how did Granny and you get together?'

'She told me that Joe was smitten with her and as much as he was a decent, lovely man, he wasn't for her.'

'And did Joe know how she felt?'

Pete shook his head. 'Hetty was too kind to break his heart, but she never encouraged him either. She was his friend, and to her that's all it was. Hetty was friends with everyone, the life and soul of the party, and fitted right in. But Joe had become fixated on her, always waiting for her when she came out of the tearoom or we would bump into her down by the beach.'

'But you struck up a relationship with her, without Joe knowing? To save his feelings?'

Pete nodded. 'We even kept it from Betty because we wanted to just enjoy each other without anyone else knowing. We also wanted to work out a way of telling Joe without hurting him too much. The last thing I wanted was to hurt Joe, he was my best friend. And I'm not proud of having kept it secret. I could see the look in Joe's eyes whenever Hetty walked into the room.'

'Or when she sang. Everyone paid attention then,' added Betty with a smile.

Pete looked towards Verity. 'That song you heard me singing, I wrote it for Hetty and she's the only person I've ever sung it to.'

'That's where I've heard it before! Granny used to sing it whilst she was cleaning or in the garden!'

Pete's eyes glistened with more tears. 'I'm glad to hear

that. Hetty is the only woman I ever wrote a song for. We were head over heels in love but now I'm not sure what to believe. I didn't know there was someone waiting for her back home.'

Verity dared to glance towards Betty.

'Hetty was my friend and whatever she told me was in confidence.'

Verity turned back to Pete. 'How did it all end?'

'Hetty left the night Joe died.' Pete struggled to get the words out.

'What happened that night?' asked Verity, as an uneasy feeling swathed her. The mood in the room had suddenly turned very sombre. Pete stood up and placed both hands on the oak beam above the fireplace, his head bowed low. After a moment he lifted his head, and stared at his reflection in the mirror. He locked eyes with Verity through the glass.

'I was responsible for Joe's death. It was my fault.'

Silence sliced through the room. Pete's gaze fell to the floor.

Chapter Nineteen

Pete looked fragile, exhausted.

All Verity could think was that Sam's gut feeling had been right. 'You killed Joe? How?'

Verity knew her question was direct but a man had lost his life here and it seemed some kind of secret had been covered up for decades. There was no way to pretty up the questions that were burning inside her.

Suddenly aware of a figure standing in the doorway, Verity swung her head in that direction then briefly closed her eyes. Sam had arrived to make amends with Pete, to put the past behind them. She wasn't sure whether his timing was the best or the worst it could be.

'Now *that's* a question I've wanted answered for years.' There was a coldness to Sam's tone, his eyes darkening.

Betty was up on her feet in an instant, grasped Sam's arm and guided him to a chair. 'Take a seat. This isn't exactly what everyone is thinking and as much as you've been beating yourself up for years...' She glanced towards

Pete and moved closer to him. 'Pete, I know you from old. And from what you've told me today, it was a set of unfortunate circumstances. I just wish you'd told me years ago.'

Verity could tell from Sam's face that though Betty might be content to talk about 'unfortunate circumstances', he was going to take some convincing.

Betty took a deep breath. 'By my reckoning, if anyone is to blame for the unfortunate set of circumstances that played out that night, it's probably me. I pushed the first domino that toppled onto the next, creating the chain reaction of events.'

'You, Betty?' asked Verity, confused.

'But I promise I didn't know that Hetty had chosen that night to leave.' Betty gave Pete a reassuring look.

Verity glanced towards Sam, who looked even more confused than she felt, and rushed to fill in the blanks of what he'd missed. 'It appears my granny had men falling all over her. Your grandfather fell for her and Pete did, too.'

Sam looked like he was about to say something but Pete cut in. 'To be clear, Joe never had a relationship with Hetty. He was just smitten from the moment he saw her.'

'But then you swooped in and took her? You were his best friend. Why couldn't you have stayed away from her? It's not as though the girls weren't swarming around you. Why would you want to pick the same one my grandfather had his eye on?'

'It wasn't quite like that. Hetty and I were attracted to each other straightaway and of course I felt shitty about it. Joe was my best mate and we tried to deal with the situation the best we could without hurting anyone's feelings, but it seemed Hetty had other secrets that even I didn't know about. We made each other promises that we were going to be together forever and I was going to sit down with Joe soon, so I was devasted when she left. I still don't fully understand what made her choose that night to flee. I know she was your granny but she was also my whole world. If I'd known from the start that she had a life waiting for her back home, things might have been different.'

'Do you mean you wouldn't have got involved with her?' asked Verity.

Pete nodded. 'I sit here every day thinking what we had was so real and pure, hoping she would walk up that hill towards the cottage. I'd welcome her back with open arms. But now I know I was just a footnote in her story, and that the forever we talked about was nothing more than a dream.'

'Hetty didn't lie to you, Pete, and I do think she sincerely cared for you. She was just confused. She came for the summer because she needed space to work out what she wanted from the future,' said Betty, kindly.

'Apparently me and Puffin Island were just not enough.'

'That simply wasn't the case. Hetty loved it here, I know that, but there were circumstances that led her to leave.'

'What circumstances?' asked Pete. 'What is it you aren't telling me?'

Betty briefly closed her eyes. 'Hetty left me a letter when she left. I didn't know about you and her, so I assumed it would be Joe who was broken-hearted at her departure. I didn't want him to hear the news from someone else so I headed towards the coastguard hut, as I knew you were both on shift that night. That's when I saw you and stopped to tell you Hetty had left. I was so worried about breaking the news to Joe, I didn't really take in your reaction, and then you took off in the opposite direction before I could say anything else.'

'I did. I ran from the jetty all the way to the causeway to try and stop her, but it was too late. I couldn't find her.'

'I carried on to the hut to see Joe, and when I arrived, he was pacing up and down, extremely agitated, waiting for you to arrive. He told me that he thought he'd seen you and Hetty the night before, up on the cliff top together. He was waiting to confront you.'

Pete looked bewildered. 'Why didn't you ever say?'

'Because what was the point? It wasn't going to bring Hetty or Joe back after…'

Verity looked towards Sam, who hadn't said a word. She guessed he was remaining quiet on purpose, not wanting to interrupt and cause Pete and Betty to clam up. He had waited a long time to know the truth of how his grandfather had ended up in the water that night.

Betty carried on. 'I assured Joe that was impossible because surely I'd know if something was going on between you both. I thought at least one of you would have told me. Thinking he'd just got the wrong end of the stick, I gave him the letter that Hetty had left me, so he could see her goodbye for himself, but in hindsight…'

'Why in hindsight?' probed Pete.

Betty reached for her bag, and pulled out an envelope. 'The letter made everything ten times worse.'

'What's in the letter?' asked Verity, immediately

recognising her granny's handwriting as Betty leaned towards Pete and handed him the envelope.

'I'm so sorry, Pete.'

Pete took the envelope then reached for his glasses, balanced them on the bridge of his nose and sat back in the chair. Tension hung in the air and Verity watched his eyes flit up and down over the cream-coloured paper. He eventually gave a tiny gasp and then his watery eyes locked with Betty's.

'Hetty was pregnant?' Pete turned the paper over but the other side was blank. 'It says she was pregnant.'

Betty nodded. 'I've always thought that that had to be the reason she went home, to marry her fiancé and give her baby the family it deserved. Her future was decided for her.'

'But how do you know the baby wasn't mine?'

In that second a million thoughts exploded in Verity's mind. Betty's answer could change everything she had ever known or thought about her past. Glancing back at Pete, she saw he was staring at her. She suspected that they were having exactly the same thoughts. But as much as she stared, she couldn't see any physical resemblance between them.

'Because Hetty was throwing up most mornings from the day after she arrived. My own mother pulled me aside to ask whether she was sick, as we'd often heard her. It was only after reading the letter that I realised she was suffering from morning sickness.' Betty looked towards Sam. 'All the letter said was that she was going back home to have the baby, so when Joe read it he put two and two together and made five. After seeing Pete and Hetty up on the cliff he thought Pete had stolen his girl and the baby was his.'

Pete looked distraught. 'But this is the first I'm hearing about this.'

'Joe thought you hadn't shown for your shift because you had a guilty conscience. You were his best friend and he'd confided in you how much he liked this girl, and how, after his previous relationship breakdown, he was taking his time to get this right. But having spotted you together on the cliff, he was angry. He kept looking out of the window waiting for you to arrive. I told him I couldn't see that it was possible for you two to have been having a secret relationship, and I was just about to tell him about her marriage proposal, when a call came in. A tourist had alerted the coastguard that they'd spotted someone in the water. I told him not to do anything daft when you arrived, and that I'd come back in an hour, after the rescue was completed. I'm not even sure Joe heard me though, as he'd already started to race towards the jetty.'

'But there was no one found in the water, according to all the reports, and believe me, I've combed every article, every logbook. Where were you at this point?' Sam cut in, staring at Pete accusingly.

'I was making my way back up Lighthouse Lane. Joe wasn't at the hut when I arrived, but the rescue had been logged and the phone was ringing. The caller on the other end of the line was apologetic, saying he'd rung in only moments earlier, but the tourist had made a mistake. What he thought was a person was actually a huge log that had been washed up in the waves, wrapped in some sort of material. I hurried after Joe.' Pete was trembling, his face pained. 'You've got to believe me, I didn't mean for it to happen...' His voice was earnest.

'Didn't mean for what to happen?' pushed Verity.

'When I arrived at the jetty, there was pandemonium, a crowd huddled together, screaming and shouting. I waded through the people to get a closer look and saw someone had thrown a life ring in, but it was too late. Joe's body was being battered by the waves and was heading out to sea fast, taken by the rip current. I saw it in his hand...he was clutching my cap. The cap I wore every day without fail, come rain or shine. When I took off to try and stop Hetty from leaving, it must have dropped over the side of the jetty into the sea. He thought it was me in the water,' Pete gasped on a sob. 'My whole world was plunged into despair. Everything came crashing down around me. In the matter of an hour, I'd lost Joe and Hetty both, my best friend and the love of my life.'

Betty cupped her hand around Sam's.

Tears were flooding Pete's cheeks. 'My hat lost him his life – and now I've just discovered that even though he thought I'd been the worst friend in the world, he still jumped into the water knowing he mightn't survive the rip current. We were quick to get the boat launched but it was too late. When we pulled him from the sea, he was already gone.'

Sadness bled through the room. Everyone was hurting, each for a different reason.

Verity wrapped her arms around her. It was such a brutal catalogue of events that had led to the awful tragedy. She took in the despair and hurt in Pete's and Betty's eyes.

They had both suffered from holding onto their parts of the jigsaw until now.

'One day, I hope you find it in your heart to forgive me,' Pete said to Sam as he mopped his brow with his handkerchief. Profound sadness and tiredness were engraved on his worn face. Verity hoped that Sam understood the depth of Pete's pain, which had no doubt engulfed him every day since that catastrophic night.

Hopefully, now that the truth was out, the guilt and the black cloud that had hung over them all would finally begin to lift.

As they watched, Sam stood up and walked out of the cottage without saying a word.

Turning towards Pete, Betty urged, 'Let him go and make sense of it all. He'll be okay.' She stood and opened her arms. 'I think we both need a hug.' Pete nodded and hugged Betty tight.

'I'm so sorry,' he whispered. 'I should have told you.'

'And I should have told you. I'm sorry, too.'

Verity watched with tears in her eyes as they parted. 'Pete, when did you send the postcard?' she asked.

Pete and Betty sat back down.

'The next morning. I just wanted Hetty to come back. The night of the accident, I came over to your cottage.' Pete looked at Betty. 'You and your mum made me a drink and there was a moment when neither of you was in the room and I noticed your mum's rental book on the dresser. Inside were Hetty's personal details, including her home address, so I took a punt and quickly scribbled it down on a piece of paper. I honestly thought she would get in touch and come back if she heard about Joe's death.'

'I suppose we'll never know whether she knew or not. All we know is that she chose to get married and have the baby,' Verity added tentatively.

Pete nodded and turned towards her. 'You have the same laugh. That's why you took me by surprise, that day up on the cliff, when you laughed about the mooing puffins.'

Verity smiled. 'Will it be difficult for you if I did stay around?'

'You mean on the island?'

She nodded.

'Of course not. If anything, you lit up my life again. I felt like you've accepted me for me. Not many people can make me smile the way you do. Over the years I lost the zest for living.' Pete looked around the room. 'This room is still exactly the same as the last day Hetty was standing here. I've been stuck in a time warp, waiting for a return that was never going to come. I was so focused on the past that I forgot to live in the present...and I've certainly not looked after myself.'

Verity stood up and touched his arm. 'That can all change now. I'm sure when Sam processes everything, he'll come around. I do know he was coming today to talk to you and hopefully put things to bed before the vigil.'

'Timing is everything,' murmured Betty.

'I'm glad you don't mind me staying, Pete, because I've enjoyed puffin counting and working alongside you in the vet's. Let's hope I get the job and can find a home before winter sets in.'

'Job? What's this?' asked Betty.

'I've applied for a job with Cooper.'

'Oh, Verity, that's brilliant. I've got everything crossed for you.'

'Me, too,' added Pete.

Verity smiled at them and pointed to the door. 'I'm going to leave you both to it.' After hugging them tightly, she made her way back to the van, wondering whether her granny would have stayed on Puffin Island if she hadn't been pregnant. Sadly, that was a question that was never going to be answered.

Chapter Twenty

It was nine a.m. on voting day when Verity woke to the sound of puffins and gulls, and sunshine bursting through the curtains of the van. Last night it had taken her ages to get to sleep, the circumstances that led to Joe's death running through her mind, all of it so sad. If her granny hadn't left the island that day, things might have been very different. She knew she couldn't change any of it, but she couldn't help wondering what she would have done in her granny's circumstances. It was a difficult one.

From the way Pete had spoken, Verity knew that he'd thought he and her granny had a future together. You could hear the love for Hetty in his voice, and he'd waited all these years hoping she would walk back into his life. Verity was in no doubt that her granny had loved her grandfather, but she was more than likely in love with Pete too, given the stories she'd told about Puffin Island and the picture hanging in her favourite room in the house, constant reminders of what could have been.

Discovering the pregnancy would have cemented the need to go home and marry her baby's father, but had she had regrets? Verity would never know. She still had so many questions. She wished she could have one more conversation with her grandmother about her summer on Puffin Island.

Verity thought about going over to see Sam, but decided it was best to give him time. He would still be coming to terms with all yesterday's revelations. She hoped the feud that had festered for many years between Sam and Pete would one day be abandoned, but today wasn't likely to be that day, as they were going to go head-to-head again when the island voted on the safety barriers. Voting booths were being set up in the church hall, Betty was in charge of issuing the ballot papers, and Cooper had been roped in as a fair adjudicator to count the results. An announcement was due to be made at three p.m. that afternoon at the bay.

Reaching for her phone Verity was amazed to note she had slept for eight hours. She saw a text from Kev and swiped the screen.

> The new tenants are in and your absence has just been clocked. I've been accosted!

Verity quickly typed back.

> Tell me more.

Almost immediately Kev's name flashed on to the screen. Verity swiped the text message and burst out laughing.

> I told him it was top secret and I wasn't allowed to tell anyone. But in case anyone asks, you won the lottery, have bought a house in the South of France and are now dating a celebrity and couldn't be happier!

Verity could picture Kev furtively spilling the untrue secret, and no doubt making it extremely believable. As she climbed out of bed and slid open the van door, she was swathed with a feeling she had missed – happiness. In a way, she *had* won the lottery. If she were still in that mundane relationship, there was no way she would be waking up with this view.

> You're such a fibber!

She quickly typed back, still with a smile on her face, glad she could always rely on Kev to set the cat amongst the pigeons. As she slid her feet into her trainers, she looked across towards Cliff Top Cottage.

'Wow! What's all this?' she asked, walking over towards Pete, who was battling with an old rug that he eventually threw onto a pile of rubbish that was accumulating outside in the garden. All his windows were wide open and colourful hanging baskets bursting with blooms were hanging on each side of the cottage door. On the table outside there were tins of paint and dustsheets.

Pete turned towards her. 'It's a brand-new day and a brand-new start.' He gave a her a warm smile. 'Would you like a cup of tea?'

'Yes, thank you.' He disappeared back inside and soon returned carrying a tray with a pot of tea and two mugs.

He gestured towards the new bistro set that had been set up overlooking the cliff top.

'Is this new, too?' she asked as she sat.

'Picked it up this morning from Puffin Pantry. They were selling off their old sets as they have new ones outside on the street.'

'It looks pretty and new to me.'

Pete poured the tea. 'Have you spoken to Sam since yesterday?'

Verity shook her head. 'I thought I'd give him some space whilst he comes to terms with everything. How are you feeling about it all?'

'It was a complete shock to discover your granny was pregnant...' He hesitated. 'I know it's going to sound daft, but she was the only woman I ever truly loved. I honestly hoped she would stay on Puffin Island with me, even if it meant I had to face Joe. If only I could see him one last time to have the conversation. If only my cap hadn't been in the sea.'

'I know,' replied Verity.

'The one thing I can take away from all this is that she still had our puffin picture. That means a lot to me.'

'She did, and she hung it in her favourite room in the house.'

'We bought that picture together on our first date. In fact, we bought two. We sat on the top of the cliff watching the puffins whilst we wrote on the back of them, both wondering what the future was going to hold. We were so full of hope. I still have mine hanging on the landing at the top of the stairs.

'It's a funny old world, isn't it? Every single day I

thought about her and hoped she would walk up that cliff path with her curls bouncing off her shoulders and her wide smile smothered in red lipstick. She melted my heart from the very first moment.'

'Would you like to see a photo of her? I have loads, but there's a special one I carry with me in my purse.'

'That would be lovely.'

Verity hot-footed it back to her van and soon returned. 'It's one of both of us, sitting in the garden.'

Pete took the photograph and his eyes instantly teemed with tears. 'She's just as beautiful as I remember.'

'Do you know what I think?'

Pete looked towards her.

'I think it was fate that I discovered that postcard.' Verity looked up at the sky. 'My reckoning is that she'll be looking over us right now, glad we've met. I needed this, Pete.'

'This?'

'This new adventure, a change.'

They both sipped their tea.

'Did Hetty have a good life? Was she happy?' asked Pete.

'She was a jolly granny, always singing and smiling. She taught me how to bake, ride a bike, tie my shoelaces, and she told the best stories about this island. Even though she never mentioned you specifically, out of loyalty to my grandfather, it's clear she never forgot you, and I think she'll be very pleased I've found my way to this island and applied for a job here. All the upset I've been through in the last few months now feels well worth it.'

'Cooper would be mad not to hire you.'

'Then all I'll need to do is find a house. This was

definitely fate. I've got a good feeling it's all going to work out somehow.'

'And is everything okay between you and Sam?'

Verity shrugged. 'I hope so but I'm trying not to overthink it.' She felt herself blushing a little, remembering the night they'd spent together. No one had evoked such passion in her before. That night had been playing on a loop in her mind ever since. She hadn't come on this adventure looking for love, but as Pete had recently said, when you know, you know. And there was something about Sam Wilson that she couldn't shake off.

'He's a good lad and a hard worker, and he has been dealt a rough hand. But he has his grandfather's spirit and talent.'

'When I heard him sing in the pub, I honestly thought he was a recording artist.'

'He has the same tone as his grandfather. It takes me right back to those band days when I hear it.'

'He's made it clear he's only looking for fun.'

'That really isn't Sam's style. Like I said, he's protecting himself.'

'I can understand that. I'll just have to keep living in hope that there's a decent man out there for me.'

'Talk to him. It might be easier now the truth is out about Joe.'

'Why didn't you ever tell Sam about your hat being in the water?'

'I suppose because Sam was so angry, and because it meant I'd have had to go into the whole story about Hetty and why I was late for my shift. Even after all these years, the memories still feel too raw.'

'And now?'

'I thought I'd done something wrong to make her leave, and then, with Joe's passing, my sadness and grief consumed me. But now I know the reason she left, I understand. I just wish I'd heard it from her.'

'It may all have been too difficult for Granny too.'

'I get that...and she probably assumed Betty would tell me the truth at some point.'

They finished their tea and were lost in their own thoughts for a while, Then a voice bellowed from the cliff path, 'Pete, why aren't you down at The Island Hall?'

Betty was standing on the cliff path, waving her arms. She hurried towards them.

'Get yourself down to the bay. You've had a hell of a lot to say about the barriers in the last six months...' She trailed off as she glanced towards the cottage. 'Nice flowers, and thank God you're chucking away those dusty old rugs. What's brought all this on?'

'Closure, new start.'

'Glad to hear it. Welcome back, Pete!' She pressed a swift kiss to his cheek. 'Now come on, I'll see you down there.' Betty disappeared as quickly as she'd appeared.

Pete chuckled. 'Despite everything, friends are the best thing that can ever happen to anyone. Even though she's bossy and we have our differences, Betty does make the best lemon drizzle cake and the finest breakfast I've ever tasted. I'd best show my face.' He stood up.

'How are you feeling about the vote?'

'This is not to be repeated, as I don't want people thinking I'm softening in my old age, but I can see it from both sides. I just want everything to be settled and drama-free.'

'I understand that feeling. I hate to tell you, but you're already a softie. I could see that from the moment I met you, even though you shouted at me to remove myself from the cliff top.'

'I'm sorry about that.' He gave her a smile.

'What's your plan for later?'

'I'm going to sand and paint these windows and get this cottage back to life, and at three o'clock I'll make my way to the harbour and hear the result.'

'Do you want any help? I'm not the best at painting but I can't go wrong with the sanding.'

'Are you sure?'

'Absolutely. It'll stop me checking my emails every two minutes or waiting for the postman to find my van.'

'Cooper will interview you, without a doubt.'

'I hope so,' replied Verity, crossing her fingers. 'Give me a second. I'll get changed and come with you to The Island Hall.'

Ten minutes later they wandered across the bay. The wheels of democracy were fully in motion, the islanders filing towards the temporary voting station. The whole thing was being taken very seriously. Betty was holding a clipboard and checking everyone's ID at the door, even though she knew them all. Verity was greatly amused.

'Good morning!' she called to Clemmie and Amelia, who were walking down together.

'There she is! We've heard rumours that you're applying for a job with Cooper?' Clemmie linked her arm through Verity's. 'How blooming marvellous.'

Pete leaned in and whispered, 'That's the joy of living on a close-knit island. Don't think your business will ever be your own again.'

'I won't!' Verity laughed.

As they approached the door Betty greeted them in an official manner and ruled a thick biro line through their names on the list. 'ID, please.'

'I'm your granddaughter! Surely you don't need to see my ID?' protested Clemmie.

'This is official island business. I'm not leaving anything to chance or having any votes disqualified on my watch.'

'Are you being serious?'

Betty held out her hand and a bemused Clemmie handed over her ID. Once Betty was satisfied, she turned towards Verity. 'Unfortunately, you're not a resident of the island...yet.' She gave her a heart-warming smile. 'So you can't vote this time.'

Verity smiled and held up crossed fingers. 'Next time!'

As the others went inside, Verity turned to find Sam approaching. Strangely he wouldn't meet her eye but walked straight into the building without so much as a hello or a smile. Perplexed, she sat on a nearby bench. The morning had started well but now her mood slumped. Why had he blatantly ignored her? Was he lashing out at her because of her granny, thinking that if she hadn't left the island when she did, Joe would still be alive? Surely he couldn't now be blaming *her*? She managed to persuade herself not to jump to conclusions. She would wait and talk to him as soon as the vote was over.

Within seconds Pete walked out of the hut. 'All done.' He stood by the bench with his hands on his hips. 'And now I'm ready for a day of spring-cleaning.' He glanced at Verity. 'What's up with you? You suddenly look glum.'

'Sam has just totally ignored me and I'm not sure why. Did you see him inside?'

'I did,' replied Pete. 'Surprisingly, he nodded in my direction, which I wasn't expecting.'

'Why's he ignoring me then?'

'I'm not sure, but there's only one way to find out.'

'Do you mind if I wait for him before I follow you back up to the cottage?'

'Of course I don't mind. But first, put on your best smile.' Pete had dropped his voice to a whisper.

Verity looked over his shoulder and saw Cooper walking towards them.

'Good morning, Pete. I bet you'll be glad when this vote is counted,' said Cooper, warmly.

'As long as it goes in my favour. Can I introduce you to Verity?' Pete gestured towards her and she immediately stood up and shook Cooper's hand.

'It's a pleasure to meet you. I've been hearing good things about you,' stated Cooper. Verity took a sideward glance at Pete, who tipped her a discreet wink. Had he put in a good word for her? Her suspicions were immediately confirmed. 'Pete has been telling me all about you and your incredible work helping to save local dogs that have tested their flying skills...and about you getting involved in the puffin count. That's very brave.'

'It was a real endurance test,' said Verity with a grin, holding out her arm to show off her puffin wounds.

'Ouch! They did like you, didn't they? It was funny, just after Pete finished telling me how wonderful you are, I checked my inbox to find I had a job application from you.'

Verity blushed.

'I'd like to formally invite you for an interview.'

'You would?' Verity's eyes widened.

'I would. How about this afternoon? Four p.m. at Cliff Top Veterinary Surgery? I know it's a bit soon but if it's inconvenient we can rearrange.'

Verity clasped her hands together. 'In the words of the Jackson Five, I'll be there.'

Cooper smiled at her enthusiasm. 'Great! In the meantime, I have a ballot to count and a result to announce, and I also need to somehow try and fit in an appointment with the estate agent.'

'Are you moving?' asked Pete, clearly surprised.

Cooper shook his head. 'I've decided to rent out the living accommodation above the surgery. It's a good space, all appliances are working and the electrics have been checked, so all it needs is a fresh lick of paint. It would be great to have someone permanently on the premises once we're up and running.'

At this, Verity exchanged a loaded look with Pete, who nodded towards Cooper.

'What's going on between you two?' asked Cooper.

'I could save you a trip to the estate agents,' said Verity, 'as I'm actually looking for accommodation. I'm currently living in my travelling van and even if I don't get the job, I'd make a brilliant tenant.'

'What are the chances of that?' said Cooper looking at them both.

'I'm heading back up to Cliff Top Cottage with Pete. Maybe I could have a look around?' Verity asked hopefully.

Cooper delved into his pocket and retrieved a set of keys, a huge smile spreading across his face. 'I've already read your references and I'm sure we can come up with a fair rent.'

'Thank you!' She took the keys. 'I know I'm going to say yes before I've even seen it. I'll bring back the keys when I meet you for the vote result at three p.m., if that's okay with you?' Cooper nodded and Verity took off. She didn't even wait for Pete – she was just too excited to see the flat and couldn't believe how neatly her life was falling into place.

As she rushed towards the cliff top she heard Pete shouting, 'I thought you were waiting for Sam?'

'I'll catch up with him later!' she called over her shoulder.

'New home and an interview. Could this day get any better?' Verity murmured to herself, determined not to let Sam's cold reception ruin her happy mood. As soon as she'd checked over the flat her plan was to find Sam, on the pretence of checking in on Jimmy, before helping out Pete with the cottage.

Five minutes later she was standing outside the surgery. She waved at Nathan, who was pottering about in his garage. She unlocked the door and stepped inside. The flat was open-plan with a living and kitchen area, and at the back of the room were bifold doors. Verity opened them and found herself on a small balcony. People would pay millions for a view like the one before her, the sea stretching for miles and the cliffs guarded by thousands of puffins. She couldn't believe she was standing here. She had been lucky that Cooper mentioned the flat to her before anyone else, and she thanked whatever higher power was looking after her for putting her in the right place at the right time.

The bedroom was a decent size, with built-in wardrobes and a dressing table. A door led to the bathroom. It was everything she needed to settle into her new life. Verity could already picture herself walking the small distance to work and sitting out on the balcony with a glass of wine in the evening. She could easily make the flat feel like home. She couldn't wait to negotiate a rent with Cooper.

Full of excitement, she locked the door of the flat and headed back to the bay, which was a hive of activity, full of rowing boats and kayaks, children running in and out of the water, tourists set up for the day with picnic blankets and windbreakers. She noticed The Island Hall was locked up and Betty wasn't standing guard outside the door anymore, which probably meant the islanders had voted. Sam too was nowhere in sight, and since there seemed to be no activity at The Sea Glass Restaurant, she assumed he must be keeping Jimmy company.

Five minutes later, feeling a little apprehensive, Verity knocked on the door of Cosy Nook Cottage. Seconds later the door opened. She gave Sam a huge smile. 'And how's the patient?'

'He's asleep.' He made no effort to invite her in.

'Umm, okay,' she replied. 'Is everything okay, Sam? I'm feeling a little tension. Have I done something to upset you?'

Sam was quiet, and could barely meet her eye. He inhaled. 'Verity, I can't do this.'

Even though Verity knew in her heart what Sam was trying to tell her, she still needed to understand why. 'Do what?'

'This.' He wafted his hand between them both.

Verity forced a brightness into her voice she wasn't feeling. 'Can we talk about this? I really don't want to be in a situation where it's uncomfortable when I see you, like it feels now.'

Sam sighed and opened the door. Verity walked in and Sam gestured towards the sofa. 'Would you like a drink?'

She shook her head. 'Don't go waking up Jimmy.'

Sitting at the other end of the settee, Sam looked pensive.

Verity decided to begin. 'I know you said it was nothing more than a bit of fun, but I'm confused because your actions towards me suggest that it's not just that. The way you looked at me when we were together...I could see you cared.'

The second she'd laid eyes on Sam she'd been captivated by his smile, his sparkling eyes, the way he dressed – the whole package. The connection she'd immediately felt between them had taken her by surprise. She was prepared to do anything to make Sam admit that he felt it too.

'I do care but...'

There was silence.

'What's stopping you from letting go? Why have you built these gigantic walls around yourself? I'm not that bad, you know.'

He smiled. 'I know you're not, and that's the problem.'

'Huh? So you'd like me to be horrible?'

'It would make it a lot easier for me.'

Verity took the plunge. 'Is this anything to do with Alice?'

'How do you know about Alice?'

'No one has been speaking out of turn. I like you and so I asked Amelia and Clemmie whether you had a girlfriend. They mentioned Alice in passing but didn't give any details. Are you still in love with her?'

'I'm not in love with Alice.'

'Because I see before me a gorgeous, successful man who deserves to be loved.'

Sam was quiet for a second and, as Verity watched, blinked back tears. 'It's not quite as simple as that.'

'Tell me then. Help me to understand what exactly is going on here.'

'Everyone leaves me,' he blurted. 'I'm a bad omen. No one sticks around.'

Verity narrowed her eyes. 'Do you mean Alice?'

'My grandfather, my mother, my father, Alice. I'm all alone in the world. Everyone leaves sooner or later and I just can't go through it all again.'

'Do you mean with me?'

Sam nodded. 'The second I saw you outside that greasy spoon there was something about you. I hoped we would be on the same ferry and I searched high and low for you.'

'You did?' Verity was secretly chuffed.

'I did. And then when you turned up here I couldn't believe it. It felt like maybe we were meant to keep finding one another. But experience has taught me that eventually everyone leaves. I'm never enough.' Sam's voice faltered and Verity reached over and took his hand.

'You are enough. Everyone on this island loves you, and hopefully, now the truth is out about your grandfather's death, you'll have a bit of closure and the weight will be lifted.'

'There was a lot to take in, but I definitely don't feel any animosity towards Pete, anymore.'

'That's good. I genuinely believe Pete wants to be here for you, just like I do. Sam, I have no intention of leaving.'

'But you will. You'll go back home just like—'

'Alice?' Verity finished his sentence. 'Is that what happened? Will you tell me about Alice?'

Sam took a breath. 'Alice was here on holiday, I didn't even notice her at first but she began to eat at the restaurant night after night. She flirted and everywhere I went she turned up. Cutting a long story short, we fell in love and Alice decided she was going to stay on the island. She said it was so different from the hustle and bustle of the city where she lived, and she loved the fact that everyone knew everyone and we were such a close-knit community. Of course, we talked about the future, about making a life together and starting a family. It was the first time I ever began to think I was a part of something, and that I'd found someone who wasn't going to abandon me as everyone had before. It was hard to let myself be vulnerable – and then it all came crashing down.'

'What happened?'

'On February 29th, Alice had gathered everyone on the bay. I finished my shift at The Sea Glass Restaurant, and walked along the jetty wondering why all the islanders were congregated on the sand. There was a massive cheer when everyone saw me, and from the middle of the crowd appeared Alice, with a microphone in her hand. Then, in front of all my friends and neighbours, she asked me to marry her. I said yes. I was the happiest man alive. Cora and Dan had arranged a fireworks display and we had drinks on the beach. The whole island danced and celebrated until the early hours. I thought that was it, my luck was changing, but a week later she was gone.'

'Gone? Where did she go?'

'She left me a note – she couldn't even tell me herself – saying that Puffin Island and I weren't enough for her. She wanted to travel and see the world and wasn't ready for marriage yet. But it was she who asked me! I can't even begin to tell you how humiliated I was. I had to go and tell everyone she'd left and the engagement was off. I just don't understand how someone could change their mind so quickly.' Sam briefly closed his eyes. 'It's one of the reasons I got a dog, because at least they love you for who you are and don't let you down.'

'Have you spoken to anyone about this?'

'Do you mean a therapist?' Sam shook his head. 'Men cope.'

'I'm going to stop you right there. Men need to talk. You're just as human as I am, and it really helped me to talk to someone objective when I was going through my separation. It's a safe space and it's good to get things off your chest. Try it. Give it a go.'

Sam nodded.

'And we aren't all like Alice, you know.'

'You say that, but I just can't get closer to you because I

know it'll hurt when you go. I can't deal with any more upset.'

'So you like me a little bit then?' Verity teased.

'Of course.'

She leaned towards him and rested her forehead against his. She smiled. 'Someone very wise once told me that sometimes in life, you have to just let go, go with the flow and see what happens. We may get our hearts broken – but what if we don't? I truly believe it was fate that I found that postcard and it brought me here, to you. No matter what happens, meeting you, spending time with you, has been one of the greatest joys of my life. No matter what happens, I'll have the best memories.'

'But that's just it, you'll leave, go back to Staffordshire and all that will be left are the memories—'

'What if I tell you I love Puffin Island?'

'I've heard it all before.'

'What if I tell you'—she moved away from him, slowly reached inside her bag and pulled out the keys of the surgery flat—'that these are the keys to my new flat… hopefully?'

Sam's eyes widened. 'New flat?'

'My new flat *on Puffin Island*.'

Verity watched the expression on Sam's face as the penny dropped.

'Where?'

'Above Cliff Top Veterinary Surgery. And not only that, I also have an interview this afternoon for the position of veterinary assistant.'

'That's brilliant, Verity!'

'I'm doing everything in my power to stick around.'

'You're being serious, aren't you?'

She nodded. 'Deadly.'

'Cooper would be mad not to take you.' Sam stood up, pulled her in for a hug and squeezed her tight. When he let go, he cupped his hands around her face. 'I'm so glad you're staying.'

'Me too.'

He bent his head and kissed her softly on the lips.

'What's happening here?' she asked.

He pulled away slowly. 'I think, just like Pete, Betty and yourself, I'm making a fresh start.' He smiled. 'And I promise I'll go and talk to someone, because I don't want to mess this up.'

'This?' she queried, moving her finger between them.

'Yes, this,' he said, mimicking the motion.

'I don't want you to mess it up either.'

'I think I'd be an idiot not to take a chance with you.'

'I think you'd be an idiot not to, too.' This time Verity leaned in and kissed him first. 'I have got one thing to say to you, though.'

'Which is?'

'Luckily for you, it's not a leap year.'

Sam grinned. 'You're not funny.'

'Just a little,' she replied.

Chapter Twenty-One

I t was just before three p.m. and everyone was gathered at Blue Water Bay. No one knew what the result of the voting would be, except Cooper, who'd counted the votes. He was standing at the edge of the sand talking to Pete. As soon as he spotted Verity, he gestured for her to come over.

'What did you think of the flat?' asked Cooper.

Verity took the keys out of her bag. 'To be honest, Cooper, I just have one major complaint.'

Cooper's smile dropped as he looked at Pete then back at Verity. 'Complaint?'

'The view through those bifold doors was just terrible. I really couldn't put up with it on a daily basis!' She laughed.

'For a minute there…'

'I'd love to take the flat if that's okay with you, and if the rent is manageable.'

'Glad to hear it, because I have this for you.' He handed her an envelope. 'Pete and I had a discussion and we think this is a fair monthly price.'

Verity opened the envelope and looked at the figure written on the piece of paper within. The rent for the flat was a few hundred less than her own home that she was renting out. With her wage from the new job – if she got it – she would be able to manage perfectly. She held out her hand to Cooper. 'Deal.'

'Fantastic! I'll get the contract drawn up and we can have it signed by the end of the week.'

'Perfect. I'll see you at four p.m. for the interview.'

'You will. Speaking of the time…' Cooper checked his watch and said goodbye before walking off towards the microphone stand that was positioned on the jetty.

Pete leaned in and whispered, 'I think the job is in the bag.'

'I hope so,' replied Verity. 'I can't believe this is happening. And by the way, I need to apologise to you. I didn't make it back to the cottage to help you out.'

'Where have you been?'

She grinned.

'You made everything okay with Sam?'

'Yes.'

'I'm glad to hear that.'

Their conversation was interrupted by Cooper switching on the microphone. Verity spotted Sam at the front of the crowd and caught his eye. He grinned at her, the two of them sharing the secret that only minutes earlier they had been wrapped in each other's arms and had almost forgotten the time.

Cooper began to speak and Verity and Sam both turned towards him. 'We all know why we're here today. The safety of our islanders and visitors is paramount and we want to do what's best to stop vehicles being trapped on the causeway when the tide turns. Ideas have included posters on the ferries, TV campaigns, radio campaigns and, of course, barriers. Islanders have strong opinions both for and against the barriers, and so the only way to settle this was by an island vote. All votes have now been counted and verified, and inside this envelope is the result.'

Verity noticed a look pass between Pete and Sam.

Cooper opened the envelope. Verity was reminded of the BAFTA awards.

'In total we have one hundred and sixty residents over the age of eighteen who were eligible to vote. One hundred and sixty votes were counted. The total number of islanders for the barriers is eighty; the total number of islanders against the barriers is eighty.'

There was a groan all around. It was a draw?

'What happens now?' whispered Verity to Clemmie, who was standing next to her.

'God knows,' she replied.

Cooper held his hand up to silence everyone. 'Can I make a suggestion?'

All eyes were on him, while his own were searching the crowd. Then they found and fixed on Verity. She gulped, not knowing what he was going to say.

'This morning we had one hundred and sixty residents on the island, but this afternoon we have one hundred and sixty-one.'

Again, there was chatter all around.

'Oh my gosh, he's not going to make me choose, is he? Please tell me he isn't going to make me choose,' Verity mumbled to herself.

'Verity Callaway.'

All the islanders turned in her direction.

'My suggestion is that Verity has the deciding vote. She'll soon be moving into the flat above the veterinary surgery and so she is Puffin Island's newest resident.'

What the heck was she meant to do now? She supposed she could refuse but then the debate over the barriers would continue to cause unrest. It was an impossible situation as either way she was going to upset Pete or Sam.

Thinking fast on her feet, Verity began walking towards Cooper. She took the microphone from him and gazed out at the islanders. 'Hello! I can't believe how much has fallen into place for me during my time on Puffin Island. I've fallen in love with the place. But I have to say – if it wasn't for me getting stranded on the causeway, I'd be in Amsterdam right now. I was the latest idiot to be rescued from the causeway, when the clock in my van stopped and I read the time wrong and misjudged the tide. If barriers had existed, they would definitely have stopped me driving across the causeway and getting swept up by the tide.'

Sam smiled. Verity knew he was hoping she would sway the vote in his favour.

'But I'm actually glad there were no barriers…'

The smile dropped from Sam's face.

'…Because my destiny was diverted down another path. However'—she took a breath—'I can see both sides of the argument and I really can't vote on this.'

Both Pete and Sam looked confused. She invited them up to join her. As soon as they were by her side, she continued, 'I have an idea. I don't know if it's possible, but surely we can all work together to see if we can make it happen.' She looked towards Sam. 'I do think the barriers are a good idea and will help to save lives, but also'—she turned towards Pete—'I understand your argument fully. So, how about we combine the two ideas? Would it be possible for the barriers to be installed but with an override function that the coastguard on duty can operate? Could there be some sort of key that could manually operate the barriers in case of an emergency?'

All the islanders were quiet and watched Pete and Sam, who were looking at each other. Sam's face broke into a smile first. 'I'm up for discussion on that, if Pete is?'

Pete nodded and extended his hand.

Watching them shake hands, Verity was ecstatic. She couldn't have hoped for a better result. She handed the microphone back to Cooper, who was clearly impressed with her diplomatic skills.

'I'm going to go and get ready for my interview.'

Cooper nodded and Verity left the jetty to a round of applause.

'Ever thought of running for prime minister?' Sam asked, appearing behind her.

'Ha ha. That certainly wouldn't be my dream job. It's been difficult enough keeping you islanders in check since my arrival.'

Sam swept her off her feet and kissed her full on the lips. 'You're just the best. I've got to go over to the restaurant, but come and tell me all about the interview when you've finished. There will be a drink waiting for you.'

'I shall do just that.' She kissed him again before he headed off.

She turned to find Clemmie and Amelia standing with

linked arms in front of her. 'Er, excuse me.' Clemmie wafted her hand between Verity and Sam, who had paused a few feet away and was deep in conversation with Pete. 'What's going on here?'

'Just going with the flow,' replied Verity with a wink. 'But I'll catch up with you both later. I'm just off for a job interview.

'Good luck!' they trilled in unison as Verity hurried off towards the cliff path to get ready.

Chapter Twenty-Two

One week later

Verity straightened Sam's tie before they left for the bay. Today was the fiftieth anniversary of Joe Wilson's tragic death, a loss that had rocked Puffin Island both in the past and the present.

It was early evening and as a mark of respect for Joe all businesses had closed their doors so that every resident could attend the vigil.

'How are you feeling?' asked Verity, slipping her hand into Sam's as they walked down Lighthouse Lane.

'It's been a hell of a week but for good reasons.'

Verity smiled. 'I have to say it's been one of the best weeks of my life.'

'I suspect the next one will be even better. You'll be starting your new job and moving into your flat.'

'I can't wait.'

Verity's interview with Cooper had been successful and

two days later the postman had wandered up the cliff top path and headed straight for her van.

> 'Miss Verity Callaway?'
>
> 'That's me,' she'd replied, taking the envelope from his hand and immediately noticing Cooper's logo stamped on the front. After ripping open the envelope she'd quickly scanned the words and taken off towards Cliff Top Cottage without shoes on, waving the letter in the air.
>
> Pete had opened the door to a very excited Verity.
>
> 'I got the job! I actually got the job! I can't quite believe it!'
>
> But Cooper had offered her a lot more than the position of veterinary assistant. He'd asked her to be the Practice Manager as well, because instead of a part-time surgery he wanted the practice to be open full-time.
>
> 'Congratulations!'
>
> Verity had hugged Pete then turned and begun to run from the cottage. 'I need to tell Sam!'
>
> 'Put some shoes on first!' Pete had shouted after her.

'And you and Pete are friends now. I'm happy about that.' Verity squeezed his hand.

'I am, too. It did us good to all sit in the same room and talk through everything – Pete, Betty and I.'

'Have you forgiven Pete for falling in love with my granny?'

'You can't help who you fall in love with.' Sam gave Verity a heart-warming smile and lightly nudged her shoulder with his.

'I like the fact that you both met with the company that's designing the barriers.' Verity was delighted to see Sam and Pete working together. All animosity had lifted.

'A genius suggestion by yourself.'

'I wouldn't go as far as genius, more like common sense.' She grinned.

When they reached the bottom of Lighthouse Lane, Verity could not believe her eyes. She stood still and looked all around. 'Wow! I wasn't expecting that.'

'It's an amazing sight, isn't it?' Hundreds of fishing boats were lined up as a mark of respect, and dotted all around the bay were firepits, and fairy lights hanging between poles hammered into the sand.

Parked at the side of the bay was a fish and chip van. Sam pointed. 'On this night, every islander eats fish and chips from the van as a mark of respect, because my grandfather was the best fisherman of his era around these parts.'

All of the islanders were gathered at the bay, and as Sam walked onto the sand all heads turned towards him. He didn't let go of Verity's hand as they made their way towards the front of the crowd. Betty walked over to meet them and enveloped Sam in a hug, and, as soon as she let go, Pete stepped forward and shook Sam's hand. Verity swallowed the lump in her throat. Even though she'd never known Joe, it was heart-warming that all the islanders would come together to remember him in this way. She slipped in next to Pete as Sam stood in front of the crowd and Cooper passed him the microphone.

'Thank you all for coming to pay your respects to my grandfather, Joe Wilson. He was a huge part of this community and on the fiftieth anniversary of his death we have come together once more.' Sam glanced at the photograph of Joe on the nearby easel. 'I really wish I'd got to meet him...' He swallowed then paused to compose himself. 'There are people standing amongst us today who knew my grandfather and they only ever have good things to say about him. It's no secret that Pete was my grandfather's best friend, and I'm pleased to say that, thanks to Verity's arrival on the island, the rift between myself and Pete has started to heal. I hope that one day we too will become the best of friends.'

Pete nodded his agreement and Betty placed her hands on her heart. Verity knew she must have hoped for years that they would bury the hatchet, but had thought this day would never come.

'As usual, we have the fish and chip van waiting to feed you all, and Cora and Dan have set up a drinks tent, so please help yourself. But before you grab your refreshments, I'd like to tell you a story...'

Verity knew that Sam and Pete had agreed that the truth of the night Joe died should be shared. Sam explained the tragic chain of events. There wasn't a dry eye in the place when the islanders realised that Joe had jumped into the sea thinking he was saving his best friend. Pete joined Sam at the front of the crowd as the story concluded, and together they unveiled a brand-new plaque that had been engraved and mounted on the harbour wall, honouring Joe and his sacrifice. Just before Sam was about to wrap up his speech, he glanced at Betty. Verity saw her disappear from the crowd and wondered what she was up to.

'I've got one more thing to share with you all.' Betty had reappeared, holding two guitars.

'As we all know, my grandfather was in a band called The Men from Puffin Island. Eric, John, Joe and Pete became quite famous in their day, but the opportunity to take the world by storm was tragically taken from them when my grandfather passed. I know that the band never played together in public after that fateful night, but I'm hoping that on this very special day of remembrance I can persuade the remaining members to join me, right here, right now, to perform in my grandfather's honour.'

All the islanders began to clap and cheer as John suddenly appeared with a keyboard and Sam and Pete took their guitars from Betty.

'Sam didn't even tell me about this. Did you know?' Verity asked Betty as she rejoined her.

Betty smiled. 'I caught them rehearsing.'

Sam turned to Pete and John. 'I'd love to become an honorary member of your band for one night only and I can't think of a better time to perform with you guys.'

The crowd was encouraging, the sound of cheers and clapping growing louder until Pete held up his hand and instantly everyone fell silent. Cooper placed three microphone stands on the sand and they took their positions.

'This song is dedicated to Joe and a wonderful woman who brought sunshine to our lives and this island, back in the summer of 1972... It's called "Puffin Compares to You".'

Verity's body erupted in goosebumps as they began to play the song that Pete had written for her granny. The whole community was clapping along as Betty took hold of

Verity's hands and began to dance with her, Clemmie and Amelia quickly following suit.

It was over an hour later that the band finished playing and were given a standing ovation.

Tears in her eyes, Verity looked all around her. There were people in fishing boats waving torches in the air, others drinking and eating fish and chips, or sitting on deckchairs enjoying the music. There were even islanders paddling at the water's edge. This was what community was all about. Verity was moved that she had been accepted so readily by everyone. Her new life on Puffin Island had begun in the best possible way.

As soon as Sam finished playing, he put down his guitar, ran towards Verity, swept her off her feet and spun her round. She giggled. 'You were amazing! You were all amazing!'

He kissed her and she realised everyone was watching as they began to clap. He pulled her in for a hug. 'The postcard from Puffin Island brought you here and I'll always be grateful,' he whispered.

Pete handed Sam a beer. 'You play and sing well. With a talent like that you could go far.'

Sam shook Pete's hand. 'I enjoyed every second of playing with you. I hope it won't be the last time.' The smile on his face said it all.

'I've got a feeling it won't be.' Pete winked.

'Would you both excuse me for a minute whilst I say thank you to a few people?' said Sam.

Standing next to Pete and Betty, Verity realised that this was the happiest she'd felt in a long time. Everything had slotted into place for her.

'I want to thank you,' said Pete, looking at Verity. 'For finding the postcard and coming into our lives. It's because of you the whole truth has come out and we can all finally start to move on. You know, when Betty told me you were Hetty's granddaughter I immediately thought there was a possibility you could be my granddaughter.'

'The thought crossed my mind, too,' admitted Verity.

'There's a part of me that wishes you were.'

Verity took hold of Pete's hand. 'We may not be biologically related, but if I could adopt you as my grandfather that would make me very happy.'

Immediately the tears welled up in Pete's eyes. 'That's the nicest thing anyone has asked me for a long time. It would be my absolute honour.' He hugged Verity tightly.

'You daft pair of buggers,' cut in Betty, teasing, but her eyes were filled with happy tears.

Sam was suddenly back at Verity's side. 'What have I missed?'

'Nothing,' replied Verity, slipping her hand into his. 'All of you are very lucky to have each other.'

'And we're lucky you came into our lives. Do you fancy some fish and chips?'

'I do!'

As they walked towards the fish and chip van, Sam smiled at Verity.

'Why are you smiling at me like that?'

'I was just thinking what an incredible woman you are.'

'I can't argue with that!' She grinned, leaning in and kissing him on his cheek.

They stood for a moment and gazed at all the islanders gathered on the beach.

'I used to wonder what life was all about, but it's this community right here in the bay. No matter which way the tide turns, true friends are never apart. Can life get any better than this?'

'Oh yes,' replied Sam with a glint in his eye. 'I promise you that it can.'

Acknowledgements

Welcome to Puffin Island!

I'm super excited to be bringing you the first book in my brand new series, *A Postcard from Puffin Island*. This series was inspired by two things. Firstly, a trip to Holy Island (Lindisfarne), which is situated off the Northumberland coast in the north east of England, just a few miles south of the border of Scotland and secondly, a postcard I discovered in an antique shop in the heart of Staffordshire. Written on the postcard was a cryptic message which led to the creation of this story.

I really can't believe this is my twenty-second book to be published and there is a long list of truly fabulous folk I need to thank who have been instrumental in crafting this novel into one I'm truly proud of.

The clever team at One More Chapter, who are utterly fabulous. I still pinch myself that I am a part of this fantastic publishing family. I'm hugely grateful for everyone's hard work and especially to the gorgeous Charlotte Ledger who turns my stories into books. You are the best.

My editor, the wickedly smart Laura McCallen, when she's not rubbing shoulders with royalty, Laura is working hard on my books to make them as best as they can possibly be.

My copy editor, Tony Russell, who has been with me

throughout my Love Heart Lane journey and has now packed his suitcase and is spending his vacations on Puffin Island.

Love and thanks as always to my family, Emily, Jack, Ruby and Tilly.

A special mention to my daughter Ruby Barlow who designed the map of Puffin Island which you will discover in the front of this book! We had great fun coming up with all the names of the places you can visit on the island as well as walking around graveyards to discover characters names.

Of course, I have to thank my two writing partners in crime, Woody, my mad cocker spaniel and Nellie, my loon of a labradoodle. I couldn't never imagine being without either of you.

My amazing best friend Anita Redfern, who is simply the best and makes me a happier human. I love you dearly.

Big love to Julie Wetherill, you rock!

A special thank you to Bella Osborne, who brainstorms with me often … very often! And is always at the end of the phone when I need her most, usually when I'm near the end of my novel and I'm convinced I don't actually have a story!

Thanks to Deborah Carr & Glynis Peters for the great laughs in Jersey. The word of the weekend was yumnuts and a wonderful time was spent touring the stunning coves whilst talking all things bookish.

Thank you to all the book bloggers, booksellers and library staff for reviewing and recommending my novels. And of course, a huge thank you to my lovely readers. I wouldn't have the best job in the world if it wasn't for you choosing my books to read.

I have without a doubt enjoyed writing every second of this book and I really hope you enjoy hanging out with Verity and Sam on Puffin Island. Please do let me know!

Happy reading!

Warm wishes,

Christie x

YOUR NUMBER ONE STOP
ONE MORE CHAPTER
FOR PAGETURNING BOOKS

The author and One More Chapter would like to thank everyone who contributed to the publication of this story...

Analytics
James Brackin
Abigail Fryer
Maria Osa

Audio
Fionnuala Barrett
Ciara Briggs

Contracts
Sasha Duszynska
Lewis

Design
Lucy Bennett
Fiona Greenway
Liane Payne
Dean Russell

Digital Sales
Lydia Grainge
Hannah Lismore
Emily Scorer

Editorial
Arsalan Isa
Charlotte Ledger
Bonnie Macleod
Janet Marie Adkins
Laura McCallen
Jennie Rothwell
Tony Russell

Harper360
Emily Gerbner
Jean Marie Kelly
emma sullivan
Sophia Wilhelm

International Sales
Peter Borcsok
Bethan Moore

Marketing & Publicity
Chloe Cummings
Emma Petfield

Operations
Melissa Okusanya
Hannah Stamp

Production
Denis Manson
Simon Moore
Francesca Tuzzeo

Rights
Vasiliki Machaira
Rachel McCarron
Hany Sheikh
Mohamed
Zoe Shine

The HarperCollins Distribution Team

The HarperCollins Finance & Royalties Team

The HarperCollins Legal Team

The HarperCollins Technology Team

Trade Marketing
Ben Hurd

UK Sales
Laura Carpenter
Isabel Coburn
Jay Cochrane
Sabina Lewis
Holly Martin
Erin White
Harriet Williams
Leah Woods

And every other essential link in the chain from delivery drivers to booksellers to librarians and beyond!

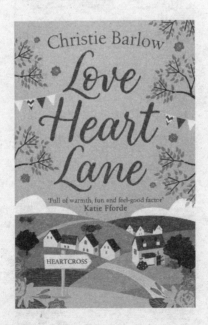

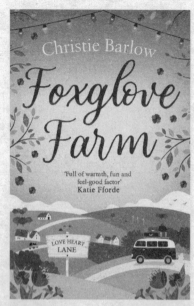

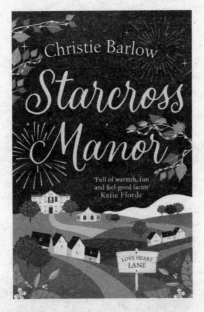

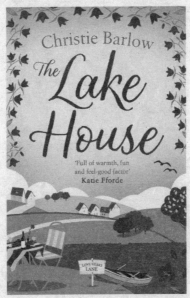

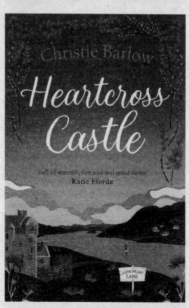

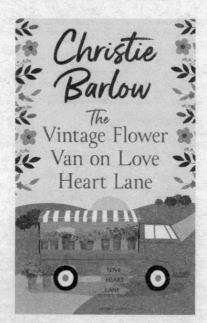

YOUR NUMBER ONE STOP

ONE MORE CHAPTER

FOR PAGETURNING BOOKS

One More Chapter is an
award-winning global
division of HarperCollins.

Sign up to our newsletter to get our
latest eBook deals and stay up to date
with our weekly Book Club!
<u>Subscribe here.</u>

Meet the team at
<u>www.onemorechapter.com</u>

Follow us!
 <u>@OneMoreChapter_</u>
 <u>@OneMoreChapter</u>
 <u>@onemorechapterhc</u>

Do you write unputdownable fiction?
We love to hear from new voices.
Find out how to submit your novel at
<u>www.onemorechapter.com/submissions</u>